Syd Parker

Secrets of the Heart

For Sarah, who I love more than chocolate!

"The face is the mirror of the mind, and the eyes without speaking confess the secrets of the heart."

--St. Jerome

Prologue

Chase Berkley pedaled as fast as her thirteen—year old legs would go. She covered the distance between the road and their secret hideout in record time. Avery had slipped her a note in math class, asking her to meet at the tree house immediately after school. They had found this old tree house the summer after third grade. They came to the tree house anytime they needed to get away from the outside world. It kept their secrets safe. The summer they found it, they had done a goofy blood sisters ritual. They cut their fingers and held them together, swearing on each other's blood, they were sisters for life. They would always tell each other everything, and keep each other's secrets safe.

She pushed back on the brakes and jumped off before the bike came to a stop. She raced up the tree, popped her head through the door and smiled at her best friend—Avery Carson.

"What's…the…emergency?" Chase choked out between gulps for air.

Avery's eyes twinkled mischievously. "I asked Michael to the Sadie Hawkins Day dance."

Chase stared at her incredulously. "Michael? Michael who picks his nose and eats it?"

Her nose wrinkled. "Gross!"

Avery laughed. "Chase, shut up! He hasn't done that since third grade. Besides he is the only boy that said yes. "

"Well, I don't see why you want to go with a dumb boy to the dance anyway. I thought we were going together." Chase's bottom lip jutted out and she started to pout.

"We can't go together, stupid. You have to ask a boy." Avery smirked. "And I know who wants you to ask him."

Chase shook her head. "I don't care. I don't want to go to the dumb dance anyway." She thought about missing a night with her best friend and suddenly changed her mind. "Okay, who?"

Avery squealed and clapped her hands together. "Oh, this will be so awesome! We can double date."

Chase shot Avery a look that said you better talk now.

"Okay, fine. Kyle likes you. He told Michael that he wanted to go to the dance with you." Avery watched hopefully for Chase's reaction.

"Kyle? Cootie Kyle? Are you crazy?" She stood up and started to pace back and forth in the small tree house. "I'm not going."

"Please!" Avery jumped up and stood in front of Chase. "You have to go, and you have to ask Kyle. That's the only way Michael will go with me. Pretty please, with cream and sugar on top."

Chase stared into Avery's eyes. She had never been able to say no to her, and this looked like it wouldn't be the first time. She rolled her eyes and acquiesced. "Fine, whatever. I'll go."

Avery grabbed her hands and started to jump around in a circle. "Okay, now for the *big* emergency."

Chase stopped jumping and looked at Avery. "What do you mean, now for the *big* emergency? Wasn't that asking me to go to the dance with a yucky boy?"

"Well, not exactly." Avery began to wring her hands together. "I'm afraid to ask you. It's kinda big."

"Avery, just ask. I don't see how anything could be worse than going out with Kyle."

"Well, you know this is like my first real date. Michael's more experienced. I mean, he was going with Ashley all through sixth grade. What if he wants to you know?"

"No, I don't know."

"What if he wants to kiss? What should I do? I don't know how to kiss? I've never kissed anyone before."

"Ugh, I say tell him no way. That is gross."

"Come on, Chase. I don't want to be the dork who couldn't kiss a boy." She twirled her hair around her finger, a sign she was trying to work up the courage to say something big. "Maybe you could, I don't know, practice with me."

Chase choked, her eyes widened. "Practice kissing…you? I, uhm, Avery, I don't know. You're a girl."

"So? It doesn't mean anything. It's just practice. Pleeaaassseeeee!"

"Okay, fine." She watched Avery's face. "How are we supposed to start?"

Avery giggled nervously. "I don't know exactly. My dad always puts his hands on my mom's face and sorta pulls her towards him. Then boom, they just kiss."

Chase cupped Avery's cheeks with her palms. She leaned towards her and puckered her lips. "Like this?"

Avery smiled. "I think so. Okay, now kiss me."

Chase narrowed the distance between them, closing her eyes at the last second. She felt Avery's breath on her face.

"Ouch!" Chase jumped back and rubbed her nose.

Avery laughed out loud. "That never happens on tv. Maybe you're doing it wrong."

Chase was doubled over, shrieks of laughter escaping her lips. "Maybe *I'm* doing it wrong? I'm just doing what you told me to do, dork."

"Okay, okay. We have to try it again." She covered her mouth and tried to stop laughing.

"You stop laughing first." Chase poked Avery in the stomach, which only succeeded in causing her to laugh louder.

Avery stopped laughing and put a very serious look on her face, but her eyes still twinkled. "Okay, are you ready?"

Chase shook her hands and took several deep breaths. "Okay, okay. I'm good." She stepped towards Avery, tilted her head and leaned towards her. She made the mistake of looking at her, and burst out laughing again.

"Come on Chase." Avery choked out between laughs. "I'm serious. Stop messing around."

"Okay, okay. I'm ready." She cupped Avery's face in her hands, and gently tilted her head to the side. She leaned in slowly, eyes closed, knowing she couldn't look in Avery's eyes without losing it. Chase gently touched her lips to Avery's. Avery ignored the brief jolt she felt in her stomach. She liked the feel of Chase's lips against hers. They were soft. She grasped Chase's arms with her hands and pulled her closer. She felt light—headed, and her stomach felt kind of queasy, but in a good way.

Chase suddenly pulled away, an odd look on her face. "Was that okay?"

Avery swallowed. "Ahh, yeah, that was good. Maybe we should try one more time."

Chase stepped back. She looked confused. "I don't know Avery." Still conflicted, she stepped closer to Avery and leaned in to her. Suddenly, she shook her head. "I can't. You're a girl. I, I have to go."

Avery shook her head, trying to deal with the influx of strange emotions that were racing through her mind. She watched Chase pedaling away from the tree house. Immense sadness washed over her. Sometime later, she left the tree house. She glanced up before she rode away. *Well, this is one secret that will definitely stay here.*

Chapter 1

Twenty Years Later

"…regret to inform you that the current economic conditions have forced TransAir to cease operations."

Chase stared open—mouthed at her CEO, unable to believe him. TransAir, the regional airline she had worked for since she graduated eleven years earlier, was going out of business. It happened overnight. She had watched the major airlines try to stay afloat by laying off hundreds of employees and cutting flights.

For the months leading up to the surprise closing of TransAir, she had reminded herself she was glad to be a pilot for a smaller airline. So far they had been immune to the rising fuel costs that were threatening to bankrupt larger airlines. She flew the same route everyday--Indianapolis to Chicago. Some people had considered this routine a study in monotony, but Chase never thought that. She loved to fly and it didn't matter that she saw the same scenery everyday.

She struggled to come to terms with the finality of the announcement. There was no warning of impending layoffs or a decrease in flights, no chance to brace for the impact. It was what it was--the end. Finito. TransAir, a presence in Indianapolis for close to thirty years was closed--past tense. Her job with TransAir was gone. *Hell, not just my job, everyone's job is gone.*

She should have figured something was up when they had requested that all the employees attend a mandatory meeting an hour before her regular flights started. She sat back in her chair and finally focused on her surroundings. She heard small pockets of conversation around her, mostly whispered words of disbelief and worry about finding employment. She tried not to think too much about tomorrow. Fortunately, she had a little money in savings and with the severance package, albeit small, she would probably be okay for a few months.

Chase stood up and made her way out. She said a few brief good--byes, commiserated that yes, indeed, the timing was horrible. She jogged to the employee parking lot, aware of the early morning chill that lingered in the air. She sat in her car waiting for it to warm up, still reeling from the last half an hour. Finally, her heartbeat returned to normal and she willed herself to leave. She glanced in the rearview mirror as she was leaving, one last look at the only real job she had ever had. *Well, what do we say, Scarlett? Tomorrow is another day.*

She drove blindly for the next hour, not sure where she wanted to be. She didn't want to go home, not yet anyway. She meandered aimlessly, at times looking up and seeing some familiar landmark and not realizing how she got there. Finally, she settled on a late breakfast. Pointing her car north, she headed to Bub's Café for coffee and their famous Bub Holes, large hand—made donut balls.

Before she got out, she grabbed the Maine Mid—Coast Guide Avery sent her months before. While Chase waited for her Bub holes and yogurt parfait, she sipped her coffee and thumbed through the guide. She found the section for Boothbay Harbor and leafed slowly through it. She smiled when she got to the section on lodging. There in all its brilliant glory was her and Avery's Victorian—Serendipity. Three years ago, Avery had talked her into being her partner, albeit silent partner in the century old Victorian turned bed and breakfast. So far, her only contribution was financial, her life too busy to afford much else. She had seen pictures, from the moment they bought it and all throughout the restoration. The finished home was truly magnificent.. While the majority of the outside was white, Avery had chosen to paint the trim shades of purple, red, yellow, and green. There was a large porch that wrapped around the home. A person could sit anywhere on the porch in a rocking chair and smell lilacs mingled with the salty, ocean air. The house sat on a large lot that faced the bay on three sides. The grassy yard sloped towards the ocean and afforded residents a wonderful view of the surrounding inlet. Chase remembered that Avery had once described it as heaven on earth. Avery had been bugging her for two years now to come to Boothbay Harbor to see their creation. *I guess this is as good a time as any to visit the old B and B.* She shook her head, knowing that she should have gone to visit already. *Some best friend I am. Get a room ready Avery—I'm on my way.*

Chapter 2

Chase flopped down on the bed. She'd been home long enough to pack clothes for a couple of weeks in Maine. She made reservations for a flight to Portland and a car. Rather than call Avery and let her know she had finally decided to visit, Chase planned on surprising her.

Chase pulled a bottle out of the six—pack she picked up at the liquor store. A lost job coupled with the memory of sharing this bed with her ex before she'd caught him cheating was as good as excuse as any to tie one on. She twisted the cap off and took a long swig. She leaned back against the headboard and closed her eyes, finally allowing the events of the day to sink in. She thought about calling Avery to vent, but knew if she did, she would blow the surprise and she didn't want to do that. Instead she decided to drink today away, and start fresh tomorrow.

She pulled her phone out of her pocket, turned it off and chucked it onto the nightstand. She looked at the bottle in her hand. *Looks like it's you and me tonight.*

Sometime during the night, Chase woke up from a dead sleep. She bolted up in bed and tried to adjust to the darkness. Momentarily disoriented, she waited for her eyes to adjust to the dark.

She wasn't sure what had woken her up, but she had a feeling something wasn't right. She glanced at the clock on the nightstand. 10:28 PM. She reached for her cell phone and turned it on. When no message notification popped up, she let out a sigh of relief. *Must have been a bad dream.* Chase turned the ringer off and laid the phone down. She pulled the covers back up and willed herself to sleep.

Chase woke up to light filtering through small gaps in the curtains. She squinted, blocking her eyes from the bright shafts of sunlight. Her mouth felt like a desert, dry with cactuses imbedded in her tongue. She glanced at the empty bottles on the night stand and groaned. *A pounding headache this morning is definitely not worth that!*

It suddenly dawned on her that her bladder was about to burst. She grabbed her crotch and ran to the bathroom. When she finished the business at hand, Chase looked at her reflection in the mirror. The dark circles under her eyes were a testament to her night of imbibing. Now that she was moving around, waves of nausea tickled her stomach. She put her hand to her mouth and willed it down. Throwing up had never been something she enjoyed.

Chase sat down on the edge of the bed and checked her phone. The message button was flashing, indicating she had new messages. She rolled her eyes. She punched in the number for her voicemail and waited for the impersonal voice to let her know she had new messages.

The first one was from Avery's mom. *"Chase, it's Barb. Avery's been in a car accident. She was airlifted to Mercy General in Portland. I'm not sure how bad it is yet. I'm catching the red—eye to Portland tonight. Call me as soon as you get this message. Hopefully, I'll have an update then."* Chase's breath caught in her throat. She suddenly knew her *bad* feeling last night was more than a bad dream. *Oh Avery, I'm coming sweetie, please be okay.*

The second message was from her mother. Chase's parents were retired snowbirds who wintered in Boca Raton. They had left last week, and as Chase listened to her mother's voice, she realized just how much she missed her. *"Chase, honey, it's your mom. We just heard the news about TransAir. That's horrible! Are you okay, honey? Your father is pacing all over the place worrying about you. Please call us as soon as you can. We love you honey."*

The third message was Avery's mom again. Her voice was quivered, and Chase could tell she was choking back sobs. Chase sat up and braced herself for the words she almost knew were coming. *"Chase, Avery's...gone. The doctor... said there was too much...internal bleeding. They tried... to save her. Oh Chase...I don't know...what I'm going to do...without her. Please call me."* The sound of her disconnecting the call rocked through the silence like a cannon.

Chase dropped the phone, her stomach heaving angrily. She ran to the bathroom and when she vomited violently, it had nothing to do with her hangover.

Chapter 3

Chase felt the plane start to descend and she looked out the window. As she watched the clouds separate, she saw the jagged shoreline come into view. She watched the blue—green of the Atlantic Ocean as it meandered along the rock—lined coast. No matter how many times she flew, it always felt different on this side of the cockpit.

Absentmindedly, she rubbed the small scar on her forefinger. She looked down at the small white line and smiled, remembering her reaction when Avery showed up at the tree house with a pocket knife.

"You want me to do what?" Chase stared at Avery incredulously.

"You have to cut your finger. It's the only way to be blood sisters."

Chase sighed. "I don't know. It's gonna hurt. Are you sure?"

"Positive. I saw it in a movie. You just have to cut it a little bit. Don't be such a wimp." She pushed the point of the knife along her finger, wincing when she broke the skin. "See, it's not so bad."

Chase took the knife from her fingers and pressed it against her finger. She was nervous, and she smiled at Avery for reassurance. Taking a deep breath, she pressed the knife into her finger. When she felt the blade pierce the skin, she dropped it and immediately stuck her finger in her mouth. "Ouch, that really hurt!"

Avery smiled ruefully. "I'm sorry." She held her finger towards Chase, and signaled for her to press their fingers together. "Okay, now we have to pledge to be blood sisters for life."

"Okay, how do we do that?" Chase waited, watching Avery's face scrunch up in concentration.

"All right, repeat after me. I, Avery Elizabeth Carson, do solemnly swear to be a blood sister for life."

"I, Avery Elizabeth..." She paused, catching the glare she got from Avery. She smirked, enjoying the fact that being a smart—ass annoyed Avery as much as it did. Chase cleared her throat. "I, Chase I do not like my middle name Berkley, do solemnly swear to be a blood sister for life."

Avery giggled. She knew Chase hated her middle name. She was named after her great—grandmother Josephine, whose French name was too antiquated to fit her. "I promise to share all my secrets, keep all of yours, take care of you always and love you more than a sister."

"I promise to share all my secrets, keep all of yours, take care of you always and love you more than a sister." Chase smiled. "Is that it?'

Avery shook her head yes. "Now we are joined for life. We won't keep any secrets from each other and nothing will ever come between us."

Chase jumped as the plane touched down, jolting her back to reality. She swiped at the tears that were forming in her eyes. She felt her heart gripped with immense sadness at the loss of her best friend. She hadn't let herself cry yet, and the enormity of her feelings threatened to burst through her fragile exterior like swollen flood waters over a weakened levee. She shook her head, willing the tears away and plastered a smile on her face. She would let herself cry soon, not today, but soon.

Chapter 4

Chase stared out over the waters of Linekin Bay. She watched the waves crash against the rocks and felt the cold November wind whip around her, effectively chilling her to the bone. She stood between Avery's parents, her arms linked with theirs. She wasn't sure how she would have survived this day without Joe and Barb Carson standing beside her.

As if knowing Chase needed strength, Barb leaned over, kissed her on the cheek and smiled understandingly. Chase thought it odd that Barb was providing strength and support to her, when in reality it should have been the other way around. She could not begin to fathom the heartache a parent would feel at losing a child. She felt the beginnings of anger start to well up inside her. Anger at the unfairness of the whole thing. Anger that her best friend was gone and she didn't get to say goodbye. Anger that someone as wonderful as Avery had been cut down in her prime. *Why does life have to be so fucking unfair?*

She tried to pay attention to the pastor that was leading the memorial service for Avery. Her church was the Boothbay Unitarian Universalist Church, which welcomed people of all beliefs. Chase had been surprised that Avery had attended church with any regularity, and that she hadn't ever mentioned it to her. *Or did she, and I just don't remember?* She mentally chided herself for the distance that had come between them. Life and work and the B & B and a plethora of unnamed reasons had kept them so busy the past few years that they hadn't had a real conversation in months.

She heard her inviting Barb to speak. Barb patted her hand gently then went and stood beside the pastor. Chase took in the serene look on Barb's face and it immediately calmed her. Chase watched her pull a piece of paper out of her pocket and unfold it against the wind.

"When Avery was little I used to read to her every night and then when she learned how to read, we took turns. One of her favorite authors was Walt Whitman. I remember the first time she read *Leaves of Grass,* she became fascinated by death." She gestured to the urn that held Avery's ashes. "I probably should have stopped letting her read Walt Whitman after that." This brought a chuckle from the few people assembled around her.

"But if I had stopped her, she never would have read her favorite poem. Those of you who were close to Avery..." Barb caught Chase's gaze and held it briefly then turned to Tess and smiled softly at her. "...know what a romantic she was." Barb paused, brushing a tear from her eye.

Chase didn't know what to make of the look Barb had given Tess. Hell, Chase really didn't know all that much about Tess Monahan. She was introduced as the woman that ran the bed and breakfast with Avery. Good friends perhaps, they had worked together for almost two years, but could she really be considered *close* to Avery. Chase decided to worry about that later.

Barb was silent for just a moment before continuing. "Avery was romantic at heart. She dreamed from an early age of meeting her soul mate and spending the rest of their lives together. I remember the day Avery found this poem. She came running home after school one day, yelling that I just had to read something. I did and I couldn't imagine what Avery had found so beguiling about it. So she explained it her way. I want to share it with you all today, for Avery. Then I will tell you why it was her favorite poem." Barb cleared her throat.

"OUT of the rolling ocean, the crowd, came a drop gently to me,
Whispering, I love you, before long I die,
I have travel'd a long way, merely to look on you, to touch you,
For I could not die till I once look'd on you,
For I fear'd I might afterward lose you.
Now we have met, we have look'd, we are safe;
Return in peace to the ocean, my love;
I too am part of that ocean, my love—we are not so much
separated;
Behold the great rondure—the cohesion of all, how perfect!
But as for me, for you, the irresistible sea is to separate us,

As for an hour, carrying us diverse—yet cannot carry us diverse for ever;
   Be not impatient—a little space—Know you, I salute the air, the ocean and the land,
   Every day, at sundown, for your dear sake, my love."

Barb allowed the words to sink in. To Chase, it sounded tragic and sad. Lovers that only had seconds together then one was tragically taken away, leaving the other one to forever stand at the ocean longing for another second. Chase couldn't help thinking that Avery had never found her one true love. She would never have her chance to stand at the ocean and long for the one she loved.

Barb folded the paper up and stuck it in her pocket. "I know it sounds sad. But Avery made it sound so wonderful, even as a child. She told me that it was romantic the thought of loving someone so much it was perfect. Even if you only had a moment with that person, it was the most amazing love you would ever know. Then after it was over, you always remembered that love and knew, just knew that someday you would be reunited. That's the love Avery always wanted. I'm happy to know she found it, even for just a brief moment." Barb looked at Tess and smiled softly at her.

Chase's stomach churned. She heard Tess whimper and turning she saw tears streaming down her face. She wasn't even sure she had heard correctly. Her mind was reeling, questions running through it. Had she heard right? *Were* Tess and Avery lovers? She'd suspected that Avery was a lesbian for sometime but to have it confirmed was entirely different. Shaking her head, she realized that the answers weren't coming. She looked to Barb for something to set her mind straight and her eyes pleaded with Chase to understand. She glanced at Joe and although he squeezed her arm, he would not meet her gaze.

Chase stared forward. She went through the rest of the memorial service in a daze. She half heard Barb say that Avery would have wanted her ashes sprinkled in the ocean so she could wash up day after day to see her lover and the life they had briefly shared. Avery had found peace and love with this woman and she wanted to be near her forever. Chase didn't know how to respond to the words *Avery's lover.* She was overwhelmed with sadness that she had allowed them to drift so far apart. Sure, they had a business together, but when was the last time they had talked, really talked? She couldn't remember. *I guess I took silent partner a little too literally.*

Chase watched as they sprinkled her ashes over the ocean, tiny fragments of them carried away on the wind. She said her own goodbye to Avery. She wondered at how little she really knew Avery and how long it would take her to come to terms with the secrets she had kept. She wondered if she would ever know why Avery kept pieces of herself private. She made her way back up to Serendipity with little more than a mind filled with confusion and a heart filled with aching sadness.

Chapter 5

Chase jumped at someone knocking on the door. She got up to answer it and faced Barb.

"Here, I thought you could use this." She handed Chase a glass of red wine.

"Thanks. Did you happen to bring the whole bottle?" Chase took the glass and pushed a lock of strawberry blonde hair behind her ear. "Wanna come in?"

Barb pulled a bottle from behind her back and smiled ruefully. "Please. I figured I better bring more than just a glass as a peace offering."

Chase sat down on the bed. "Yeah, that was a crappy way to find out about Avery."

Barb saw the hurt in her eyes. "I know. I'm so sorry. There just didn't seem to be a right time to tell you before the service. And then before I knew it, today was here and…"

"…and boom! There it is dropped in my lap just like that. Here you go Chase. Here's quite possibly the biggest part of Avery's life that she didn't share with you. Deal with it." Chase spoke without rancor, her words only hinting at the pain she felt.

Barb sipped her wine, watching Chase closely. The anguish in Chase's voice cut deeply. "I can only imagine how hard this must be for you. Maybe even harder than losing your best friend is finding out you didn't know her as well as you thought. Or thinking she purposely kept something from you."

Chase held her glass out for a refill. "I guess I just don't understand why she couldn't tell me."

"I don't think she purposely kept it from you. I think the relationship happened so fast that it even surprised her. I think she was worried about telling you, worried about your reaction. Then before she knew it, weeks turned into months and there just never seemed to be an opportunity to tell you. You both seemed to be traveling on separate paths and you didn't talk everyday like you used too."

Chase looked away and picked at an imaginary spot on her jeans. "I know, I was really busy the last couple of years. I take full responsibility for our chats being fewer and more far between. But why was she scared to tell me? I wouldn't have cared. I'm happy she found her soul mate, it doesn't matter that it is a woman."

Barb sat quietly, thinking of how best to answer that question. Revealing the answer meant letting Chase know that Avery shared *everything* with her mother, adding to the hurt of knowing there was a big part of Avery that she hadn't shared with Chase.

Barb took a deep breath. "Remember the Sadie Hawkins Day dance in seventh grade?"

Chase put her hand on her forehead and groaned. "Oh don't tell me, you know about that. I can't believe she told you."

Barb put her hand on Chase's shoulder and smiled. "She did tell me. And I will tell you the same thing I told Avery all those years ago. I couldn't have asked for a better friend for Avery. You grounded her. I never worried about the choices she would make because I knew she always considered what you would do in the same situation. You know Avery looked up to you. She loved you so much. I wondered if you ever suspected. I now know the answer to that is no."

Chase looked at Barb, confusion in her eyes. "Suspected what? I don't get it."

Barb patted Chase's hand softly. "No, I don't imagine you do. Avery was in love with you. All those years ago in the tree house when you kissed her, she felt something. Perhaps it was just a crush at first, but as you got older, I believe it developed into love for you." Barb chuckled softly. "Poor thing, I remember how incredibly confused she was that night. She came home rambling about a kiss and feeling something and girls. Honestly, I was just as confused as you are now. I made her sit down and tell me the whole story."

"I never knew. Why didn't she ever tell me?"

"Do you remember what you said when she asked you to kiss her again?"

Chase closed her eyes and transported herself back to that moment. She could feel the heat rise in her cheeks when she imagined Avery's lips on hers. *You're a girl.* The words came crashing back to her, no longer buried deep in her subconscious. "Oh."

"I don't think Avery ever understood why it mattered to you that she was a girl. But it did, and for that reason she never told you how she really felt. She resolved that night to never bring it up again. You didn't and soon life was back to normal. Or at least back to where you were before the kiss. That was so hard for her. But she wouldn't risk losing you as a friend. That she couldn't bear. It was easier for her to hide what she felt from you."

Chase looked chagrined. "I'm so sorry that I ever said that. I wish she would have told me."

Barb shook her head no. "Woulda, coulda, shoulda. Would it have made a difference?"

"I," Chase paused. "I don't know. I don't know if it would have changed things." Pain flashed in her eyes. "I guess we'll never know."

"Chase, don't beat yourself up. If the fates wanted her to tell you, she would have. I think you two were destined to be friends. She needed that more than anything. And you were the best friend she ever had."

"Well she is…was the best friend I've ever had. I'm sorry I went AWOL the last few years. I'm sorry I didn't get to hear her tell me about Tess. I would have liked to know Avery in love."

"Oh honey, you did know her in love. It was a different time and a different person, but she was the same Avery. She did miss you, but I can tell you even today, you are firmly imbedded in her heart."

Chase smiled somberly. "The same goes for me. Thanks for telling me about…you know. It helps." She gestured at the bottle in Barb's hand. "Better finish that up. No sense in wasting good wine."

Barb divided the remaining wine between the two of them. "You know, we'll get through this together. That includes Tess." Barb caught Chase's raised eyebrow. "She's a good girl, Chase. If you give her a chance, I think you will see what we all see in her and why Avery fell in love with her."

"I know. I'll try." Chase cocked her head and smirked at Barb. "So tell me, just how did Avery and Tess get together? I see she forgot about me quick enough." Her wink belied any hurt feelings.

Barb laughed. "That's easy enough. Well *my* take on it is easy enough. For a better perspective you will have to ask Tess. Tess started working here about two years ago right after you and Avery bought the place. For the first six months everything was great. Avery and Tess worked well together, despite neither of them having any experience. You know Avery's background and Tess, she escaped here from California, but that is another story entirely. Anyway, I'm straying. At the six months mark, Avery called me and asked me to come visit. She had a rather perplexing issue she needed help handling."

Chase couldn't remember Avery telling her anything about a *perplexing issue* eighteen months ago, but then again, she didn't tell me she was gay. "What was it?"

"Better to ask me *who* was it?" Barb smiled cryptically.

"Okay, who was it?"

"Tess Monahan. I know that doesn't make any sense, but it will when I am done. About six months after Avery officially opened Serendipity, Tess went from sweet, free—spirited, carefree Tess to Oscar the Grouch."

Chase tried to picture the woman being anything but kind. Chase had done her best to avoid Tess, not sure of herself to give her a fair shot considering the circumstances. But she had observed her, and knew she was one of the kindest people she had met. "Tess? Oscar the Grouch?"

Barb rolled her eyes. " Oh very much so! She was Oscar on trash day. Anyway, Avery wanted me to come visit. She wanted an opinion other than her own. After all, they worked together in close quarters and maybe she was just reading her wrong. I mean when you see someone day in and day out, even the best of friends can get on each other's nerves. Hell, Joe and I fight like cats and dogs sometimes. It's gotten a bit better now that Joe went through the *men*—opause." She held her fingers up in quote signs to emphasize her point.

Chase laughed out loud. "Barb, you are not right."

Barb laughed and shook her head in agreement. "You got that right."

"So what was your conclusion, doctor?"

"Well I visited for two weeks. I watched those two girls together. They were both so jumpy anytime they were around each other. Trying so hard to avoid one another, but making sure the other was aware of her. Since they didn't speak to each other except for work related issues, I got to spend a lot of time with both of them. I had a lot of one—on—one conversations with Tess. She's got a good head on her shoulders. And of course, Avery talked my ear off any chance she got. As an outside observer, it was easier to pick up on the subtle nuances that they were missing in each other. I've never seen two more expressive people, and yet they both missed it."

"Missed what?"

Barb put her hand up. "I'm getting there. Avery wanted to know my take on it. Did Tess tell me what was wrong? She wanted to know if it was something she had done or was doing? You know Avery was a fixer. She never wanted anything broken, and if it was, she wanted to know how to fix it. In this instance it was a little more difficult than just putting some duct tape on it. I told her it wasn't anything she had done, although if she wanted to make it right, there was lots she could do. I remember her words that night to me. *Tell me what's wrong. Tell me what I can do to fix it.*"

Chase smiled. "Avery always had a hero complex. Funny, maybe she needed fixing most of all."

Barb smiled cryptically. "You could be more right than you know."

"So what did you tell her?" Chase was anxious for the answer. It was one piece in the puzzle of Avery's life that was now laid before her.

"I looked her square in the eyes and I told her the issue is Tess is in love with you and if I know my daughter as well as I think I do, I would say you are in love with her."

Chase was quiet for a moment, absorbing this piece of information, trying to fit it in the whole picture. When she finally spoke, her voice was low. "What did Avery say?"

"Well when she picked her jaw up off the floor, I could tell she wanted to argue with me. Some nonsense about being so far out in left field that I couldn't see home plate. Funny girl. It was obvious it was going to take a little while for her to realize what I knew two days into my visit. I told her this is the situation, your heart will tell you what to do to make it better. And trust me, Tess is feeling as lost as you are right now. Don't shut her out."

"So what happened? Well I mean I know what happened, duh, but what happened then?"

Barb shrugged her shoulders. "I don't know. My plane left the following morning. She must have figured it out, because Avery called me three days later and said that she was taking Tess out on a date. And the rest, as they say, is history." Barb rose and walked to the door. "Tonight is Joe's last night here. He has to go back to work on Monday so he is flying out early tomorrow. Will you please have dinner with us?"

Chase smiled warmly. "Of course I will. I do want to spend some time with Joe before he goes."

"And Chase?"

"Yes?"

"Please don't be upset with Avery. She really did love you and never meant to hurt you. I hope you can accept that and give Tess a chance. And remember, now that Avery is gone, Serendipity is officially yours. She's probably scared that another part of her life is going to get stolen from her."

"I know." Chase waited till Barb shut the door then she leaned back on her pillow. She felt the first tears trickle down her face. She covered her face, hoping that they wouldn't hear her sob. She had finally let herself cry.

Chapter 6

Chase threw a sweatshirt on over her t—shirt and followed the smell of fresh coffee. She ended up in the kitchen, which ran the length of the back of the house. Looking out the windows past the enclosed solarium that acted as the dining area for Serendipity, she watched the angry waves crashing into the rocky shoreline. The fog hadn't yet rolled in enough to block her view of the tiny islands that dotted the water throughout the bay. She knew the white caps indicated a change in the weather and she shivered at an imaginary breeze.

"They are forecasting rain this afternoon. It's a perfect day to curl up with a good book and a great bottle of wine."

Chase turned to Barb and smiled brightly. "I'm game. Good morning."

"Good morning, dear. Did you sleep well?"

"Mmm…actually yes. I slept like a rock. There is something about hearing the ocean at night that lulls you into a deep sleep. I know why Avery loved this place." Chase raised her arms over her head and stretched. "There is something so peaceful about the ocean. I just wish I would have made it out here before…" The words trailed off, she couldn't bring herself to say before Avery passed away.

Sensing the loss for words, Barb just nodded in agreement. "Yes, there is, but be ware, the winters are rough. Fortunately, when Avery was redoing the house, she had them install central heat."

"But what about the old steam heat radiators in the rooms?" Chase looked confused.

"Ambiance, nothing more. Avery figured that added to the charm of this house." She winked at Chase. "Obviously fooled you pretty well."

"Yes, she did. I couldn't have asked for a better partner to handle the details and play with my money." Chased teased.

"Too true. Well, can I get you a cup of coffee? It's a fresh pot. We are in between seasons right now, so the only guests you will be fighting for coffee are Tess and me. Still cream only? We have this yummy Tiramasu creamer."

"Yeah, just never could do it black. Too strong for my blood." Chase watched as Barb poured flavored creamer and coffee into two mugs. She inhaled, appreciating the aroma of good coffee. She reached for the mugs of steaming coffee as Barb handed them to her. "Joining me?"

Barb shook her head and picked up her own cup off the counter. "Uh—uh. But I think someone else could use a cup." Chase followed her eyes outside and saw Tess standing at the edge of the yard. "She could use a friend right now."

Chase shifted uncomfortably, not sure she was emotionally ready to face Tess. So far, Chase had done a great job avoiding her. The hurt of losing Avery coupled with the sting of finding out she hadn't told her about Tess was still close to the surface. She would have liked some time to let the wounds heal. She tried to accept that it was not Tess's fault. She was probably hurting just as much, if not more. "Yeah, okay."

Chase walked quietly across the yard, balancing the mugs of coffee. She looked at Tess standing alone, her long blond hair buffeted by the strong wind. She had a heavy blanket wrapped tightly around her shoulders, but Chase could see she had not changed out of her pajamas. Her feet were bare against the cold, wet ground.

Sensing someone behind her, Tess turned to face Chase. She tried to smile, but it stopped at her mouth. Her light blue eyes were tinged with red and immense sadness was reflected in her face. She took the mug Chase held towards her and gripped it against her body, allowing the heat to warm her body. "We used to have coffee out here every morning. I was always up early, waiting patiently for her to finish her beauty sleep and meet me out here. I keep expecting her to come bounding down the steps, yelling I'm here." Tess absentmindedly rubbed her cheek. "She would always kiss me on the cheek, laughing about not subjecting me to dragon breath first thing in the morning."

Chase willed her body to move and she put her hand lightly on Tess's arm. "I'm sorry for your loss. You must have really loved her."

"I do, more than life itself. She is the light of my life. I know that sounds so cliché, but before I met Avery, I was lost, only I didn't know I was. I was floundering around in the dark, existing, not really living. She showed me what life is really about. It's not about a job, or how wealthy you are, or what you have, it's about love. Pure and simple. Avery taught me how to love. She lit up a whole world that I had forgotten was there. She brought me home again. I came half way around the globe to get there."

Chase looked at Tess, slightly confused. "I think there is a story behind that statement, maybe you will tell me. I wish Avery had told me about you. To be honest, you both are strangers to me." She said it without rancor, just sadness.

Tess smiled warmly. "I'm sorry for that. I wish you could know just how much Avery struggled with not telling you. No matter how happy we were, there was always something missing. Some piece of her life that wasn't in harmony. I know she wanted to tell you, and I'm certain she would have soon...if she were here." Tess stopped, her words catching in her throat. She swallowed and tried to hold it together. "I feel like I know you so well. Avery talked about you all the time. I hope you decide you want to get to know me. I think we could both use a friend."

Chase was quiet for a moment then turned and looked at Tess. She saw her own pain reflected in Tess's eyes. She linked her arm through hers and nodded. "I know we could both use a friend."

It was a tenuous start to their relationship, but a start anyway. They stood quietly, two women joined by heartache and loss. They watched the waves crash over the rocks, water churning violently. The foam caught on the wind, spraying them gently with droplets of moisture. In their hearts, they said a silent hello to Avery, feeling her presence all around them and in that moment, began to heal.

Chapter 7

Chase put the car in park in front of the United Airlines gate and turned to Barb. "Are you sure you don't want me to park and come inside with you? You still have two hours till your flight. I can keep you company."

"Don't be silly, I'm fine. I brought the latest Mary Higgins Clark mystery. I'm dying to read it. Besides, you need to get back to the house. Tess is probably going nuts right now. Poor thing, she can't cook worth a lick. If it weren't for Avery, I think she would have starved by now. If you let her plan the meal for Thanksgiving, you will probably be eating a tv dinner."

"Great. So I guess I'll be the resident chef for awhile. How long will you be gone again?" Chase's blue eyes looked desperate and Barb had to laugh.

"Just a week. I am sure you two can survive that long. Joe and I will spend Thanksgiving with the family then we will be back up here for a few weeks. As much as I don't want to think about it, we have to start thinking about the will. Avery made her father and I the executors. I spoke to Avery's attorney, Jude Stafford, yesterday to get an update on the proceedings. She has already filed a petition to probate the will in the Probate Court. She doesn't expect there will be a hearing, since Avery's will and testament will be uncontested. Now we just wait to hear from the court. Then the fun starts."

"Fun?" Chase regarded her curiously.

"Oh yes, my dear, the fun. You've never settled a will before, especially with property involved, I gather. Let's just say it's a good thing Avery didn't have any brothers or sisters. There's nothing like family fighting over a dead loved one's hundred year old pocket watch that doesn't keep the right time." Barb's eyes twinkled.

Chase chuckled. "You are not right. I'm going to miss you." She leaned over and gave Barb a quick kiss on the cheek. "Give Joe a hug for me and Happy Thanksgiving to you both."

"Happy Thanksgiving to you. Try to make sure Tess gets fed something more than chicken nuggets." Barb winked at Chase. "You're a good woman, Chase. Thank you for being here for me. That means a lot." She stepped out of the car and grabbed her bag out of the back seat. "We'll see you in a week. I love you, kiddo."

Chase smiled at the endearment. Barb had called her kiddo from the first day she met her twenty—three years ago. "I love you too."

She watched Barb walk through the automatic doors and waived when she turned around one last time. Sighing softly, she shifted the car in drive and pulled away from the curb. She found her way back to I—295 and started the trip back to Boothbay Harbor.

She scanned the radio stations and stopped when she heard "1999" by Prince. Her thoughts flew to the summer after third grade. The first summer she had spent with Avery. Chase's parents had given her a small boombox for her ninth birthday and in truth, probably should have invested in Energizer stock at the same time. Chase could still remember the first time they heard the song.

"Chase, let's party like it's 1999." Avery spun around the tree house, her body bouncing to the fast beat. She grabbed Chase's hands and pulled her up, making her dance right along with her. "What do you think we will be doing in 1999? That is sooo far away."

Mentally Chase calculated the years. They would both be twenty—five years old. "I don't know. I guess we will be married and have a house and kids and a dog. We will be twenty—five after all."

Avery giggled hysterically. "Twenty—five. We will be ancient. What do you want to be when you're old? I want to be an actress. I'm gonna be just like Jo from *Facts of Life*. She is so cool. She isn't girly and she gets to ride a motorcycle. I bet she is just as cool in real life. Yep, that's what I am going to be. What about you, Chase? What do you want to be?"

Chase thought for a moment. "A pilot. I want to fly airplanes."

Avery wrinkled her nose up. "Ahh, you only want to be that 'cause you just got to fly in one. Besides, girls aren't allowed to be pilots, silly. Only boys can be pilots. That's what my Uncle Mitch said. You could be a flight attendant. You'd still get to go everywhere."

Chase shook her head. "Who says I can't be a pilot? Just 'cause your dumb uncle says it, doesn't mean it's true. I can be whatever I want. You just wait and see. Besides, how do you know you're going to be an actress?"

Avery lip jutted out and she glared at Chase. "I say so. And don't call my uncle dumb…only I'm allowed to do that."

Chase laughed. "Okay fine. I'm still gonna be a pilot. You can be an actress."

Avery stopped dancing and looked into Chase's eyes. "Are we still going to be best friends? We're supposed to be best friends for life."

Chase smiled. "Of course, dummy. We'll always be best friends. When you're rich and famous and you have your own plane, I'm gonna fly it for you. That way we'll see each other all the time. Of course, you will have to pay me lots and lots of money."

Avery raised her nose in the air and acted like a snob. "But of course. I will be the most famous actress ever and I will be rich so I can afford to pay you a gazillion dollars."

Chase doubled over laughing. "I thought you wanted to be Jo, not Blaire."

Chase caught herself smiling at the memory. She had followed her dream of becoming a pilot, and wouldn't have changed it for anything. She loved flying. Loved the exhilaration she felt when the plane picked up speed and the wings caught the air, in that first second when the wheels leave the ground she truly felt alive.

Of course, Avery had changed her mind several times about her intended career by the time she left for college in the fall of 1993. She finally graduated with a degree in Marketing from the University of Notre Dame. Avery's ability to think outside the box gave her a competitive edge and she got hired right after college by a large marketing firm in Boston. She worked her way up to a corner office and handled several well known, multi—million dollar accounts.

To an outsider, she appeared happy--a woman that had made it big in a man's world. Then one day three years ago, she quit her job. She moved to Maine and fell in love with the coast. She convinced Chase to buy into an old bed and breakfast named Serendipity, which at the time was not much more than a run—down house on a great piece of coastline. Anyone that knew of her spontaneous decision couldn't have been more shocked. It appeared Avery had gone a little crazy, but she wouldn't be detoured, and Chase would give her friend anything. It took a year to completely overhaul the property, and when it was finished Avery had reopened it under the original name, ready to take on boarders. At that point, everyone decided she *had* completely lost her mind.

Chase felt guilt start to overwhelm her. In the three years that they'd owned Serendipity, she hadn't made it there to visit one time. Avery kept her up to date on the progress and when it opened she had invited her to the grand opening, but Chase had been too busy. Now, Chase was too late. If only she could have slowed down for just a minute. Maybe that's why Avery had wanted her to visit so much, besides wanting to see her best friend. Avery had finally figured out how to slow down and really live life and perhaps she wanted to share that with Chase.

Chase shook her head realizing that though she hadn't chosen to get out of the fast lane, life had made the choice for her. Life had grabbed her by the collar and forced her to stop and look at her life. Unfortunately, when Chase looked around she didn't see what she had wanted to see. She wanted her best friend now. For the past few years, she had only caught glimpses and now it seemed to Chase, glimpses were all she was left with.

Chase slowed the car down and pulled onto Maine Road Twenty—Seven, the road that went to Boothbay Harbor. She had left I—295 and driven up US 1 without seeing any of it. Shaking her head, she realized she was still on auto—pilot. It was ironic that when she was in the air, Chase processed even the most minute detail. She didn't miss anything. How could it be so different all of the other times? Determined to honor Avery's memory, she forced herself to focus and to appreciate everything around her. *Avery I let you down so much the past few years. I promise you that no matter what it takes, I'm going to find what you did. Forgive me for being so late.*

Chapter 8

Chase put the rest of the turkey away, grabbed two beers and joined Tess in the large living room that served as the common area for guests at Serendipity. There was a large fireplace with a stone mantle that went all the way up to the ceiling. Mounted above it was a large flat screen tv, that could be viewed from both couches as well as the oversized recliners that were scattered around the room. The refinished hardwood floors had a distinctively vintage squeak when you walked across them. Avery believed that retaining some of the original charm of the Victorian helped guests feel like they were lost in time when they visited Serendipity, and that added to the experience of the whole stay.

Chase plopped down on the couch beside Tess and handed her a beer. She watched her twist the top off and take a long swig. "Thanks. And thank you for dinner. I have to admit you might almost cook better than Avery…almost." Tess looked up. "Sorry babe."

Chase rubbed her stomach and groaned. "I'm stuffed. I don't even think I can have another slice of pumpkin pie for my bedtime snack. What are we watching?" she asked, gesturing to the tv.

"It's the end of the Seahawks—Cowboys game. I can change it if you want." Tess reached for the remote.

"Nah, this is fine. I don't think I have actually watched a whole game since I was a kid. My granddad and I used to hide out in the basement and watch them together. You know, come to think of it, I think he still owes me a Big Mac from the 1983 Super Bowl."

Tess chuckled. "I'd say it is way past time to collect."

"Well, besides the statute of limitations on Super Bowl bets expiring, my time ran out a couple of years ago." Chase caught the look of confusion on Tess's face. "He passed away two years ago."

"I'm sorry." Tess was silent for a moment. "How did he die? Not like that's any of my business."

"No, it's fine. Alzheimer's disease. He got really bad towards the end. That was really hard for me. He and I were always close. When I would go visit, he had no clue who I was. He thought I was my mom towards the end, but only because I think he remembered her as a kid. I try to remember him as the granddad I watched football with twenty—five years ago." Even as Chase talked about it her voice quivered a little. "Anyway that was the really long way to tell you that football is fine."

Tess laughed softly. "It's okay. Thank you for telling me."

Chase smiled. "So what about you? Any childhood bets someone still owes you for? We could hire someone. You know, put out a hit. Break a few fingers."

"My, my Chase. This is an entirely different side to you. I had no idea you had ties to the mafia. And a little evil streak to boot. I think I'll get you that Big Mac, just to stay on your good side." Tess held her bottle out to Chase and toasted her. "Cheers to being the resident bad girl."

Chase laughed out loud. "A bad girl? Hmmm, I don't know about that. Apparently, Ms. Carson did not share some of her more, ahhh, adventurous stories with you. I think it may be time to open up some of her case files."

Tess's eyes twinkled mischievously. "No, I think she didn't share those with me, or at least not all of them. Do tell."

"Hmm, where can I start?" Chase's forehead wrinkled in concentration. "Okay, did she ever tell you the story of how we met?"

"Yeah, you met in school. Third grade right?"

"Yes, but I wouldn't exactly say we met on amicable terms." Chase spoke cryptically.

Tess narrowed her eyes and cocked her head. "I'm confused…"

"Let's just say your little Avery wasn't always the sweet and innocent girl she purported to be." Chase smiled and winked. "She was, uhm, enterprising enough to make her introduction my first day there."

Tess smiled mischievously. "My Avery? Anything but sweet? I can't imagine that."

Chase laughed out loud. "Man, I could tell you some tales that would make your toes curl. She may have been sweet most of the time, but she had a mean streak in her that more than made up for it."

"And let me guess, it all started in third grade?" Tess stood up and went to stoke the fire. She glanced at Chase, her eyes filled with curiosity. "So tell me the story."

Chase drained the rest of her beer and set the bottle down on an antique chest that served as a coffee table. She waited until Tess sat down again before starting her story. "It was the spring of third grade. My dad got transferred for work. I wanted to stay and finish the year out, but with us moving states, that wasn't an option."

"What does your dad do?"

"Did. He is retired now. He was a team physician for the Colts. When they moved to Indy from Baltimore, we made the move too. It was hard for me to start a new school in the middle of the year, but I was determined to make a go of it. My first day we watched a film in science class and that is when Avery decided to welcome the new kid."

Tess rolled her eyes. "Oh lord, what did she do?"

"I was sitting there minding my own business. Had my feet up in the chair in front of me just chillin'. I guess Avery saw this as the perfect opportunity to initiate me. When the movie was over and I started to get up, my shoelaces were tied around the chair. I yanked it out, lost my balance and fell flat on my face in front of the whole class."

Chase caught Tess snickering. "Don't laugh, Monahan. That was traumatizing for a nine—year old. Basically, my life was over after that." Chase glared at Tess.

"I'm only laughing because I'm picturing Avery crawling around on the floor, trying to tie your shoes to the chair and not getting caught. I don't know how she kept her big mouth shut long enough to do it."

Chase burst out laughing. "Yeah, I guess I didn't think about it that way. She did have a big mouth."

"Our Avery had the biggest mouth east of the Mississippi and that includes a lot of New Yorkers." Tess wiped tears of laughter from her face. "So, what did you do to pay her back?"

Chase put her hand on her chest and stared agape at Tess. "Me? Do something to pay her back? Why I'm too good to do that." She smiled innocently at Tess.

Tess waved her hands at Chase to stop. "Quit making me laugh or I'm going to pee my pants. I may have just met you, but I think

I've got you pegged enough to know that you wouldn't have taken that *lying down.*" She smirked at Chase.

Chase glared at her. "Oh, lying down, real funny, Monahan. All of a sudden you're a freakin' comedian." She cocked her head and squinted at Tess. "Fair enough. I did get her back. Once I got myself untangled, I chased her down the hall and punched her right in the nose. Sure as hell surprised the shit outta her. Next thing I know, we are in the principle's office waiting for our parents to get there. Our punishment was after school detention. I think Avery must have respected me for standing up to her because after an hour in detention we were cool. We've been best friends ever since."

"Man, I would have paid money to see you two stuck in detention. I'm sure that made up for some of the stunts you guys pulled later on." Tess stood up and reached for Chase's empty beer bottle. "Want another one?"

Chase shrugged. "Sure, why not?" She stood up slowly. "I think I'm going to be bad and have another slice of pie...with extra whip cream. You in?"

Tess rubbed her belly and smiled wickedly. "You're killing me, Berk. You know I can't say no to pie."

Chapter 9

Chase wiped the extra whip cream off her plate and licked it off her finger with an appreciative groan. "Mmmmm, I think I outdid myself with this one."

"You okay over there? You sound like you are having an orgasm." Tess shoved her last bight in her mouth. "Although, I will admit it is some good shit."

"This is way better than any orgasm I've ever had, and it doesn't come with a side of drama either."

Tess smiled warmly. "Honey, it's good, I'll give you that. But if it's better than any orgasm you've ever had, you haven't been with the right person. It's time you started to live a little. Now that you are done with that boy of yours, you need to find a man that will rock your world."

Chase shrugged. "I don't know, maybe I need to follow Avery's lead and try a woman. Wanna help me find one?" She chuckled at Tess's shocked expression. "I'm kidding."

"You know we are always trying to recruit new members, but being a card carrying member of the rainbow coalition isn't something you just do at random. You're either gay or you aren't. Simple as that."

Chase's eyes narrowed thoughtfully. "How did you know you were gay?"

"From my first crush on our next door neighbor when I was four years old."

Chase looked surprised. "Are you serious? You remember that?"

"Sure. I came out of the womb carrying my card. I'm gay for life."

"I imagine that was somewhat painful for your mom, especially if it was laminated." Chase laughed at herself when Tess groaned.

"Sorry, way too much alcohol. After a few beers I start to think I am actually funny."

"Uhhh, yeah, alcohol will do that. I think it would be better if you keep your talent limited to the kitchen."

"Ouch, below the belt. Keep drinking, pretty soon even you will think I'm funny."

"Looking? I already think that." Tess said with a smirk.

Chase glared at Tess, trying to keep from laughing. "You are evil, Monahan. I am starting to reverse my previous opinion of you. I think Avery must have corrupted you. Certainly you weren't this mean before you met her."

Tess took a pull of her beer and regarded Chase thoughtfully. "On the contrary, I'm way nicer now. I was a ruthless bitch before I met Avery. Nothing like the love of a good woman, or in your case a man, to put you on the straight and narrow. I think we mellowed each other out. Before Avery, if I wanted to chill, it would take at least half a joint." She caught Chase's shocked expression. "Hey California man, that's what we do. When I felt a little uptight, I hit a vending machine on the corner and five minutes later, everything was cool."

"Are you serious? You got pot from a vending machine." Chase stared at Tess incredulously.

"Well I may have exaggerated a tad, but it is really easy to come by, which was a good thing most days. I was so wired living out there."

"Man, what had you so wired? Job or relationship? And how on earth did you get to BFE, Maine?" Chase rattled the questions off like a machine gun. She gestured to her beer and her eyes registered an apology. "I'm sorry, that's really none of my business. Besides thinking I am really funny, this stuff makes me talk way too fast and say things I shouldn't say."

Tess dismissed the apology with a wave of her hand. "Please don't apologize. If I let a little thing like no tact," she said with a wink, "bother me, I would have to go back to smoking pot, and I gained way too much weight doing that. Always had the munchies. That's the one thing they don't lie about. Do you want the unabridged version?"

Chase glanced at her watch. "Yeah, of course the long version. I've got nothing but time. Ahh, a life of leisure."

Tess drained her beer. "Okay, but I'm going to have to have another one of these to get through it. You want another one?"

Chase nodded yes and watched Tess leave the room, only to return a moment later with two fresh beers. "Now where was I? Let's see, I'm originally from Connecticut... Hartford. Your typical WASP. I graduated in 1987 with a degree in biomedical engineering from Yale and after all of that, I decided infectious diseases just weren't my bag. All of a sudden, I was twenty-two and I didn't have any idea what I wanted to do with my life."

Chase raised her eyebrow and looked at Tess. "Engineering? Damn, woman, you didn't tell me that you're a genius. I'm impressed."

Tess snorted. "*Was* a genius. I killed a lot of the brain cells over the last twenty years. I probably couldn't tell you a thing I learned in college. So much for a hundred thou in tuition."

Chase looked confused. "Twenty years? How old are you?" Chase shrugged and smiled ruefully. "I know, I know, but we've already established I have no tact."

"I'm forty—three. Not exactly old...yet."

"Wow! I had you pegged at like thirty—five. You look really good."

Tess smiled. "Thanks. It must be all of my clean living. And they say pot is bad for you." She took a pull of her beer and jumped when some of it dripped out the side of her mouth and dribbled down the front of her sweater. "Shit! That's cold." She glared at Chase when she started to laugh. "Shut it, Berk! Damn bottle must have a hole in it."

Chase struggled to catch her breath as she doubled over laughing. "Yeah, must be the bottle. I'm sure it's not the user at all." She snorted when Tess gave her the evil eye. "Okay, okay. I'll stop. So, before you killed all your brain cells and forgot how to drink out of a bottle, how did you get to California?"

"Before I tell you that, I have to clarify that I wasn't bottle fed, I was breast fed." She smiled wickedly. "And despite my issues with a bottle, I have no problem with nipples." Tess laughed when Chase groaned loudly. "Yeah, I know, that was pretty bad. Anyway, there I was, twenty—two years old, and didn't have a fucking clue about anything. I was pretty lost. The only thing I had managed to do with some finality was come out of the closet. Yale may be known for academics, but let me tell you, the campus is full of some beautiful women. Add smart to the package and I am done."

"You didn't come out before? Why not…especially if you knew all along?"

Tess shrugged. "I was scared I guess. My family is super religious. Being gay didn't exactly fit the plans that my parents had for me. My dad was a minister in a Protestant church and when I came out to my family, they gave me an ultimatum. Shape up or ship out."

"Shape up? What was their definition of shape up?"

"I guess I should have said *straighten* up. They told me I couldn't be gay so I left."

"To California?"

Tess nodded. "Yes, San Francisco to be exact. One of my roommates from Yale had moved out there and was always trying to get me to move out there. It seemed like a great time to do it. Of course, I didn't have much choice and at the time, I had to get away from my family or go crazy. They wouldn't let my sisters talk to me. It was really rough the first couple of years."

"I can only imagine how hard it must have been. I don't even want to think about what it would be like to have my family disown me. My mom and dad are all I have."

"The first few months I didn't think I would make it. I came close to picking up the phone a hundred times and begging to come home. I would have done anything to get them back, even pretend to be straight. But Shane stopped me every time."

"Shane? Who is he? Someone you met in California."

"*She* was my roommate, and off and on again girlfriend. She was pretty out and proud and wasn't going to let me go back in the closet. So bottom line, I never called and never ducked back in the closet. Besides Shane's influence in my personal life, she gave me some direction in my professional life, or should I say she pulled me in her direction. Shane was crazy about video games, from the first time she played Pong to surviving college on MS. Pacman. Her favorite movie was *Tron*."

"So Shane turned you into a gamer and you traveled around the world and won Super Mario brothers championships?" Chase smiled, amused with herself for being so clever.

Tess's jaw dropped. "Wow, yes, exactly! How did you know?"

Chase looked surprised. "Really? That was right?"

"Uhm, no, not really. Do I look like that big a dork? Actually, Shane went to work at SEGA, developing gaming software. The company was fairly new and the battle for the next, greatest game system was raging, so they hired pretty much anyone that had some wits about them. I had a degree from Yale, so they figured I must be pretty smart. The next thing I know, Shane and I are working on the team that is developing some pretty kick—ass games."

Chase looked impressed. "That's cool. Which games?"

Tess smiled mischievously. "I could tell you, but then I'd have to kill you. Let's just say it was a certain mammal that gave Mario a run for his money." Tess saw Chase's blank expression and laughed. "Sorry, I guess you have to be into video games to know that one."

Chase shook her head in agreement. "I guess so. It's kinda cool though. I've never known anyone that invented video games."

"Well, I'm glad to know I rate pretty high in the Chase Berkley book of cool."

Chase smiled warmly. "Yeah, you're up there. I should have figured Avery would pick someone spectacular to fall in love with. Speaking of you and Avery, how did you happen to end up here from San Francisco?"

"Hmm, that is my *man, it's a really small world* story. The marketing firm that Avery worked for in Boston handled all of our advertising. When she came on board, she took our account over from some guy that had just made partner. We didn't spend a whole lot in advertising and she was new, so it made sense to give the rookie the smaller accounts. Avery and I talked a few times over the next few years, but it was always work related. Then one day about three years ago, she resigned. Just dropped off the face of the earth. A year later, she sent out a mass email announcing the grand opening of the Serendipity bed and breakfast, with an invitation to be among the first to stay there."

Chase smiled, reminiscing about Avery. "Yeah, that sounds like Avery. She probably copied her contacts before she left the firm just so she could market Serendipity when she got it up and running."

Tess smiled. "Yeah, that was our Avery. Always networking. I was intrigued by the email. I had struggled through fifteen years of ups and downs with SEGA. More downs than ups I think. Hence the little issue." She pinched her thumb and forefinger together and held them to her lips. "But I never inhaled."

Chase laughed out loud. "No, Bill, I'm sure you didn't. Just like I'm sure Monica didn't swallow."

Tess made a face. "Ooh, gross. That is one of the reasons I am glad I am not into guys. Just couldn't quite get my head around *that* head. Anyway, I think I was ready for a break. I decided to fly out here and stay for a couple of weeks. Avery and I got to know each other outside the office and found out we got along pretty well. I joked about quitting my job and living here full time, of course, I was just teasing. Avery didn't think so. She said she thought that was a great idea. She realized running a B and B was a little more work than she thought and she was looking for a partner to help out with the business side of it. I must have smoked enough to be slightly delusional as well, because I flew back out to San Francisco and quit my job. I gave up my apartment, said goodbye to life in the fast lane and hello to Boothbay Harbor."

"Wow. You just gave it all up, no questions asked. Left everything that you knew. Talk about a leap of faith." Chase stared at Tess incredulously. "I don't know if I could ever do that."

"Well I had already done it once, not by my choice of course, but I had first—hand experience with walking away from the only life you know." Tess was quiet for a moment, as if trying to decide what to say next. "I don't know if this one was a leap of faith. I think it was more a leap of hope, if that makes sense. I already knew wherever I ended up, I would be all right, but this time I *hoped* for something better than all right. I wanted wonderful. It took six months, and not six easy months either, for us to figure out that wonderful meant running this place as life partners and not just business partners. I went to bed one night just existing and woke up the next morning really living. I felt at home for the first time in twenty years. I lived more in the eighteen months I was with Avery than any of the forty years leading up to that." She swiped at a single tear that threatened to roll down her cheek and smiled sheepishly. "Sorry, I can't talk about it yet without getting a little emotional."

Chase wiped her own eyes and tried to laugh. "Don't be sorry. I miss her too. You can't expect to get over Avery in less than a month. I hope I find love like that one day." She smiled warmly at Tess and then snapped her fingers, an epiphany hitting her. "Don't you think it's kinda ironic?"

Tess cocked her head and looked quizzically at Chase. "What's ironic?"

"Serendipity." Chase announced assuredly, as if Tess should be able to read her mind. "It's ironic that this place is named Serendipity and that you stumbled, quite by accident, onto the most wonderful relationship of your life. You weren't even looking for it."

"Hmmm, interesting." She looked away and pondered the sweet irony of it all. "Yeah, it is ironic. The one time in life I think irony worked in my favor. So, what about you? What brings Chase to this exact moment and place in the universe?"

"Excuse me." Chase said around a yawn. "And there is the last side effect of beer, it makes me sleepy. You know I might have to get back to you on that one. I'm not really sure exactly *where* I am right now."

Chapter 10

Two weeks later, Chase sat with Tess and Joe and Barb Carson in the waiting room at the office of Jude Stafford, Estate Attorney. Chase and Tess sat in two weathered leather chairs facing the receptionist, at a right angle to a couch where Joe and Barb waited. Chase tapped her foot nervously on the floor, anxious to get the meeting over with. For some reason, anything to do with the will made her nervous. Or maybe it was just a reminder that Avery was gone.

Chase turned at the sound of footsteps. She watched a tall woman stride confidently into the room. She had short, blond hair that was tucked behind her ears and flipped out at the nape of her neck. She wore a navy pant suit that accented her long legs. Chase was taken aback when she saw a man's tie knotted tightly against her throat. She watched as the tall stranger exchanged familiar greetings with Tess and the Carsons.

Chase tried not to stare and she blinked momentarily to clear her head. She found herself held captive by emerald green eyes that were regarding her curiously. A thought so foreign to Chase came crashing from the recesses of her subconscious and she found herself admitting she was one of the most beautiful women she had ever seen. *Now, where in the hell did that come from?*

The woman broke into a smile and extended her hand towards Chase. "You must be Chase. I'm Jude. Jude Stafford. Avery's attorney. Welcome to Maine."

Chase stood up and grasped Jude's hand and she felt it enveloped in soft warmth. She felt her breath catch and her stomach jumped wildly. Somehow she managed to get herself together enough to stammer out a greeting. "Yes. I'm Chase…Chase, uhm, Berkley. It's nice to me…meet you."

Chase felt her heartbeat quicken. She looked at Jude's hand capturing hers, holding it longer than politeness dictated and quickly withdrew it. Her mind worked frantically to try to attribute her reaction to Jude as an extension of her anxiousness about the will, but she was frightened to think that it wasn't the will at all.

Jude smiled warmly at Chase. "It's a pleasure meeting you. Avery told me so much about you. We got to be pretty good friends after she moved up here. I handled the estate that she, well you both bought Serendipity from. Between that and preparing her will, we spent quite a bit of time together."

Chase smiled wryly. "I wish I could say the same about you. Avery didn't mention you at all."

Jude chuckled nervously, apology registering in her eyes. Eager to get past the awkwardness of the moment, she turned to Joe, Barb and Tess, who had stood up to join them. "Why don't we head back to my office and I will fill you in on the latest details."

Jude waited till they were all seated around the large oval desk that took up half of the room she called her office. She opened a folder, pulled on black wire—rim glasses and scanned several documents. Chase watched Jude closely. She liked the way Jude looked in her glasses—sexy and smart. She thought it was cute when Jude bit her bottom lip while she was reading. *Chase Berkley, get a freaking hold on yourself. It's a woman for god's sake.* She tore her gaze away from Jude and forced herself to look out the window.

Chase jumped at the sound of her name. She met Jude's bemused expression. "I'm sorry. What did you say?" She glanced away quickly, unable to breathe when Jude's green eyes bore into her.

Jude pulled her glasses down slightly and peered at Chase over the rims. "I was just saying that everyone here was pretty much caught up except you. I was going to give you a brief rundown of everything."

Chase gripped the arms of the chair and took a deep breath to calm her nerves. "That sounds good. Shoot."

"As you know, we are all here because of Avery's last will and testament. As part owner, Serendipity automatically becomes solely yours."

Chase rubbed her chin, deep in thought. "So what happens now?"

"Let me bring you up to speed then we can all go over the process from here on. I prepared Avery's will, but with the caveat that a living trust would be a more efficient way to handle her estate." Jude saw Chase's confused expression and answered the unspoken question. "Basically, a living trust is set up so that a person's assets would be transferred into the trust prior to death. He or she would appoint a trustee and at the time of death, the trustee could distribute those assets in accordance with the deceased person's wishes, without having to probate the estate. This doesn't include the house of course, just her remaining assets. Unfortunately, we didn't get the paperwork done before…before Avery di…passed away. Now, we have to proceed with the will, and sometimes that process can be somewhat lengthy. That pretty much brings you up to date. Any questions before we forge ahead?" She paused and looked at Chase, measuring her reaction. When she didn't see one, she turned to the Carsons. She handed them copies of paperwork she had in the folder. "Good news. Probate has been initiated and the court has issued letters of authority appointing you both as the executors of the will."

Joe and Barb took the papers and scanned them quickly. Barb looked at Jude, her eyes brimming with tears. "I'm sorry, this just makes it even more final that my baby isn't coming back." Joe put his hand over Barb's and squeezed it. He didn't say anything, just silently comforted her.

Chase stole a glance at Tess. Her head was down, and Chase could see a single tear streaming down her face. She wanted to reach out to Tess, to comfort her, but despite the time they had spent together, Chase didn't feel like she was ready to step across that line. For the time being, she just smiled warmly at Tess and hoped she could share her strength in her time of heartache.

She knew everyone handled their grief differently, including herself. Lately, her way of dealing had been long runs in the chilly December weather. As her feet covered the distance, her mind struggled to process everything that had happened in the last month. From losing her job and boyfriend, to losing the best friend she ever had. The time alone let her think about how much she really thought she had known Avery. She wondered if she was just as much to blame as Avery for keeping her relationship with Tess a secret. The answer she kept coming back to was she didn't have an answer.

Jude waited a few moments in deference to the family then she continued slowly. "Barb, I'm so sorry. I can imagine how difficult this must be for you, for all of you. I'll do whatever I can to make the whole process easier on you."

Joe leaned forward. "We know you will Jude. You've been wonderful to us. We all knew this process would be difficult. Some days just hit home a little more than others." He held up the letter and fixed his gaze on Jude. "What happens now?"

"As you know, when Avery died, a notice of her death was published in the local paper. We also had the same notice put in the Portland Journal. This served as a notice to the public including any creditors that Avery may have accounts with. In Maine, there is a four month creditor period where anyone that feels like they have an interest in Avery's estate can come forward. I know from the sale of Serendipity that the purchase and renovations were paid for with cash. She doesn't have a mortgage on the property, so that shouldn't be an issue. Tess, you would probably know better than me if she had any other loans or credit cards with balances on them."

Tess shook her head no. "Other than one credit card, which we paid off every month, she didn't have anything. The Honda is paid off." Her voice started to quiver. "Avery was always good with her money, and she hated paying interest to anyone."

Jude smiled. "Good. That should definitely help. In the mean time, we will begin to compile a list of the assets that Avery had. She had an appraisal done on Serendipity not long after the renovations were completed, so we have a general idea of the value of the property. Tess, I'm assuming she had any retirement and life insurance policies changed to list you as the beneficiary. I can help you submit claims on those…if you'd like." Jude smiled when Tess shook her head in agreement. "The other matter we will have to work on besides getting a total value of Avery's estate will be handling some of the expenses that generally arise as a result of disbursing a person's estate. Joe and Barb and I have already discussed my fee, and per the original agreement with Avery, we have agreed on the amount. We will need to pay income taxes for Avery for the year. As long as no other outstanding bills are submitted by any creditors, everything else will go to the persons named in the will, specifically you four. So aside from getting everything together, it's pretty much a waiting game for the next three months."

Chapter 11

Chase watched Tess out of the corner of her eye. She glanced at the speedometer and knew she was just enough over the speed limit to grab a passing cop's attention. Adding to the fact that Tess was driving a little too fast for the curvy road heading back to Serendipity, she was swiping tears from her eyes. All in all, it made Chase just a little bit nervous. "You okay? Want me to drive?"

Tess turned to Chase, her expression confused. "What? Why would you need to drive?"

Chase leaned over and pointed at the dash. "No reason, other than it looks like you are trying to set a new land speed record."

Tess looked down. "Oh shit! Sorry, I really wasn't paying attention."

Chase put her hand over Tess's and squeezed it. "You want to talk about it?"

Tess smiled, comforted by the gesture. "I guess I thought this would get easier. No matter how much time passes, I still ache." Tess sniffed softly, her voice shaking. "I keep expecting her to come walking through the door and say April Fool's or something."

"That sounds like Avery." Chase laughed softly thinking about her friend's slightly twisted sense of humor. "I know how hard this has been for me. I can only imagine how much more difficult it has been for you. I wish I could make it easier."

Tess smiled and nodded. "I know. I'm just not sure how to do that. I don't know if I'll ever get over Avery. I would like to get to the point where I don't go to bed and wake up crying everyday. I'm just so…" Tess fell silent. Chase squeezed her hand again and looked out the window, letting Tess talk when she was ready. "I'm scared too."

"Scared? Of what?" Chase looked at her, confusion evident on her face.

Tess pulled the car in the driveway, put it in park and shut the engine off with her left hand. She sighed softly. "Scared, overwhelmed. I don't know. I had this wonderful life and home with Avery. Now she's gone, and I am not sure of anything. I don't have a say in the house, which means I'm at your mercy. And even if we work things out and I'm still here to run it, how will I do that? I can't run this place by myself. This is the only place I've ever called home. There isn't another one. Running home to my family to pick up the pieces isn't an option."

Chase tightened her grip on Tess's hand. "Don't be scared of your life here, I'm not going to take Seren…"

Tess jerked her hand away from Chase. "Damn it, Chase! I didn't tell you that so you could try to fix things. I'm just telling you how I feel. I'm not asking you to feel pity on the poor homeless, family—less woman. I'm just scared. This is the only thing left of Avery that I have."

Chase watched helplessly as Tess fled from the car and ran towards the beach. She watched her back until she disappeared below the rocky shoreline. Chase wasn't mad or offended by Tess. She knew that her fear and anger were part of her heartache.

Chase leaned back against the seat and closed her eyes. Her thoughts returned to Jude. Even as Chase pictured Jude's deep, emerald green eyes, her stomach jumped and her heart started to beat faster. Her confusion grew when she realized she couldn't remember a time that she had met anyone who made her react that way. She hadn't felt that when she met Tess. Lord knows, she absolutely did not feel that way with her ex. With him, it had never been more than a warm, safe feeling. No, it was completely different with Jude. Chase's body responded to her in a totally new and very confusing way. She made her feel things she was sure she didn't want to feel. Chase's mental gaze dropped to Jude's lips--her very soft, very full lips. She felt a stirring between her legs and she jumped. *Oh shit! That cannot be good.*

#

Chase knocked softly on Tess's door, still not sure what she was doing here. She smiled when Tess opened the door, not surprised to see her eyes were red and puffy. "Can I talk to you a minute?"

Tess opened the door all the way and stepped aside to let Chase enter.

Chase waited for her to say something, but when she didn't, Chase forged ahead. "I've been thinking about what you said earlier."

Tess looked chagrined. "I'm sorry I shouldn't have gone off on you like that. It's not your fault." She smiled sadly. "Unfortunately, I've used Barb as a punching bag so much lately, I figured it was time to spread some sunshine elsewhere and…lucky you, you are the winner." Tess emphasized her point by dropping a light punch on Chase's arm.

Chase chuckled at Tess's informal apology. She stepped forward and caught Tess in a bear hug. "It's okay. I'm pretty tough."

Tess sniffed. "Thank you for not, you know, punching back. I don't think I would bounce back as well."

Chase shook her head. "No. I figure you could use a little good news right now…which brings me to the reason I wanted to talk to you. At least I hope it's good news."

Tess cocked her head to the side and searched Chase's face, trying to anticipate what she wanted to say. All she saw there was a slightly cryptic smile. "What?" She asked suspiciously.

"Well, I've been thinking about this whole thing with the house. Avery obviously wanted us to meet for a reason. I'm willing to find out what that is…if you're game."

"Hmph!" Tess snorted loudly. "So even though she is gone she could continue to wield her magical powers over us, forcing us to battle the dragon and…"

"…rescue the Princess!" Chase shouted, her voice tinged with laughter. She caught Tess's surprised look. "Okay, so maybe I know a little bit more about video games than I let on."

Tess laughed out loud. "Berk, I knew you were more dangerous than you let on. I'm impressed."

"Good. Now if you could run with that feeling. Here's what I am thinking we should do. As you know, I'm kinda jobless at this particular juncture. I was thinking maybe I could stick around awhile. Maybe help run Serendipity. I'd like to keep it open, keep Avery's dream alive."

Tess's eyes lit up. "Are you serious? Don't be messing with me." She glared at Chase. "Or I'll punch you for real this time."

Chase covered her arms quickly. "No, no, that is entirely unnecessary. Your little love pat earlier was just fine." She smiled sarcastically at Tess. "All joking aside. I'm as serious as a heart attack. I may not know anything about running a bed and breakfast, but at my last count, you were down a chef, with no, ahh…viable candidates in sight."

"Ooh low blow, Berk. I might not be so eager to *hire* a smart—ass young pup like yourself to run my kitchen."

Chase smiled wickedly. "You might change your mind when the new vacation review comes out and the talk of the town is how bad the food is at Serendipity. I question your integrity…if you're willing to take such an unmitigated risk."

"Well far be it from me to have my integrity impuned." Tess was silent for a moment, her eyes squinted in deep concentration. She stuck her hand out towards Chase. "Very well then, I accept your generous offer."

Chase grasped her hand and pumped it up and down vigorously. "And if I decide I can't work with your demanding ass as a boss, I'll grab my horse and ride off into the sunset."

Chapter 12

Chase waited patiently in the reception area at Stafford Law Office. She didn't have an appointment to see Jude, but Barb had mailed her some statements belonging to Avery and she thought she would drop them off while she was out. She drummed her fingers nervously on the arm of the chair and smiled apologetically when the receptionist lifted her eyes to Chase then dropped them to her fingers. "Sorry."

"Can I get you something while you wait? Water? Pop?"

Chase was going to refuse since she would only be here a minute, but she was so nervous about seeing Jude, that she figured she better have something to occupy her. "Sure. Water is fine thanks."

Chase watched her disappear down a long hall. Seconds later, she heard footsteps and looked up to see Jude coming towards her. Jude broke out into a smile, and Chase thought that if it were possible, she was even more beautiful today.

"What a pleasant surprise. I wasn't expecting you." Jude extended her hand and Chase reached out to shake it.

Chase felt the electricity shoot through her and blushing, she looked away hoping Jude didn't see the way that she made Chase react. "I just wanted to drop some statements off that Barb sent. I hope that's okay." Chase finally looked at Jude, and was surprised to see her pull her gaze from her breasts back to her face. Rather than be embarrassed at being caught, Jude flashed her a little smirk. "It's more than okay. Why don't we go into my office and take a look at what you have."

Chase had just sat down in front of Jude's desk when her receptionist came in with her all but forgotten bottle of water. "Oh, yeah, thank you."

"Jude, can I get you anything?"

"I'm fine, Beth. Thank you. Will you please shut the door behind you?" She watched her walk out then turned to Chase and smiled. "She's a wonderful woman. I think she runs this place, not me. I'd be lost without her." Jude shook her head. "Damn thing is…she's always trying to feed me. That would be a great way to waste a perfectly good crew scholarship."

"You crewed? Heavyweight?" Chase asked referring to the taller, heavier crew teams. Quad or eight?"

Jude looked impressed. "Wow, you know crew?"

Chase shrugged. "Sure, well not that much really, only from watching the Olympics."

Jude raised her eyebrows and peered at Chase. "And I pegged you for a bowman."

"Huh?"

"The man, or woman, at the bow, or front of the boat. Kind of like the crew coach. To answer your question, I rowed for Brown in under—grad and then Harvard. Usually eight man teams. I was part of the engine room or power house, which is made up of the four women in the middle. They call it that because the four rowers in the middle are always the strongest, the speed of the team. My nickname in college was the Hulk."

Chase's gaze traveled over the parts of Jude's body she could see above her desk. "You don't look like the bulging muscle type, but I wouldn't mind seeing you rip your shirt off in front of me." Chase gulped, realizing that she had said the second part of that sentence out loud. She felt her face burning, and wished she could crawl under the desk. "I am so sorry. I didn't mean to say that out loud."

"Not at all, the fact that you thought it is quite flattering." Jude smiled suggestively. "I must admit that I do find you very attractive, and the fact that you feel the same, is quite a turn on."

Chase felt her mortification quickly replaced by something else, something much different than embarrassment. A feeling that was very close to what she felt right before she climaxed. This sudden realization scared her, and she started rambling in a totally ineffective attempt at denial. "No, that's not what I meant at all. I just meant you must be in very good shape. I admire that, I'm sure it's even attractive…to some people."

Jude raised her eyebrow and studied Chase. "But not you?"

Chase shook her head side to side furiously. "Well, no, of course not."

"Hmm, that's interesting."

"What's interesting?" Chase inquired.

"Oh nothing. Just if you expect me to believe that, you are going to have to stop looking at me like that."

Chase tried to act innocent. "Like what?"

"Like you want to rip my clothes off." Jude stated matter of fact. "You may be telling me one thing, but your eyes are speaking volumes. And right now they are saying you want me."

Chase shook her head no again and pushed her chair back. "My eyes aren't saying anything, other than I think it's time for me to leave." She tried to get up, but Jude locked eyes with her and she was frozen. She watched as Jude stood up and slowly came around the desk. She grabbed the arm of Chase's chair and spun it around so she was facing Chase straight on. Jude's voice was deeper when she spoke again.

"Counselor, your witness. Bailiff will swear the witness in."

Jude picked a book up off her desk and held it in front of Chase. *"Place your right hand on here. Do you swear to tell the truth, the whole truth and nothing but the truth so help you God?"*

Chase giggled. She put her hand up to stop the smile when she saw Jude glare at her. She cleared her throat. "I do solemnly swear to tell the truth, the whole truth and nothing but the truth so help me God."

Jude placed the book back on the table. When she spoke, it was the same sexy voice that made Chase's heart skip a beat. "Ms. Berkley, on the day in question, did you contact the plaintiff, Ms. Stafford?"

Chase looked into Jude's green eyes. She bit her lip nervously. "Yes, I did."

"What was the purpose of your visit?"

Chase licked her lips. "I was dropping off paperwork."

"Didn't you think it was somewhat suspicious to be dropping paperwork off without an appointment?"

"No, I thought it was appropriate given the time of the visit."

"And didn't you, during this visit, allow yourself to be locked in the office with the plaintiff? Behind closed doors with someone who is obviously gay? I can only imagine what went on behind closed doors."

"*Objection.Conjecture.This is all speculation.*"

"*Sustained.*"

"You do admit you were locked behind a closed door with the plaintiff?"

"Yes."

"And would you agree that the plaintiff has the most beautiful eyes you've ever seen?"

"*Objection! Irrelavent. What bearing does this have on the case?*"

"*Overruled. Let's get to the point.*"

"Your honor, if you will just bear with me, I'm sure you will see this has bearing on our case."

"Ms. Berkley, please answer the question."

Chase looked away nervously. When she spoke, her voice was low. "Yes, I do think she has the most beautiful eyes I have ever seen, but that doesn't mean…"

"A simple yes will suffice. Now, Ms. Berkley, on said date did you or didn't you tell the plaintiff you would like to see her rip her shirt off in front of you? Yes or no."

"Well, yes, but…"

"May I remind you again that this is a yes or no answer. Did you or didn't you gaze longingly at the plaintiff? And wouldn't you admit that it is obvious you are attracted to the plaintiff?"

"*OBJECTION! Leading!" Your honor, she is clearly putting words in the witness's mouth.*"

"*Overruled. Counselor, you may continue with your line of questioning.*"

Jude put her hands on the arms of the chair and leaned towards Chase. "Ms. Berkley, are you attracted to Ms. Stafford?

Chase felt her stomach flip—flop. She couldn't tear her eyes from Jude's face. Her gaze dropped to her lips and she felt herself getting aroused. Jude ran a finger lightly along Chase's jaw, down her neck and along the vee of her sweater, her finger just grazing the top of her breast. She leaned in closer and stared intently at Chase. "Yes or no?"

Chase couldn't breathe, she tried to tear herself away from Jude's magnetic force, but she was helpless. She lost herself in Jude's eyes. Her face was so close Chase could feel her breath on her skin. Her head was screaming yes, but when she said the word it was barely a whisper.

"Can you please repeat that for the entire courtroom to hear?"

Chase opened her mouth to say yes and Jude tilted her chin up and captured Chase mouth against hers. She kissed her softly and Chase melted. She arched her body trying to get closer, wanting Jude to take her, to possess her. She wanted to feel Jude's tongue against hers. When Jude finally slipped her tongue between her lips and flicked her tongue softly, Chase felt wetness flood her panties.

Jude slid her other hand underneath Chase's shirt and caressed her nipple till it was a taut peak. Chase gasped when Jude rolled her hard point between her fingers and pinched it lightly. Chase groaned into Jude's mouth. The only clear thought in her head surprised her. *I could come just kissing this woman.*

Chase jumped when she heard a knock on the door. She wrenched her mouth away from Jude's and looked up at her. "Shouldn't you get that?"

Jude planted light kisses all over Chase's face. "No, they'll go away."

"What if it's important?"

Jude chuckled and caressed Chase's cheek with the back of her knuckles. "How important can it really be? I'm an estate attorney." She dipped her head down and kissed Chase again. Chase was so turned on that she thought she would crawl out of her skin. She felt a raw, primal need pierce her body and she pulled Jude's hand down and put between her legs. She completely forgot the knocking when Jude's hand started to caress her softly. Jude's finger found her clit and massaged slow circles around it. Chase ground her body against Jude's hand, aching for release.

Chase's mind was a hazy fog, her focus dimmed till there was only Jude. A slow, persistent noise pushed at the door, threatening to bring her back to reality. It was a dull, rhythmic pounding in her head. Trying to focus, she remembered the door. Someone was knocking at the door.

Then a voice broke through the haze. "Hello? Chase? Are you awake in there?"

Chase bolted upright, confused and more aroused than she had been in forever. She rubbed her eyes and tried to focus. She put her hand over her mouth as the reality of what happened hit her. She looked around her room, she was alone, there was no Jude, only a dream of Jude. *Oh fuck!* Chase could not believe what had just happened. She'd had an erotic dream about Jude. An erotic dream about another woman. She tried to convince herself that it was just a random dream, it didn't mean anything. She wasn't gay and she wasn't attracted to Jude. Or was she? *Answer the question, Ms. Berkley. Are you attracted to Ms. Stafford.*

"Chase? You awake?"

Chase shook her head and ran her hand through her hair. "Yeah, Tess. I'm up. Hang on." She swung her feet to the floor and heaved herself out of bed. Opening the door, she tried to look normal. "What's up?"

"It's snowing. I wanted you to see our first snow together." She grabbed Chase's hand and tried to drag her out of the room. "Come on! I've got coffee all ready."

Chase grabbed her robe and slippers and followed Tess, all the while trying to convince herself she wasn't attracted to Jude.

Chapter 13

Chase stared out the window, squinting in the morning sunlight. She glanced over her shoulder at her mother and father drinking coffee in the sunroom. "It's hotter than hell down here. I don't know how you guys can stand the heat and humidity."

"Unless I'm mistaken dear, you haven't been to hell so I'm sure you can't say whether it's hotter here than in hell." She said the words with just enough sarcasm to make them almost funny.

Chase stifled a smile, and rolled her eyes at her mother, Constance Berkley. Connie, to everyone close to her. Chase was used to her dry humor, growing up as an only child with a stay at home mom had given her plenty of exposure. She had picked up quite a bit of her mother's humor, among other things. Chase sat down and looked into brown eyes that resembled her own. They were twinkling with laughter. "Honestly, I don't know why you have to be so literal. It's freaking hot down here. I'm sure that hell isn't this warm, whether I've been there or not."

James Berkley laughed at the exchange and patted Chase on the hand. He was used to his two girls bickering back and forth. A mother and daughter that were that much alike couldn't manage not to bicker sometimes. "Honey, your mom is just teasing you. She knows it's hot, even for Boca. Why don't you jump in the pool to cool off?"

Chase glanced over her shoulder at the glistening water in their backyard pool. It was surrounded by a large screened lanai, but the early morning sun was shining directly onto the pool and she knew it would be hot. "Ugh, I'd melt before I made it to the water." She groaned when she saw the large plastic snowman sitting on the patio. "Christmas just isn't the same down here. It seems sacrilegious in ninety—five degree weather. Even Frosty is melting out there."

Connie laughed. "In case you forgot, you used to complain about the cold. Remember how bad some of those Indy winters were? And forget Baltimore, frigid is putting it nicely." She squeezed James hand and smiled. "I was so glad when your father retired and decided to spend winters down here. Do you know how bad the cold is for someone my age?"

Chase snorted. "Someone your age? Mom, you're only fifty—eight. You make it sound like you are ninety."

"Fifty—eight, ninety, it's all the same."

James cleared his throat loudly. "Connie, don't make us older than we are." He winked at Chase. "Next thing you know, Chase will be locking us away in an old folk's home. I plan on spending another twenty years here before I let them put me out to pasture."

"You guys are both nuts. I've never seen two healthier people. I'll probably be stuck with you till *I'm* ninety—five."

"You will if you keep making us wait for grandchildren. You know, your father and I aren't getting any younger." Connie's tone suggested she didn't want to hear more excuses from Chase about settling down and having children. "What about Derek? He's so handsome. You would have beautiful babies together."

Chase hated this conversation. They had it at every holiday, and most phone conversations in between. Now on top of having her mother harass her about giving her grandbabies, she had to tell her she and Derek were no longer together. "Mom, you have to stop with the settling down and having babies thing. I'm just not ready, I haven't met anyone I want to settle down with and have kids." She paused and took a deep breath. "Besides, Derek and I aren't together anymore."

"What? When did that happen? Why aren't you with him? He was such a sweet man."

Chase looked at her father, silently begging him for help. James put his hand on Connie's arm. "Honey, why don't we leave Chase alone about it? I'm sure she will talk about it when she is ready."

"Chase honey, you know I'm just concerned about you. I'm your mother, it's my job." Tilting her head to the side, she studied Chase closely. Deciding Chase needed to talk woman to woman, she sent James out to pick up supplies for lunch. When they were alone, Connie asked Chase if everything was all right.

Normally, Chase talked to Avery about stuff like this, but Avery wasn't here anymore. Chase shrugged. "I don't know. I'm lonely. I miss Avery. I don't really miss Derek, I think I miss the idea of being with someone. As nice as he was, we were never really a couple. Not like a perfect couple, like you and Dad."

"Oh honey, there aren't really any perfect couples anymore. Even your father and I have had rough spots."

"But you love each other. You have passion. I haven't had that with any of my boyfriends. Not even Derek, as much as you liked him."

"You were always such a romantic. Your father and I got lucky I guess, not everyone has that. Most of the time, you find a man you can get along with and hope for the best. Once in a while, you actually fall madly in love with him and you live the storybook life. It's probably unfair that you had to have us as an example. You have your heart set on true love and when you don't find it, you break up. Just because you and Derek didn't..."

"Derek's gay, mom. He likes men. I'm pretty sure that it probably wouldn't have worked out...no matter how hard we tried."

Connie looked stunned. "Oh my, I, well, I certainly didn't see that coming."

Chase laughed ruefully. "Well, I can say I didn't let myself see it. Maybe I ignored it because I was as disconnected from the relationship as he was. First Avery and then Derek."

"I'm not one to stick my nose where it isn't welcome, but I blame her parents entirely. They were way too lenient on her."

Chase rolled her eyes and laughed. "Oh whatever, mom. You are one of the nosiest people I know. Besides, it has nothing to do with the way her parents raised her. She's always been gay. I just chose not to see it...Derek too."

"Oh honey, do you honestly believe that?" Connie pursed her lips, daring Chase to disagree. "It's not a disease like diabetes."

"Really mom? Are you serious?" Chase shook her head, angry at her mother's narrow—mindedness. "You're right, it's not a disease, but it is something you're born with. The same as I was born with brown eyes like you."

"You couldn't be more wrong. Avery, and God forgive me, I loved her like she was my own, was gay because her parents let her run wild and associate with the wrong crowd. Fortunately, we were able to save you from the same thing. Why, I'd be beside myself if you told me you were one of those, those...lesbians."

Chase was too angry to speak. Her mind flashed to Tess. Poor Tess, who's family had cut her off because she was a lesbian. She had a small inkling of how bad the rejection felt, but knew that it was nothing compared to the pain Tess lived with everyday. She realized the unfairness of it all. She got up and walked to the window, ignoring her mother's continued chatter. She was silent for a few moments. Finally, she turned and faced her mother, a solemn look on her face. "She was my best friend. I loved her like I would my own sister, and I'll stand up for her like a sister. You may not agree with me or with her preferences, but I refuse to let you malign her, especially when she isn't here to defend herself. She couldn't change who she was anymore than you can change who you are. I don't want to hear you speak about Avery that way ever again. And *if* one day I tell you that I'm a lesbian, you will just have to live with it. I would hope that as my mother you really do love me *unconditionally"*

Chase strode out of the room before her mother had a chance to respond. She was frustrated and confused. The dream of Jude was still fresh in her mind and she hoped that her mother had mistaken her blush of embarrassment as anger. She was having feelings she had never had before and they scared her. She knew that her own personal struggle contributed to her snapping at her mom. Realizing that there was a chance that she was a lesbian had her so off kilter that even the smallest thing was setting her off lately. She needed some time before she returned and made up with her mother, as they always did after an argument. Later, she would find her and apologize, but for now, she wanted to just get away and forget everything.

#

"So Jude, your father tells me that you are thinking of getting out of estate planning and going into criminal law?"

Jude raised her eyes and looked across the table at Christina, her father's latest paramour. Her parents had divorced long ago and her father was on track to break the record for most marriages *and* divorces among the Stafford men. He came by it honestly though, his father and grandfather had been married and divorced four and six times respectively, not counting numerous woman who hadn't managed to tie them down. Christina Dodson was the most recent in the long line of women. Barely forty, she was twenty—five years younger than Charles V. Stafford III. Evidence of her existence as a gold digger was obvious to Jude, from the recently died platinum blond hair to the enormous breasts that were just a little too high for forty. Jude was used to a parade of woman at her father's table, and this Christmas was no different. *Same old story, only the scenery has changed.*

Jude set her fork down, wiped her mouth, and stared at Christina with barely hidden boredom. "Did he? My father believes that if he tells that story enough he may actually will it into existence. On the contrary, I'm quite happy with estate law. I've never had my father's appetite for blood." Jude referred to his days as a criminal defense attorney, a field he tried to push Jude into ever since she had come out of the womb a girl, and not the boy Charles had wanted. She was his one last chance at carrying on the Stafford line, and as he reminded his ex—wife quite often, she had let him and his forefathers down.

"Jude!" Charles voice boomed across the table. "Watch the tone! You will show a little respect if you are going to be in my house."

Christina put her hand on Charles to settle him down. "It's all right honey." Her voice sounded syrupy—sweet and frayed Jude's nerves even more. "She's just stating her opinion." She looked at Jude and winked. "We're women dear, we understand these things. Don't pay attention to your father."

Jude rolled her eyes. She hadn't paid attention to her father in years. What little respect she did have for him disappeared when her mother left. Her twisted sense of family obligation was the only thing that made her show up for these little family get—togethers. "Charles, you and I both know that I'm not giving up my practice and going into criminal law. Unlike you, I don't like to help the bad guys get away with their crimes. I've told you that a thousand times before."

Her father snorted. "You're just like your mother. Not an ounce of fight in you. Always content to sit on the sidelines and watch life pass you by."

"Don't you dare talk about Mom that way." Jude's fists were clenched with fury. "And you're wrong. I am a fighter…when it matters. I'm not like you Charles, and I never will be. You and I will always see things differently, the least of which is the kind of law that I choose to practice."

Charles laughed out loud. "Well, you did manage to get one thing from me." He caught Jude's look of confusion. "My temper. Never let it be said that you don't have the Stafford temper. And I really wish you wouldn't call me Charles. That was cute when you were four, now it's just disrespectful." He paused as William and Maria cleared the main course from the table and brought dessert and coffee for the three of them.

Jude smiled at William and Maria Smyth. The Smyths had been with Charles since Jude's mother had left. Jude had been close to both of them, but especially William. He filled the void that her strained relationship with her father had left. Jude took a quick bite of the pecan pie that Charles always requested for Christmas. "Mmm, Maria this is wonderful! Why don't you come work for me instead of Charles? You could make me one of these everyday."

Maria winked at her and smiled devilishly. "Soon, honey. I've been slipping cyanide to your father a little at a time. As soon as he kicks the bucket, Will and I will be on your doorstep.

Charles shook his head and laughed. William and Maria had been with him long enough that this was the normal banter that they all shared. "You can't kill the devil, Maria." He turned to William and pretended to glare. "William, you need to tighten the reigns on this one. She is too feisty for her own good."

William winked at Charles and took Maria's arm. "Come on wench. There's a plank with your name on it." He smiled warmly at Jude. "Stop by and see us before you leave. We have your Christmas present."

"Oh Will, you shouldn't have." Jude looked down at her plate and when she looked up again, her face was that of a child looking for approval. "I have something for you and Maria too." She watched them leave the room and felt warmth in her heart. No matter how much time passed, they were still the couple that had raised her and given her as much love as they had given their own children. "I'll stop by on my way out."

Charles watched them leave and shook his head. He regarded Jude with interest. "If you gave me half the respect you gave them, our relationship would be so much better."

Jude looked at him askance. "On the contrary, *Father,* if you loved me half as much as they do, our relationship would be so much better. You always wanted a boy." She shrugged noncommittally. "I guess you'll just have to get used to disappointment."

"Now Jude, you are going to have Christina thinking I'm a bad father." He smiled at her, suddenly remembering she was at the table with them. "How do you like your pie, dear?"

"It's delicious." She pushed the pecan pie around her plate, in a show of eating, but she never actually took a bite. She wouldn't risk all the plastic surgery she'd had for some dessert, no matter how much she liked Charles. "I'm just too stuffed to eat."

Charles patted her hand condescendingly. As if suddenly friends with Jude, he winked at her conspiratorially. "Speaking of me being a good father…" He pulled an envelope out of his pocket and tossed it towards Jude. "Merry Christmas."

Jude opened the envelope and sneered. "Still trying to buy me off I see."

"On the contrary, I love you and I like giving you a Christmas present."

"It's a check for ten thousand dollars. That's not a present, that's a bribe." Jude wadded the check up and put it on the table beside her plate. "I'm not going to cash it…just like the last ten you gave me. Don't you think it's time you finally accept the fact that I'm not going to be the son you always wanted? I'm not going to be the lawyer you always wanted? This is who I am, and if you can't accept that, too bad."

Charles regarded Jude thoughtfully. Before he spoke, he glanced sideways at Christina and she dutifully excused herself. He fixed Jude with a hard stare that if directed at anyone else, would make them cower in fear. When Charles saw that she wasn't quaking with fear, it aggravated him more. "Damn it Jude! I blame your mother entirely for your surly attitude. It's your mother's fault your one of *them*."

"What's the matter, Charles? You in particular should like me being one of *them*." She brushed her hands through her hair and laughed. "I'm just what you wanted…a son."

Charles slammed his fist on the table. "I wanted a son, not a fucking dyke. I should have known better than to marry a low—life like your mother. It's obviously a defect she passed onto you. The Stafford bloodline is too pure to produce a lesbian." He ignored Jude, who was fuming with anger, and continued his tirade. "I've tolerated this aberrant behavior long enough. You're thirty—five years old Jude. It's time to stop this ridiculous behavior and grow up. It's time to stop whoring around and settle down. I've introduced you to plenty of eligible men and you continue to ignore me. Your sisters aren't that way, and honestly I think you choose to be that way to spite me." He sighed heavily. "Maybe I did push you to be the son I never had, and maybe that was wrong. I gave up on you being a boy a long time ago, don't you think it's time you started behaving like a woman?"

"If you are finished with your vitriolic diatribe…" Jude was on the verge of blowing up, but she had worked too long to quell her temper so that her father would never see her out of control. When she spoke her voice vibrated with barely concealed anger. "…what I do with my life ceased being your business the day I moved out. You made it quite clear that you didn't want to be a part of raising me long before that." She picked up the crumpled check and waived it at her father. "Now your guilt is getting the best of you. But let me assure you, a yearly Christmas stipend is not going to make up for all the years you were absent in my life. I made my way without you. I put myself through law school, I'm supporting myself very well without your sage advice. As far as my personal life goes, that is none of your business. You may not agree with my life, but rest assured, your model life has been an eye—opening experience. Remind me again about the sanctity of marriage. Jenna and Jessica may have opted to use your *wonderful* match—making skills, but forgive me if I don't. You keep throwing men at me and expect some miracle." She stood up and leaned towards him. "Keep dreaming. Whether you accept it or not, I like fucking women." She threw the check onto the table in front of him and strode quickly out of the room, leaving a very stunned Charles Stafford III.

Chapter 14

Chase pushed the cart, her eyes roving the shelves at Hannaford's Market. She had returned home to Serendipity after visiting her parents in Florida for Christmas to find the pantry stocked with nothing but cereal and ravioli. Somehow, Tess had managed to survive on those two staples for the two weeks Chase was gone.

Chase shook her head, thinking about Tess. She had invited Tess to come to Florida with her, but she had begged off, saying she preferred to just be alone since it was her first Christmas without Avery. Chase wanted to insist, but in the end decided that perhaps Tess did know what was best for herself. When Chase got home, Tess was quiet, but otherwise okay and she didn't push her to know how she spent the two weeks alone.

Chase started to make the turn from one aisle to the next and stopped abruptly. She saw the profile of a tall blonde standing four feet in front of her. Chase pulled her cart back, trying to escape unnoticed.

"Chase?"

Chase pretended like she hadn't heard the woman. Beating a hasty retreat, she flew down the next aisle and was about to turn the corner when her cart crashed into an oncoming cart. "Oh shit!"

"It is you. Didn't you hear me say your name?"

Chase looked up into Jude's welcoming green eyes and she blushed uncontrollably. She could almost feel Jude's lips on hers and her hand raking across her... *Oh that kind of thinking has to stop now.*

"No, sorry, I was spacing. Happens when I shop, I get into the *zone.*"

Jude laughed. "I would say so. I'm still reeling from the head on crash."

Chase smiled ruefully. "Crap, I'm sorry."

Jude shrugged and dismissed it with a wave of her hand. "You're just lucky I'm not some ambulance chaser who wanted to stick it to you." Jude smiled at Chase's mock horror. "So I heard you decided to stick around awhile."

"Oh, yeah. Who did you hear that from?"

"Tess."

"And do you talk to Tess a lot?" Chase said teasingly.

"Every now and then." Jude winked at Chase. "I have to keep tabs on you."

"And why are you keeping tabs on me again? You're not interested, are you?"

"Oh, I'm interested all right." Jude stepped closer, and Chase's heart skipped. "You happen to now own all of a rather expensive bed and breakfast. And I am always interested in my clients."

"Oh." Chase looked crestfallen. "I hoped…I mean, that's good. I wouldn't want to worry about you being *interested* in me."

Jude rolled her eyes and looked at her fingernails, apparently bored with the conversation already. "No need to worry. You really aren't my type."

Chase looked confused. "But I thought you were you know."

Now Jude looked confused. "You know what?"

Chase shuffled uncomfortably. "Well, you know…a lesbian." The last two words came out as a whisper.

"Why would you assume I was…a lesbian?" She mimicked Chase's whisper for the last two words.

Chase turned red again. She tried not to let Jude see how embarrassed she was. "Well, you are Avery's attorney, I thought maybe…" Chase stared at the floor. "Plus, you kinda look gay."

Jude raised her eyebrow. "I look gay?"

Chase shook her head, already deep in the hole she had dug for herself. She figured she didn't have anything left to lose, so she forged ahead. "Well, you know, the suit and tie, and the short hair. Plus your voice is kind of deep…for a woman."

"Okay, let me get this straight. You think I'm gay because my hair is short, I wear ties and my voice is deep." Jude rolled her eyes heavenward. "That is priceless. And to add insult to injury, you assume that because I am…a lesbian, that I am attracted to you." Jude laughed out loud. "That may just be the faultiest logic I have ever heard."

Chase's embarrassment started to turn to anger the more that Jude chided her. She opened her mouth to say something when Jude stopped her.

"Let me just set the record straight. I am…a lesbian, but not for the bullshit reasons you think. I happen to like my hair short, it's easier to take care of, plus it brings out my eyes. I wear ties because that is the one thing my old man taught me how to do…tie a tie. Plus, it makes me look like a badass. My voice, well you will have to talk to my parents about that." She put her finger up to stop Chase from interrupting. "And assuming I am attracted to you, simply because I am gay is a generalization I can do without. Just because you're straight, does that mean you are attracted to every man you see? Now, if you will excuse me, I need to get back to shopping. I wouldn't want you to think that I'm attracted to you just because I stood and talked to you so long." Jude spun her cart around and started to walk away.

"Wait…please." Chase grabbed her arm and when Jude turned, she saw green eyes looking at her expectantly then just as quickly, a mask of indifference covered her face. Chase looked chagrined. "Jude, I'm sorry, I didn't mean to offend you." She pointed at her mouth. "Sometimes the sensor doesn't work. You know, make sure the brain is engaged before you put the mouth in gear. I always get that mixed up…I put my mouth in gear, than realize I am not thinking before I speak." Chase stopped when Jude started to smile. "Sorry, now I'm rambling."

Jude shook her head. "Don't apologize, it's cute." She put her hand up fast. "But that doesn't mean I'm attracted to you."

Chase started laughing. "I deserve that. So are we even?"

Jude put her hand on her chest and pretended to be offended. "Even? Not even close honey." She pushed her cart out of the way and stepped within inches of Chase. "But I can think of a way to make it up to me."

Chase looked up into Jude's eyes and froze. She willed herself to keep her gaze on her eyes. *Whatever you do Chase, do not look at her lips.* She smiled and pretended nonchalance. "Oh yeah, what's that?"

Jude inched even closer. She wet her bottom lip and smiled. Chase was mesmerized, unable to breathe. When Jude answered, Chase's eyes went to her lips involuntarily.

"I haven't eaten all day." She winked at Chase mischievously. "If someone were to say buy me lunch, I think that would more than make up for any prior transgressions."

Chase swallowed, her heart pounding in her ears. She felt herself sway towards Jude and she tightened her grip on the cart to steady herself. She willed herself to speak, and when she did her voice was an octave higher than normal. "Lunch? That's all it will take? That's all you want from me?"

Jude searched Chase's face for several seconds before she answered. When she did her voice was low and husky. "For today."

#

Jude pulled into a space in front of The Thistle Inn, an old sea captain's house that had been turned into a bed and breakfast. Jude had been thinking about coming to the pub for a late lunch anyway, and now she was here with unexpected, but quite welcome company.

She wasn't quite sure what it was about Chase Berkley that got under her skin so much, but she was quickly warming to the idea of spending an afternoon with her. Maybe she needed a nice straight friend to give her some guidance. As an attorney, albeit an estate attorney, she was highly sought after in the limited lesbian circuit around Boothbay. Jude didn't ever want for female company, but she had long ago decided to adopt a strict no repeats dating rule. That sounded better than one night stand. She couldn't squelch a smile when she saw Chase drive up.

She hopped out of her BMW X6 and smiled as Chase pulled in beside her. She reached down and opened the door, holding it so Chase could get out. "Is this okay…since you are treating?"

"Oh yeah, I've driven by here a couple of times and wondered if it were any good."

Jude smiled. "Well, it's good…if you like great food. If not, we can try someplace else."

Chased waited while Jude shut her door then pressed the lock button on her key chain. "No, this is good. Besides, I'm always trying to find new things to serve the guests." She followed Jude inside. They opted to sit at a table rather than the bar, which was made of an eighteen—foot dory that had once sailed the waters of Boothbay Harbor.

When they were seated, their server introduced herself and took their drink orders. Chase watched Jude as she interacted with the young woman. She hid a grin when the waitress starting flirting with Jude. With Jude's classic good looks and charming personality, it was no surprise to Chase that people would flirt with her. Jude looked away from the waitress, her eyes questioning Chase. "Is that okay?"

Chase blushed when she realized she had been caught staring. "Is what okay?"

Jude laughed. "You always go Buzz Lightyear on your lunch dates?" She laughed again at Chase's look of confusion. "Sorry, nephews that love *Toy Story.* Are you always somewhere out in space on your dates?"

"This isn't a date remember…you're not attracted to me."

"I never said I wasn't attracted to you. What I said was I didn't need you assuming I was attracted to you, simply because I am gay. There's a difference there. So technically, it could be a date." Jude smirked.

Chase rolled her eyes at Jude. "Lawyers. If you must know, I didn't space out, I was shocked to see you shamelessly flirting with a helpless young woman."

"Jealous?" Jude's piercing eyes held Chase captive and she almost melted from the heat of her gaze. "Cause I can flirt with you too."

Chase shook her head no. "Ahh, no thanks. I refuse to play second fiddle, and besides, I'm not gay."

"That's never stopped me before." She smiled at Chase mischievously. "In a town this size it helps to not limit yourself. So how about it?"

Chase nearly choked. "How about what? How about me and you hook up?" She shook her head side to side furiously. "I can assure you that will never happen."

"No, silly, how about a beer? The Belhaven Scottish Ale is the bomb." When Chase nodded okay, Jude turned to the waitress and smiled an apology. "We'll have that and can we get a water as well?" Jude watched the waitress walk away then turned back to face Chase. She smiled confidently. "Believe me Chase, if I wanted it to happen, it most assuredly would."

Chase shivered despite the fact that Jude's gaze was making her uncomfortably warm. As much as she tried to refute that statement, she had to admit that Jude was probably right. Suddenly, she wanted to get back on safer ground. "So what do you recommend?"

Jude didn't bother looking at her menu. "Everything I've had is wonderful, but the fish and chips is the best. Unless you are one of those women who watches her figure."

Chase laughed. "Not yet. I am sure I will have to one day." She closed her menu. "That sounds good. I'll have that."

Jude smiled. "Me too. And you have to save room for a piece of their blueberry pie." She licked her lips and moaned. "It is beyond divine."

After the waitress brought their drinks back and took their orders, Chase looked around. "This place is really cool. Thanks for bringing me here."

Jude glanced around. "Yeah, it's pretty nice. In the summertime, the decks are open for outdoor seating. I like to come here and take an extended *working* lunch. And by that I mean, a sit outside and read a book lunch." She put her elbows on the table and rested her chin in her hands. "So, you are a pilot. Who did you fly for?"

Chase spun the mug in her hands, not meeting Jude's eyes. "No one that you've heard of, I'm sure. TransAir. It *was* a regional airline that ran between Indy and Chicago."

"Was? Oh, I understand. That's why you have been able to stick around so long."

Chase shrugged. "Yep. I would say it was unfortunate, but this place has been good for me. It's given me a chance to get to know Avery a little better. Plus, I'm learning some interesting things about myself."

Jude sipped her beer. "Oh yeah, like what?"

Chase smiled. "Hmm, not anything I am ready to share just yet."

Jude shrugged. "Fair enough. I'll be around…if you decide you want to share. So what do you think of Tess?"

"She's great. It's easy to see why Avery fell in love with her."

"You know she was pretty worried about meeting you. One of the few things she and Avery ever disagreed about was Avery not telling you. Tess wanted her too. I don't think Tess understood her decision to keep it a secret for so long. Knowing you the little bit that I do, I don't think it would have been an issue." Jude paused, her eyes questioning Chase.

Chase was silent for a moment, trying to decide how she wanted to answer that question. When she spoke, her voice was low and

Jude could hear the hurt in her tone. "I can't tell you that I wasn't hurt that I had to find out the way I did. It wouldn't have mattered though. Avery was my best friend. I loved her no matter what. I wish she could have seen that." Chase paused, her voice starting to quiver. "All that aside, I love Tess. She's like a sister to me. I'm really glad I've had the chance to get to know her. Besides, I think she could use a surrogate sister."

Just then the waitress brought their food to the table. Chase eyed the meal appreciatively. "Mmm, this looks delicious." She slathered tartar sauce on her fish and took a bite. "You weren't kidding. This is fabulous!"

Jude smiled. "One of the perks of being a lawyer. I'm always right."

Chase snorted loudly. "Whatever! You may have nailed the fish and chips, but I can name at least one thing you will be wrong about." She winked at Jude, and knew that she was thinking the same thing.

Jude put her fork down and covered Chase's hand with hers. Her thumb caressed Chase's palm softly. She increased the pressure when she felt Chase try to pull away. Her gaze was penetrating and Chase shivered. "Normally, you aren't my type, but you are so cute when you're wrong that I find myself thinking that veering from my type might be fun. Believe me, Chase, if I decided I wanted you, you wouldn't turn me down. And I can guarantee, you would love every second of it." She rubbed Chase's palm a second longer then moved her hand away.

Jude had to pull her hand away. Touching Chase and seeing the look of naked longing in her eyes did nothing to quell the growing attraction she felt for her. She still didn't understand it. Chase was not the kind of woman that Jude went after. She looked down at her plate and picked up her fork. She hoped Chase didn't notice that desire was making her hand shake. *It's nothing, Jude. You just need to get laid. Just make it through lunch then you can pick someone up tonight and work out your frustration.*

Chase put both her palms on the table to steady herself. She took several deep breaths and willed her heart to stop pounding out of her chest. Jude's hand on hers had been bad enough, but when Jude said her name, it sounded like a caress and she imagined how her body would respond to Jude's soft touch. She tried to dismiss her disappointment at not being Jude's type, attributing it to her own vanity. *Why wouldn't I be her type?* Chase looked at Jude, watching her until she looked up from her plate. "Why not?"

Jude looked up, confused. "Why not what?"

"Why aren't I your type? What is your type?"

Jude's brain screamed a warning. *Don't answer that!* She pinched the bridge of her nose and debated her answer. She decided to take the safe route, omitting any acknowledgment that she was attracted to Chase. "Let's just say I'm not the relationship type, and I get the feeling you are. To put it bluntly, I'm the one night stand kind of girl."

Chase searched Jude's face, trying to see if she was telling the truth or just trying to let her down easy. "What makes you think I can't be like you and have fun?"

Jude set her fork down and studied Chase for a moment. "Have you ever had a one night stand?"

Chase looked abashed. "Well, no, I guess not…but that doesn't mean I can't."

Jude laughed softly. "Are you seeing anyone now? Is there some heartbroken boy back in Indy? I'm sure you've left a trail of tears in your wake."

"Not hardly." Chase laughed scornfully. "I lost my boyfriend shortly before I lost my job."

"Lost him? Do you make it a habit to misplace people?" She cocked her head sideways, liking the fact that Chase was sticking her tongue out at her. "Is that a threat or a promise?"

Chase leered at her. "It's a promise. And I don't make promises I can't keep."

Jude blushed. She could feel the heat rising in her face, and effusing her whole body. She grabbed her water and gulped it down.

Chase realized her comment flustered Jude, and it made her smile. "What's the matter, Counselor? You aren't scared, are you?"

Jude managed to pull herself together and scoffed loudly. "As if. I don't scare that easily."

It suddenly dawned on Chase that she had hit the nail on the head. "It all makes sense." Chase smiled cryptically. "I've got it all figured out."

Jude swirled her beer around her glass. "Oh yeah, what do you have all figured out?"

"You." She paused, waiting for Jude to stop her, when she didn't interrupt, Chase continued. "You're afraid, that's why you jump from one woman to the next."

Jude scoffed loudly. "And what would I be afraid of?"

"You're afraid of getting hurt. That's why you never allow yourself to have a relationship. If you don't ever give your heart away, there's no chance it will get broken."

Jude winced. She looked away from Chase, unable to look at her piercing gaze. Chase was half right. But it wasn't that she was afraid of getting hurt, it was that she was afraid of getting hurt…again. Her mind flashed to her last year of law school. Myra Dawson. She was Jude's first and only love. Against her better judgment, Jude had fallen in love with Myra. Her heart had subsequently been ripped out when Myra starting dating men because she couldn't deal with the stigma of being out. That, and she would have lost her parents generous financial support had she insisted on continuing to live a lifestyle that they found "absolutely mortifying, and an abomination in the eyes of the Lord". Jude had felt betrayed and heartbroken. She swore she would never allow herself to feel pain like that again. Add to that, her father's belief that marriage was disposable, and it was the recipe for a cynical, commitment phobic woman.

When she spoke again, her voice was laced with sarcasm. "You think that you can meet me two times and have my whole life figured out? You're way off. I choose a no repeat policy because I don't want drama. I like my freedom. It has nothing to do with not allowing myself to fall in love. I like having fun. And believe me, there has never been a shortage of fun."

Chase rolled her eyes and laughed. "Whatever you need to believe to sleep at night. I'll bet money I'm more right than you will ever admit."

Jude shrugged. "Maybe…maybe not." She signaled the waitress for another beer. "You want one?" At Chase's nod, she raised two fingers. "As long as we are playing the psychoanalysis game, it's my turn." Jude tilted her head and studied Chase. "Here it goes. You've spent your whole life running away from something. My guess, some truth you don't want to face. You can't ever stop running because if you do, the truth will catch you and then you have to deal with it." Jude waited when the waitress showed up with their beers. "I wonder though if maybe the truth isn't so bad, and if you stopped running and accepted it, you might be happier knowing it."

Chase nodded in agreement. "You could be right. Maybe you should ditch the law gig." She took a sip of her beer and smiled. "I think you should admit that I was right too and we are both afraid of something, something bigger than both of us. I think Avery wanted me to run the bed and breakfast because she wanted me to learn something about myself up here. And maybe she didn't just stumble across your name in the phone book. Maybe you are in this for a reason too. We are part of some bigger master plan."

Jude laughed softly. "Sure Dorothy, and what else did you learn from the Wizard?"

"Whatever! At least my source isn't the flying monkeys."

Jude laughed out loud. "Touche." She paused while the waitress cleared their plates, and asked if they wanted anything else. "Two pieces of blueberry pie, a la mode." She winked at Chase. "Trust me on this. Even the monkeys love it!"

Chase burst out laughing. "Far be it from me to doubt the monkey."

"Oh my god!" Chase said around a mouth full of pie and ice cream. "This is delicious!"

Jude smirked. "See, I told you. I'm never wrong." She caught Chase's sarcastic look and laughed. "Okay, fine. I'm mostly right. So, you never told me how you lost your boyfriend."

Chase stuffed another bite in her mouth and set her fork down. "I guess I should say he was stolen." She caught Jude's confused look and continued. "Right before TransAir closed down, I came home to find my now ex—boyfriend Derek with another man."

Jude winced. "Ouch. That sucks. Of course, it's just one more reason I don't do relationships."

"Looking back, I don't know that it was much of a shock. I wouldn't say it was the most intimate relationship. Somehow, I don't think sex once a month constitutes a relationship. That's more like a roommate sorta thing."

"Agreed." Jude snapped her fingers. "You know something just hit me. I'm starting to see a pattern here. First, Avery is a lesbian, then your ex—boyfriend is gay. Is there something you want to tell me? Maybe it's the truth you're running from. Yep, that's it. You're gay too. And you are totally in lust with me and want to ravage me."

Chase smacked her hand on her forehead. "Oh my gosh, you're right. That's it!" She gave Jude her best whatever look. Her voice was heavy with sarcasm. "For real? That's the best you've got? I'm gay. Remind me that I need to look for different representation."

Jude raised her hand. "Very funny."

Chase looked up as the waitress approached the table. She took the empty pie plates. "How was everything?"

"It was wonderful, thank you."

She looked between the two women. "Will that be separate checks?"

Chase answered before Jude could respond. "Just one, this one is my treat."

Chase paid the bill, tipped the waitress generously, and followed Jude outside to their cars. It had gotten dark and colder in the time they were inside. Chase shivered. "I think it's time to go home and make a fire."

Jude smiled wickedly. "We can spread a blanket out in front of it and have wild, crazy sex."

Chase's mouth dropped in shock. She started stammering. Jude put her fingers over Chase's mouth to stop her from talking. The second her fingers touched her lips, her heart skipped a beat. She wanted to replace her fingers with her mouth and kiss Chase till she was begging her for mercy. Jude pulled her eyes from Chase's lips and looked into her eyes. She saw her desire mirrored in Chase's face and she jerked her hand away, scared at the ferocity of her gaze. No one had looked at her with such desire and she was pretty sure that Chase didn't realize what she was silently asking for. And she was pretty sure if she didn't break the spell Chase had on her, she would take her right now.

"I was just kidding. A fire sounds great." Jude stopped for a moment. "You should definitely get home and enjoy that…fast. Don't let me keep you."

Chase felt the intimate moment dissolve and she felt empty. Desperately, she tried to hold onto the feelings that Jude stirred in her. She smiled, but it was a melancholy smile that did little to mask her unspoken regrets. "Thanks for suggesting this. I had a really good time with you."

"No, thank you for lunch. I can't remember the last time I enjoyed someone's company as much as yours." The words didn't surprise her, but the emotion behind them did. If she wasn't careful, she knew that Chase could become a hard habit to break. Still she waited impatiently for Chase to reply. She wanted to know that

Chase felt the same way she did. That thought scared her more than she thought possible.

"Me too. I had a really nice time. Maybe we can do it again." She paused, waiting for Jude to say yes.

Jude watched the emotions play on Chase's face. She watched it change from hope to uncertainty to sadness, but still she couldn't say the words she knew she needed to hear. Jude had to keep her distance. It was the only way she would keep her heart safe. She liked Chase, but she wouldn't risk her heart for anyone.

Chase shivered and folded her arms across her chest. "I guess I better go. Thanks again."

"Yeah, me too." Jude made no move to leave, waiting for Chase to take the lead. Chase backed away, and started to turn to leave. Then she spun back around. "Hey, can I ask you a question?" Jude nodded and Chase continued. "Where did you go to law school?"

Jude laughed. "Tulane. Why?"

"No reason. I just wondered." Chase pressed her finger to her lips. "Uhm, you weren't on a crew team by chance, were you?"

"No. I'm not big on water. I played bee—ball for Tulane." Jude cocked her head and searched Chase's face. "Why are you asking?"

Chase blushed, and was immediately grateful it was dark so Jude couldn't see. "No reason, just curious."

Jude snorted. "Asking me where I went to law school qualifies under curious. Asking me if I rowed, that is more along the lines of being specific enough to warrant a reason. So talk."

Chase shook her head. "It's nothing." She started to turn, reaching for her keys. "So I'll talk to you later."

Jude grabbed her arm and held her. "Uh-uh. Talk."

Chase shifted uncomfortably. "It's nothing really. I sort of had a dream about you. We were talking about where you went to law school. You told me Harvard and that you were on the crew team." She shook her head, embarrassed. "Yep, that's about it."

Stepping closer, Jude moved her hand down Chase's arm and grasped her hand. "That's it? What was the context of the conversation? Did we do anything else besides talk?"

Chase was silent long enough to let Jude know without any words that there was more in her dream than just talking. She opened her mouth to answer, but couldn't think of a way out of the question.

Jude smiled. "You don't have to say anything. I think I know." She stepped even closer. "Was it as good for you as it was for me?"

The breath that Chase was holding came rushing out and she shivered at the closeness. "It's not like that. I came to your office to drop something off and then we were just sitting and talking. There isn't anymore to it than that."

"Oh, okay." Jude could tell from the unsteadiness of her voice that there was more, much more that she wasn't sharing. She decided not to push. If Chase had dreamed about her in that way--great. If she didn't want to share, that was even better. Jude wasn't sure she could handle knowing that Chase was feeling something for her, even if it was just lust. She smiled, her eyes searching Chase's in the moonlight. "I better let you go build that fire. I'm sure you're freezing."

Chase realized her hand was still captured in Jude's and she squeezed it. "Actually, I'm surprisingly warm."

Jude looked down and realized that she was absentmindedly caressing Chase's hand. She pulled it away quickly. "Sorry." She shoved her hands in her pockets, aware that if she didn't her hands would find a way to touch Chase again. *I have got to get the hell away from her before I do something stupid.* "Okay, well, I am going to take off. Thank you again."

"Yeah, me too." Her voice wasn't convincing enough to even believe herself that she wanted to leave. Chase pulled her keys out of her pocket and hit the unlock button. Jude reached around her and opened the door, her face so close she could feel her breath on her cheek. Chase's gaze dropped to Jude's lips and her breath caught in her throat. At that moment, Jude turned and realized how close she was to Chase. A few inches closer and…She looked at Chase and realized that she was staring hungrily at her lips. Alarms went off in Jude's head again and she stepped back and shook her head. "Don't"

"Don't what?" Chase asked nervously.

"Don't kiss me." Jude tried to sound stern, but even to her ears the statement sounded weak.

Chase inched closer. "Why not?"

"Because you're going to love it." Jude's head was spinning, her body ached to touch Chase, yet she continued to fight it. Her mind screaming at her to leave.

"So?" Chase put her hand on Jude's arm and kept her from backing up. "Is that so bad?"

"Chase…please." Jude pulled her arm away and went around to the other side of the door. "It's worse than bad. You'll love it and you will want more, and that will make me want more. And I'm not *that* person. I'm not what you want, I'm not even sure you know what you want." She shook her head. "Even if this is what you want, I'm not the right woman for you."

Chase stared at her. "Really? Then tell me you don't want me."

Jude's stomach flip--flopped. How could she look this woman in the eyes and lie to her, when she knew that the truth was written as plainly on her face as it was on Chase's face. The thought that she could give in and take what was being offered flashed through her mind, maybe it would work. Maybe Chase would be different. Just as quickly, she pictured Myra and she felt a knife in her heart. The thought sobered her. She shook her head and looked at Chase, an apology in her eyes. "I can't. I'm sorry." With that, she spun on her heels and went to her car, leaving Chase standing there, wondering how on earth she had gotten to this point.

Chapter 15

Forty—five minutes later Jude tore into the parking lot of Styxx, a gay and lesbian bar in Portland. She was on edge, her nerves still raw from the feelings Chase was bringing out in her.

She went inside and headed straight for the bar. She nodded at the bartender, and when he finally made it down to her, she ordered a double whiskey on the rocks and threw a twenty on the bar. When he brought it back, Jude grabbed it and downed it in one swallow. The initial burn made her eyes water, but as the feeling of warmth hit her stomach, she knew she had come to the right place. "Give me another."

He shrugged. "Rough night?"

She shook her head and laughed cynically. "Not yet, but if I find the right girl it might be." When he filled her glass again, she winked. "I think I just found her." She grabbed the glass off the bar and tipped it up at him. "Thanks."

Jude walked across the crowded bar towards a striking brunette, who had her hand on some woman's thigh. Jude had caught her watching her approach out of the corner of her eye and smirked. *This will be too easy.*

When she got to her table, she pulled out a chair and sat down. She leaned towards her and smiled seductively. "I'm buying you a drink. What are you drinking?"

"I'll get her drinks, she's with me." The woman whose thigh had been occupied by the brunette, glared at Jude.

Jude laughed wickedly. "Don't worry, you can have her back when I'm done." She turned to the brunette again. "Come on."

To her credit, the woman at least pretended to think about it before starting to get up. She put her hand on her date's arm. "It's cool, baby. I'm still going home with you." She kissed her on the lips and got up to join Jude, who was standing with her hand outstretched. She took the woman's hand and pulled her to her feet.

As they walked away, Jude gestured over her shoulder towards the abandoned table. "Sorry about that."

The woman smirked. "No you aren't. My name's Diana…in case you wanted to know."

Jude shrugged. "Not especially." But she smiled to temper the harshness of her words. Normally, Jude was a charming temptress. She tried hard to make her dates feel special, but not tonight. Tonight, she was hungry and in no mood for pleasantries. She wanted to drive Chase from her mind. She wanted to forget the aching need that Chase made her feel. Tonight was about her and she would fuck this woman till she forgot Chase's face. "And you're right, I'm not sorry."

They stopped at the bar. Jude ordered two more whiskeys. She felt Diana trace her fingernail along her knuckles. "So, are you going to tell me your name?"

"Does it matter?" She laughed a low, cynical laugh. "We both know this is a one time thing."

"Fine." She picked up her glass and sipped it slowly. "At least tell me what you do for a living."

"Attorney." Jude's voice was clipped. The less she shared with Diana, the less personal it would be and that was exactly what she needed.

Diana snorted. "Figures. Only a lawyer could be this bitchy and demanding."

"Hey, if you don't like it, you can leave." She hooked her foot on the bar and turned away from Diana. Her lip curled up slightly when she felt Diana's hand on her arm. *Too easy.*

"I'm fine. Besides you're hot and I'm a great fuck."

Jude rolled her eyes. "That remains to be seen." She drained her drink and motioned for the bartender to bring her another one. She threw another twenty on the bar and waited. Three drinks had done nothing to quell the desire humming through her body. Silently, she swore at Chase. She turned her attention back to Diana and forced a smile. She rubbed her thumb over Diana's lips, trying hard to forget Chase. "Where were we?"

Diana pulled Jude's thumb into her mouth and sucked it gently. She swirled her tongue around it and moaned. Jude's eyes got dark and she leaned towards Diana. "Oh, I remember now." She pulled her hand away and replaced it with her lips. She grabbed her neck and pulled her roughly against her, her mouth claiming hers hungrily. She ravaged her with her mouth until she felt Diana's body meld against hers. Wrenching her mouth away, she smirked. "You were just trying to convince me what a good fuck you are. Why don't you show me?"

Diana followed Jude out to the parking lot. She stopped at the passenger side of Jude's BMW and whistled. "BMW. Nice. The law gig must be working pretty well for you."

"I do all right." Jude hit the unlock button and opened the rear door. She extended her hand towards Diana. "Get in."

Diana slid into the car and watched Jude get in behind her and pull the door shut. "You don't mess around, do you? It's a damn good thing you are the hottest woman in this place, or you can be damn sure I wouldn't put up with your mouth."

Jude smirked. "When I get done with you, you will be wishing you had my mouth to put up with all the time."

Diana opened her mouth to reply, but Jude pushed her back against the seat and straddled her, grabbing her shirt and pulling Diana's face to hers. Her lips captured Diana's roughly and her response was lost, replaced by hungry moans.

Jude was lost, heady with power and insatiable hunger. She pushed impatiently under Diana's shirt and her hand found Diana's breast. She squeezed it roughly, her fingers pinching her nipple until Diana gasped in pain. She tried to push Jude's hand away, but Jude grasped her wrist with her other hand and pinned it against the seat. She tugged her shirt up and her mouth replaced her hand. Her tongue raked across it until it was a taut peak. Catching it between her teeth, she bit hard enough to make Diana wince.

"Ouch, shit, that hurts." Diana tried to push Jude away.

Diana's voice finally broke through the cloud in Jude's mind. She looked up and Diana saw apology in her eyes. "Sorry, I'll try to be a little more gentle, princess."

Diana picked up the sarcasm in Jude's voice and wondered if she meant it. Her questions were answered when Jude lifted her breast and began to gently suck on her nipple, raking her tongue deftly across it, teasing it until it was hard again. The sensation ran down her body, pooling between her legs and she tried to stifle a moan.

Jude relaxed her grip on Diana's arm, but she kept it pinned against the seat. She found Diana's other nipple with her mouth, swirling her tongue around it and nipping it gently. Diana arched towards Jude, her body reacting to Jude's skilled tongue. Diana knew if Jude continued, it would only be a matter of minutes before she came and she wanted to wait until Jude was inside her. "Baby, you're going to have to stop that or I'm going to come."

Jude's eyes flicked up to meet Diana's gaze. "Isn't that kind of the point?"

Diana nodded. "Yeah, but I want you inside me. I want you to feel how hard you make me come."

Jude shrugged. "Then I guess we better get to it." She put her hand on Diana's bare thigh, her thumb rubbing light circles just below her skirt. Diana reached down and tried to pull her skirt up, but Jude shook her head. "Uh—uh. Let me."

She caught Diana's breast in her mouth again, her hand slowing sliding up her thigh. Diana pushed her hips off the seat, aching for Jude's touch. Jude held her down, as she continued to slowly tease her way up Diana's thigh. She stroked the sensitive skin on her inner thigh and she jumped. Jude looked up, her eyes questioning Diana. "Ticklish?" She rubbed softly over the spot again.

Diana jumped again. "Maybe…a little.

Jude smiled wickedly. She moved against Diana again, but this time her hand inched higher and her thumb stroked the hollow beneath her panties. She could feel the heat radiating from Diana's body and she licked her lips hungrily. She rubbed her thumb along the vee between her legs and her panties were already wet with arousal. Jude felt her own clit jump in anticipation. She took her other hand and massaged it through her pants, feeling her clit harden beneath her fingers, all the while increasing the pressure of her thumb on Diana.

Diana arched her hips, her body moving against Jude's hand. Jude stroked Diana's clit with just the right amount of pressure to keep her on the edge, but not send her plunging over.

Jude could feel herself getting closer to her own climax and she put her hand inside her pants and stroked deftly. She knew she would bring them both to a climax at the same time. She pushed the silk barrier aside, and stroked her fingers through Diana's hot, wet folds.

She caught Diana's clit between her thumb and forefingers and gently massaged it until she could feel her pulsating beneath her fingers. Jude was close, and she could tell from Diana's body that she was right there with her. She slid two fingers down to her warm center and poised there, teasing Diana as she arched her hips up further, trying to guide Jude's fingers inside her. Jude pulled them away, only to return seconds later, plunging deep inside her. She felt Diana silky warmth envelope her fingers and contract around her. "Oh Chase, you're so fucking wet."

Diana was so lost in the moment, she didn't catch the slip and she continued to push against Jude's hand.

Jude realized it immediately and her hand stilled, her fingers buried in Diana. "Shit! Fuck! I can't do this."

Jude's loud cursing broke Diana out of her spell. She realized Jude was no longer touching her. She had her hands braced on the seat and she was staring out the window, shaking her head. She was thinking about Chase, right now, in the middle of all of this. It was Chase she wanted to be with, not this second—rate imitation. Jude didn't care about anyone and she certainly didn't think about any woman with fondness. But right now, she was dangerously close to having one woman break through those barriers. For some reason, that thought infuriated her and scared her at the same time. *Damn you, Chase!*

Diana put her hand on Jude's arm. "Something wrong, baby?"

Jude jerked away from Diana and glared at her. "You need to get out…now." She wasn't angry at Diana, she was furious with herself. Diana just happened to be unlucky enough to get caught in the crossfire.

"Are you fucking kidding me?" Diana rolled her eyes. "You're seriously going to kick me out in this state? You are one crazy—ass bitch."

"Save it for someone who cares." Jude opened the door and gestured for Diana to get out. "Don't make me kick you out."

Diana pulled down her skirt and reluctantly got out. She threw Jude a look of pure hatred. "You'll be sorry, you…"

Jude put her hand up to interrupt Diana and stepped out of the car. "Don't be nasty, it's really unbecoming. I'm sure you can get yourself taken care of. Just let your girlfriend finish what I started." She slammed the door, spun on her heel and headed to the other side of the car, leaving Diana standing alone, her mouth agape.

Jude started the car and sped away, a last glance in the rearview mirror revealed a thoroughly pissed—off Diana, flipping her off.

She punched the steering wheel, and swore vehemently at the self—inflicted pain. When she got home, she flung her jacket on a chair and loosened her tie. She went straight to the liquor cabinet and pulled out a bottle of Jack Daniels. She opened it and drank straight from the bottle, ignoring the burn as the liquid poured into her and warmed her insides. "Come on, Jack. Do your magic."

#

Tess stood at the doorway and watched Chase shove dishes into the dishwasher with more force than necessary. Chase was muttering to herself, but Tess couldn't make out what she was saying. She shook her head.

Tess's laughter caught Chase's attention and she spun around to see Tess smirk. "Oh hey. Sorry, I didn't mean to be so loud."

"You wanna talk about it?"

Chase shrugged. "There's nothing to talk about." She rinsed another plate and shoved it in the dishwasher, knocking it against another plate and rattling the whole stack.

Tess shoved off the doorframe and walked towards Chase. "The last time I was that mad, it was right before Avery and I got together. I remember thinking to myself how it was possible that one woman could be so damn frustrating."

Chase looked up, her face looked miserable. "Tell me about it. Women!"

Tess raised her eyebrows. "Women in general or one woman in particular?"

"Oh, I don't know." Chase sighed heavily. "Women in general. Maybe one in particular today."

Tess looked chagrined. "I'm sorry, I don't mean to be so frustrating. I thought we were doing pretty good."

"No, silly. It's not you. You are fine." Chase smiled warmly.

"Then I'm thoroughly confused. You haven't met anyone else."

Chase smiled ruefully. "Well, make that two residents in the state of confusion, 'cause I am not sure I even understand myself."

"Well, being that I am the older, wiser half of our pair, I feel it is my sworn duty to help guide you." Tess caught Chase rolling her eyes and chuckled. "Okay, fine. As the *older* half, I am here to help. First, tell me the *who* that is frustrating you."

"It's Jude." Chase's shoulders sagged, the weight of admitting that was taking its toll on her. She knew why it bothered her, but maybe those reasons didn't exist anymore. She just wasn't sure she was ready to find that out.

"Jude?" If it were possible, Tess looked even more confused. "As in our Jude, the attorney."

"Yes, as in our Jude."

"You've only met her once and that was over a month ago. How could she be frustrating you?" Tess paused, concern in her eyes. "Did she call? Is it something with the will?"

"No, no, I ran into her today and don't worry, it's nothing to do with the will." Chase hesitated, almost afraid to continue, for fear that voicing her thoughts would will them into existence. But she had already opened a can of worms, and there was no going back. "It's, ahh, personal."

Tess shook her head. "Okay, now I am beyond confused. I'm baffled, bewildered, perplexed, nonplussed, et cetera. You're going to have to explain the whole situation."

Chase took a deep breath, and smiled wearily. "I suppose I should start at the very beginning."

"Ahh, yeah, that might be a good idea." Tess said sarcastically.

"Shut up!" Chase said playfully. "I'm trying to, but someone, namely you, keeps interrupting me." She eyed the fridge. "I might need a drink and a seat to get through this."

She pulled a bottle of wine out of the fridge, poured two glasses and led Tess into the living room. Chase was silent for half of her glass, trying to build up the courage to share her innermost thoughts with Tess. When she finally spoke, her voice was so low that Tess had to lean forward to hear.

"A couple of weeks ago, no, let me go back even further. The day we went with Joe and Barb to Jude's office, the day I met Jude for the first time, I had a, I mean I thought maybe…I think I was attracted to her." Chase lowered her eyes, not sure how Tess would react.

Tess smiled. "I was wondering if you figured that out."

Chase's head snapped up. "You knew? I mean, was it that obvious?"

Tess shook her head. "No, not especially. I guess I just kind of picked up on it." She laughed suddenly. "I know that sounds funny. I suppose I've always been good at reading situations…as long as I'm not one of the people involved."

"True." Chase laughed at Tess, remembering Barb's account of how she and Avery had totally misread each other's signals when they were falling in love. "How could you tell?"

Tess's eyebrows furrowed and she tapped her wineglass. "Well, first off, you should have seen your face when she walked in the room. You lit up like you had just seen an angel."

Chase threw a pillow at Tess and barely missed her head. "Shut up! It did not."

Tess shrugged. "Okay, well maybe not like you were seeing an angel, but it did light up. I think the most obvious thing was you seemed flustered and I knew none of the rest of us would cause such a reaction, so I figured it had to be Jude who was getting to you. But that still doesn't explain the frustration today."

"Okay, fast—forward to a few weeks ago. I had a dream about Jude. It was of a particularly personal nature."

Tess raised her eyebrows. "And by a *particularly personal nature* you mean erotic?"

Chase turned bright red. "Yes. Very." She saw the expectant look on Tess's face and waggled her forefinger at her. "No, you're not getting details."

"Fine, I probably wouldn't share with you either. So, that brings us up to today."

Chase shook her head yes. "This is where it gets really interesting. I went to Hannaford's to pick up some stuff since it was obvious you didn't do much shopping while I was away."

Tess feigned innocence. "What? I went shopping. I got the essentials. Beer and Spaghettios."

Chase snorted. "And that is why you may be the older of us, but you are so not the wiser."

"Hmm, that's funny, Berk. Did you pick up a sense of humor at Hannafords?"

Chase threw another pillow and nearly knocked the wineglass out of Tess's hand. "Ha! Serves you right, smartass. Anyway, as I was saying before I was so rudely interrupted, I ran into her today. Quite literally. I ran into her with my cart, we chatted, yada, yada, yada, I almost kissed her."

"Woah, woah, woah!" Tess waived her hand, trying not to choke on her wine. "You almost kissed her? What happened in the yada, yada, yada part?"

Chase smiled mischievously. "Just making sure you were paying attention."

"Oh you can be sure you have my utmost attention."

"Okay, well when I first saw her, the only thing I could think of was the dream, and I was mortified. There was no way I could let her see me, so I tried to run the other way. Didn't work so well. As I was making my escape, she came around the corner trying to catch me and I nailed her with my cart."

Tess snorted. "Well that's one way to get a girl's attention. Although, you probably could have just said hello."

Chase rolled her eyes. "Ha, ha, that's funny. Anyway, I offended her and to make it up to her, I bought her lunch."

"And how pray tell did you offend her? She has pretty thick skin."

Chase proceeded to tell Tess the entire embarrassing story of assuming Jude was gay, why she assumed she was gay, to which Tess dutifully rolled her eyes. She conveniently left out the part about assuming Jude was attracted to her because Chase was a woman and Jude was a lesbian. She told Tess about lunch, standing in the parking lot tempted to kiss Jude and her warning not to. "It's crazy though. I've never even been attracted to a woman before. Obviously, there's some deeper meaning behind it. I'm lonely, maybe I'm impressed because she is a lawyer. It's been awhile since I've...*you know.* I'm sure it has way more to do with me needing to get some and nothing to do with me starting to like women."

Tess chuckled. "Listen honey, at this point in your life, I think it's more important to do what makes you happy. I wouldn't try to put yourself into some category society came up with to label people, or try to dismiss some intrinsic behavior because you're not comfortable accepting attraction to another woman as an inherent characteristic. So what if you haven't ever been attracted to a woman? You are now. I know from experience, the more you fight it, the more miserable you will be. You said that Avery bringing you here was part of some bigger plan. Maybe this is it. Maybe you had to come here to finally realize, or accept, something about yourself. I say give in to your lust. What could it hurt?"

"Me, for starters. Jude made it clear that she isn't the woman for me. Some crap story about how she only has one night stands, never relationships, and I am obviously the relationship type." Chase shook her head. "She doesn't know me. How does she know I'm not in it for fun?"

Tess smiled warmly. "My dear, you are not the one night stand kind of girl, and if I'm even remotely correct, neither is Jude. It's a mighty convincing cover, but it's just that. I guess you could take her at her word and not pursue her, but I think both of you would be missing something wonderful. But, that's just my opinion, and you know what they say about those."

"Yeah, I do." Chase swallowed the last of her wine and sighed. "All I know for sure is that no one has ever made me feel the way Jude does. It's raw desire. She makes me want to do bad things. I can't think straight when I'm around her."

Tess laughed. "That may be the smartest thing you have said all night." She clinked her empty wineglass with Chase's and smiled. "Here's to a successful hunt."

Chapter 16

Chase lengthened her stride and kicked out the last hundred yards of her run. She stopped at the end of the drive way and paced slowly in front of the yard for two passes, letting her breathing and heart rate return to normal. She wiped the sweat off her face with a gloved hand and smiled.

She hadn't run since the first day she arrived in Florida over the Christmas holiday. It was too damn humid for her and rather than collapse from exhaustion and dehydration after a half of a mile, she decided to curb her runs for the duration of her visit. She hadn't started again when she got home, but after spending yesterday with Jude and fighting an uphill battle against her fragile emotions, she figured the best way to deal with it was a good, long run. She pulled back her sleeve, glanced at her watch and figured she had done at least five miles. She smiled to herself. *Still haven't lost my stride.* She walked to the front porch and stretched her calves on the steps before going inside.

Chase froze when she walked into the living room. Tess was sitting on the sofa, tears streaming down her face. Chase rushed to her side and swept Tess into her arms.

"Honey, what's wrong?"

When no response came other than heart—wrenching sobs, Chase held her close and rocked her, letting Tess cry on her shoulder. Finally, the sobs stopped and Tess sniffed softly. She pulled away and looked at Chase through swollen, red—rimmed eyes.

"I'm sorry you had to see that." She shook her head and wiped her eyes on her sleeve. "You've had to deal with enough of that lately."

"Shhh, shhh. It's okay." Chase wiped a tear off of Tess's cheek and smiled. "Besides what are friends for?"

"Obviously, to take care of a big whiney baby like me. I know you didn't sign up for that." Tess attempted a half—hearted smile, but Chase could see past the smile to the quivering chin and it broke her heart to see Tess hurting again.

"You wanna talk about it?" She tilted Tess's chin up so she could see that Chase was totally sincere in her offer. "I'm a really good listener. Besides, Avery would kick my ass if I let you stay here alone and cry."

Tess started laughing and crying at the same time. "God, I'm such a mess." She looked up at Chase. "That seems to be a pattern with us, me crying and you giving me a shoulder to cry on. It's kinda one—sided."

Chase laughed softly. "Don't worry, one of these days I'm going to fall apart and I'll need you to help me put the pieces back together again. And it will probably happen more than once, so let me get a good head start while I can. Deal?"

Tess acquiesced, solemnly nodding her head. "Deal."

"So, wanna talk about it now?" Chase tilted her head, her eyes warm, willing Tess to share her pain.

"My grandmother died…yesterday."

"I'm sorry, hon." Then as if hit square in the face, Chase jumped back in shock. "What? How do you know? I mean, you haven't talked to your family in forever. Did they call you?"

"No, they didn't." Her voice started to quiver and she paused, trying to regain some self—composure. "A friend from back home did. She said she didn't think my family would call me, given our present circumstances, and she knew I would want to know."

"What are you going to do? I mean, are you going home?" Chase looked concerned, then angry as a new thought hit her. "That's your family, why couldn't they have tried to reach you? I know they basically cut you out of their lives, but this is your grandmother for God's sake. The least they could do is remember that you are their flesh and blood."

Fresh tears started to stream down Tess's face. "Please don't be mad at them Chase. They did what they thought was right. I forgave them along time ago." She swiped at the tears again. "Right now what I need is you to be my friend. I haven't decided if I am going back or not. I think I need to sleep on it. Maybe tomorrow it will be a little clearer."

Chase squeezed her hand. "Want me to make some chocolate chip cookies? That's what my mom always did when things weren't going right."

Tess nodded, and the corner of her mouth started to creep up a little. "Okay. And maybe some hot chocolate too?"

Chase jumped up. "Of course. We'll load it up with marshmallows and whip cream."

She reached out her hand and hoisted Tess to her feet. "I'll even let you lick the bowl."

Tess face broke into a wide grin and for the first time Chase thought she may be all right again. "Deal." She glanced at her watch and looked back at Chase. "Why don't you go take a shower and freshen up first?"

Chase feigned surprise. "What? Do I stink?" She lifted her arm and smelled her pit. "It's not bad at all, I hardly smell anything." She shoved her armpit towards Tess's face, laughing wickedly.

Tess ducked quickly and managed to side—step her. "Let's just say I'm glad my nose is stuffed up from crying or I might have passed out." She winked and then ran from the room, Chase two steps behind her.

#

Chase slid the last of the hot cookies off the cookie sheet onto a cooling rack. She set the pan down, reached for her mug of cocoa and took a small sip. She quickly fanned her mouth. "Ouch! That is still really hot. Be careful!"

Tess shook her head, taking a big gulp. "Uh—uh, asbestos tongue."

"Huh?" Chase looked puzzled.

"Well maybe not asbestos tongue, but the heat doesn't burn. Way too many late nights working on the latest, greatest video games and swigging boiling coffee have made my tongue heat resistant. You're lucky I can still taste food."

Chase snickered. "Yeah, how'd that work out for Avery?" She caught Tess's blank stare. "Cause I'm thinking no feeling in your tongue could be a bad thing for someone of your…ahh…persuasion, if you know what I mean."

Tess rolled her eyes and snorted. "Believe me honey, she had no complaints in that department."

"Nice." Chase stuck her fist out towards Tess and she tapped it softly. She was quiet for a moment, sipping her hot cocoa. Her somber gaze returned and she focused on Tess. "Were you close to your Grandmother?"

"Yes and no. I was really close to her when I was quite young. I'm the oldest of three and the first grandbaby. So for the first eight years, Mamo, that's what we called her, and I were really close. I think I spent more time at her house than my own. Then when I was eight, the twins were born and they quickly became Mamo's favorites. I never knew my grandfather. He died of a heart attack a couple of years before I was born, and my dad's parents lived in Ireland so we hardly ever saw them. We really only had Mamo."

"That would be so different. I had both sets of grandparents for the longest time. My dad's mom was the last to pass away and that wasn't until three years ago."

"I can't say I'm not a little jealous of you. That must have been really nice to have all your grandparents around for so long." Tess shook her head sadly. "It's crazy I know, since I've been gone so long, but I miss Mamo. Or maybe I miss being young and the innocence that went with it. I remember growing up, Mamo would make us cakes for our birthdays. It was always whatever was our favorite kind of cake for that year. She would hide money inside it. And then for Christmas, all the family, uncles, aunts, cousins would all go to Mamo's house on Christmas Eve. We would all spend the night, wake up Christmas morning and open presents in our pajamas. My family was always so close."

Chase put her hand over Tess's and squeezed softly. "It sounds like it. I'm sorry they took that away from you. I still can't imagine the hurt you must have felt...hell, still feel."

"Most of the time it's okay, I kinda push it to the back of my mind, but this really hits home. I'm sure I will get a chilly reception, but I have to go home for the funeral. I need to say my goodbyes."

"Do you want some company? I could come with you."

Tess smiled, but shook her head no. "Thank you. That means a lot. But I think this is something I have to face on my own. These are my demons." She reached up and hugged Chase fiercely. "Just promise you will be here when I come running back."

"You know I will be. Call me if you change your mind...I'll catch a flight down there."

Tess pulled back from Chase and regarded her thoughtfully. "Thank you. You really are as wonderful as Avery said you were."

"Aww, shucks ma'am." Chase looped her thumbs through her jeans and cinched them up to cover her embarrassment. Her voice was tinted with a heavy southern twang. "I'm just doing my job, ma'am. Golly gee, no need to thank me."

Tess batted her eyelids and fanned herself with an imaginary fan. "There is just one more little thing…"

Chase shuffled her feet and looked at the floor. "Shucks ma'am, anything for you."

Tess winked innocently. "Could you hitch up the wagon and drive me to the airport?"

Chapter 17

Chase jumped at the sound of the doorbell. She had dropped Tess off at the airport in Portland that morning and she wasn't expecting anyone. Being alone in the house for the first time had her somewhat unnerved. Not freaked out, but definitely not in her comfort zone. Plus, they were interrupting her old movie marathon.

She pulled the belt on her robe tighter and went to the front door. She looked out the peep hole and frowned. Whoever was at the door was hiding behind the biggest floral arrangement she had ever seen. Confusion registered on her face as she pulled the door back slowly, the tell tale creak of the old wood echoing through the narrow hallway.

Chase smiled when Jude popped out from behind the flowers, relief on her face. "Flowers for me…you shouldn't have."

Jude eyes traveled the length of Chase's body and her face broke into a lascivious grin. She raised her eyebrows and smirked. "Something slinky for me…you shouldn't have."

Chase pulled the top of her robe up closer towards her chin and blushed. "If this old thing is slinky to you, you are obviously not getting out enough." She stepped back and met Jude's gaze. "Would you like to come in?"

"Thanks." Jude shivered and stepped in quickly. "It's pretty cold outside. I hate these arctic blasts. At least we aren't getting snow with this one."

Chase's eyes roved over Jude unconsciously. She looked adorable with her rosy cheeks, tinged pink from the cold. She seemed softer that way. Her green eyes sparkled against the white cashmere scarf that opened just enough so that Chase could see the vee at the base of her neck. Jude was wearing a knee length black leather coat, and the scent of that mixed with her spicy perfume made Chase heady. *Fuck! Why does she have to get better looking every time I see her?* Chase jumped when she heard Jude clear her throat loudly. She met Jude's amused eyes and blushed again.

Jude smirked. "Looks like that honey are guaranteed to heat things up." She caught Chase's shocked look and laughed. "Breathe. I'm just kidding. Teasing among friends…since we are friends. Right?" She stepped inside and shut the door against the cold wind.

Chase shook her head and attempted a feeble smile. "Yeah, sure…friends."

"Can you hold these a sec?" Jude handed the flowers to Chase and shrugged out of her coat. She hung it on the wrought iron coat rack in the foyer and took the flowers back from Chase. "Thanks. So is Tess around? These are actually for her. I heard about her grandmother and thought these might cheer her up."

"No, she's not. I took her to the airport this morning. She's flying home for the funeral."

"No shit!" Jude snorted loudly. "Well I kept telling her one of these days she was going to have to go home and confront the family. I'm just sad it was under these circumstances."

"I know, I feel horrible for Tess. But maybe this is just the circumstance she needs. There's a lot of water under the bridge and maybe this will help all of them get over it." Chase saw Jude glance into the living room, then back. "Did you want to come in? I could make you some coffee or some hot tea? You can warm up some before you leave."

Jude accepted and followed Chase into the living room. Her eyes flicked to the tv and she laughed softly. *"An Affair to Remember?* Interesting choice…and wine. Hmm, are you nursing a broken heart?" She settled onto the couch beside Chase.

Chase snorted. "As if! My heart is most definitely not broken, besides I love the classics. TNT is playing a Cary Grant marathon today. Reminds me of growing up and staying with my grandparents. My grandmother had the biggest crush on Cary Grant."

"This definitely qualifies as a classic, although truth be told, my crush was on Deborah Kerr."

"Hmph! You would." Chase's smile tempered her words. "You don't strike me as the old movie type."

Jude picked an imaginary piece of lint off her slacks. "There's a lot about me that may surprise you." She nodded towards Chase's glass. "What's your poison?"

"It's a Reisling Tess picked up. It's pretty good. Would you like a glass?"

"Sure why not?" Jude put her hand on Chase's arm to keep her from getting up. She felt heat shoot through her fingers into her core. She jumped at the unexpected surge of electricity she felt just touching Chase. She pulled her hand back quickly and stood up. "But I can get it. Do you want me to top you off?"

"Please." Chase took a deep breath and willed her hand not to shake. No matter how hard she tried to ignore her attraction to Jude, her body betrayed her. She was going to have to figure out really fast how to be immune to Jude. "It's in the wine cooler under the breakfast bar."

"Kay, I'll be right back." She glanced at the tv where Cary Grant's character Nicky was surprised to run into Terry, played by Deborah Kerr at the ballet. "Oh good, we are getting to the good parts."

She returned quickly carrying two wine glasses in one hand and a bowl of popcorn in the other. She caught Chase's questioning look. "Figured we couldn't watch a movie without popcorn." She handed Chase her glass and flopped down beside her, their hips barely brushing. She scooted away but not before her stomach flip—flopped at the nearness.

Chase slid to the end of the couch, pulled her legs up and tucked them underneath her. "I'm guessing you must have been better friends with Avery and Tess than I imagined."

"Guilty." Jude laughed and shoved a handful of popcorn in her mouth and handed the bowl to Chase. "I hope you like butter. I melted some and drizzled it over the top." She sipped her wine. "Mmm, this is pretty good. I'm not normally a Reisling person, but this is really good."

"Yeah, Tess knows her wines. She started taking me with her to this wine tasting in Bath. I have tried some really good wines, but there are some of the reds that I think you could use to strip paint."

Jude laughed out loud and shrugged. "Yeah, Tess's taste tend to run to the harder stuff sometimes." She held her fingers up to her lips and sucked in. "Did she tell you about her little habit when she lived in California?"

"Yes, she told me pretty early on. Crazy!"

Jude shook her head. "She is a mess!" She turned towards the tv again and sipped her wine. "What about you? Any vices besides old movies?"

"Only one, and it's a bad one." She smiled cryptically.

"Oh god, don't tell me…you're addicted to sex." Jude chuckled softly. "I figured I was the only one." Jude made the mistake of looking at Chase when she said that. Chase's eyes were a window to her soul and the look of naked desire in them scared her. She hoped that her own desire was not evident. The second she said sex her mind suddenly pictured what it would be like to make love to Chase. *Oh my god! Get a freakin' grip!*

Chase's heart was about to pound out of her chest. No one had ever looked at her with that kind of longing. Her stomach was churning and desire was pooling between her legs. Alarms started going off in her head and she suddenly felt like a caged animal, ready to jump out of her skin. It took all her effort, but she managed to pull away. "Wine. Wine's my weakness. I'm gonna get some more." She jumped off the couch and fled into the kitchen, trying to regain her sanity. She put her glass down and rested her elbows on the counter. Letting her face fall into her hands, she sucked in a deep breath and counted to twenty. *You have got to chill out. You don't let anyone get to you like this.*

Jude watched Chase leave the room and shook her head. She had been attracted to women before, but never felt an intense, overwhelming need for one. She knew this was dangerous territory and she needed to do something to get back on safe ground.

Chase turned at the sound of footsteps and saw Jude standing in the doorway with her coat on, watching her with uncertainty. "I'm going to head out. I don't want to overstay my welcome."

"Don't be silly." Chase walked towards her. "I'm sure you have a standing invitation in place." She caught Jude's gaze and held it, silently telling her everything she was afraid to say out loud. She inched closer until they were almost touching. Her gaze dropped to Jude's lips and she wet her own subconsciously, a loud voice in her head urging her forward.

Jude stood mesmerized, helpless to tear her eyes away. Whether Chase knew it or not, she was offering herself to Jude. All she had to do was take it. It was as simple as that. They were both consenting adults and if Chase was finally ready to accept who she was, she could do worse than Jude for her first lesbian encounter. Jude was experienced, and knew she would make Chase's first time the most pleasurable sex she'd ever had. Plus she had explained to Chase her rules about no repeat dating. If things got ugly afterward, too bad, she had been warned. Jude rubbed Chase's arm with her palm and felt her muscles flex underneath her touch. She took a step closer, her eyes questioning Chase, waiting for her to acquiesce.

Chase's breathing was ragged. If Jude's intense gaze wasn't enough to push her over the edge, when she rubbed her arm softly, she felt herself pitch headlong into oblivion. When she spoke, her voice was a ragged whisper. "Yes."

The sweet word hit Jude square in the face. It wasn't yes she heard, it was please don't hurt me and that was more than she could take. With more force than necessary, she pushed Chase away from her. "I can't...I can't do this. Not like this and not with you."

Chase blinked, unsure where she was for a moment, the momentary spell broken. She saw the apology in Jude's eyes and cursed herself. She shook her head and turned away from Jude, unable to look into her eyes without her body betraying her. "I'm sorry."

"Don't apologize. It's my fault." Jude shuffled nervously. She had never been in this position and she felt lost. Feelings of loneliness washed over her and she tried to ignore them. "I shouldn't have come..."

"Why not? You don't need to change your life because of me. They were your friends long before I showed up, and that shouldn't change because I'm here." She turned to face Jude, her shoulders square. "Besides, you told me the rules. Why don't we just forget this happened and try to be friends?'

"I think that's a great idea." As soon as the words were out of Jude's mouth, her heart dropped. She felt like a part of her just died. "I don't see any reason why we can't be friends. We like each other..." she paused when Chase rolled her eyes, "...you know what I mean. We get along pretty well and I enjoy your company. I think you enjoy mine. We're both intelligent adults, I'm sure we can deal with the little attraction between us."

Chase smiled sweetly. "I'm sure of it. I'm not sure it's even attraction to you, so much as admiration. No sense ruining a friendship over something trivial." Her words may have almost convinced Jude if she had been able to keep the pain out of her eyes.

"Plus, any awkwardness with us is just going to make Tess uncomfortable."

"Right." Jude shook her head up and down. "And she really is the most important person to consider. It would seem strange if I stopped coming around for no apparent reason."

"Exactly. What Tess needs is to have her friends around her for support. We'll just push through this *issue* for her sake."

Jude winked. "What issue?"

"Exactly." Chase smiled ruefully. "What issue? We don't have any issues. So, friend, would you like to stay and finish the movie with me? I think *Bringing Up Baby* is on next."

Jude laughed softly. "Yes, I think I would like that." She stepped aside and followed Chase back into the living room, trying to keep her eyes from straying to Chase's perfectly rounded backside that was tempting her from beneath her robe. *Friends? How am I ever going to stick to that?*

Chapter 18

Chase rummaged around her purse trying to find her cell phone. She finally grabbed it from the bottom and checked the display. She smiled and pushed talk. "Hey Tess."

"Hey. How are you? Things okay back there?"

"Everything is fine." Chase smiled. Leave it to Tess to be more worried about her than she was about herself. "I miss you. It's lonely in this big house all by myself. How are things there? How was the funeral?"

"They are getting better. The funeral was a bit awkward. I know my family was totally surprised to see me. I'm glad I came though, it helped to say goodbye to Mamo."

"So have you talked to them outside of the funeral? Any change in the status quo?" Chase crossed her fingers, hoping that would influence the answer.

"Let's just say we are working on it. My dad actually made the first step."

"Oh yeah?" Chase slammed on her brakes and cursed.

"You okay?" Tess could hear the squeal of her tires through the phone.

"Shit. Damn it. Think you could share the road? Seriously, learn to drive." Chase blew out a breath and continued muttering.

Tess laughed. *"Route One?"*

"Yeah, how'd you know?" Chase rolled her eyes as a car ahead of her threw on a turn signal and made a right turn at the last minute. "Sometimes I freakin' hate this road."

Tess's laughter rang through the phone. *"I didn't realize how much I missed you...and your sailor's mouth."*

"Yeah, real funny fuckface." Chase switched the speaker on and put the phone on the console. "Hey I got you on speaker, kay?"

"Yeah, that's cool."

"So give me the scoop. How did dear old dad make an effort to repair the bridge? And as a sidebar, are you singing Simon and Garfunkel in your head now?"

"Actually I had a little Crosby, Stills and Nash in my head. Teach your children well...anyway, back to my news. So I show up at the funeral service right before it starts. I sat at the back so I wouldn't cause trouble with anyone."

"You sat in the back of the church?" Chase huffed loudly, disbelief in her tone. "I would have marched my happy ass right up to the front. That is your grandmother."

"I couldn't. I know it seems easy to you, but I didn't want to make waves. I sat in the last row of the church and I watched my father up there, as tall and foreboding as he had ever been. It was a beautiful service. I don't think there was a dry eye in the place. Afterwards, we went to the cemetery. I kept my distance there too."

"Why?" Chase could feel herself getting angry. "You don't owe them anything."

"Chase, please. It's not that simple. Besides, I didn't even know what I would say to any of them if I did get close enough."

"I'm sorry, I'll be nice. So what happened?"

"I stayed at the cemetery after everyone left. I just stood there talking to Mamo, telling her everything that was in my heart. From the time I was kicked out till now, how much I loved Avery and how I felt like my heart had been ripped out when she died. It was such a relief to tell someone in my family. And then I just cried."

"Oh honey, I'm sorry. I wish I had been there. I can still come you know." Chase bit her lip, she felt helpless when her friend needed her the most. "I could get a flight out tonight."

"No, it's all good. I'm actually staying at my parents."

"What?!" Chase picked up the phone and took it off speaker. "Did you just say you are staying with your parents?"

Tess chuckled softly. *"Yes."*

"How did that happen?" Chase felt her blood pumping. "You went from banned from the family for twenty years to staying with them overnight. How did that happen?"

"I know, I'm still a little surprised at the turn of events. I thought everyone was gone from the cemetery, but next thing I knew my dad was there right beside me. He said that he was sorry, that he had made a lot of mistakes in his life and letting me go was one of them. He hoped I could forgive him and my mother. He said they

would be honored if I could stay with them while I was in town. Of course, that made me start crying again. So, I'm staying there. It's a little weird but at least they are trying."

"That's really great for you. I was hoping that somehow this would help them see that life is too short to turn your back on your family for any reason."

"It's a start. We still have a long way to go, but at least they are trying."

"So are you still heading home this weekend?" Chase asked.

"If it's all right, I think I am going to stick around for a bit. Most of the family is in town for the funeral. This will give me a chance to see everyone." Tess paused, her voice expectant. *"That is, if it's okay with you."*

Chase laughed. "Of course it's okay. You don't have to ask me for permission."

"Yeah, I know. I just figured I wouldn't leave you by yourself too long."

"Please woman. I can handle it, I'm an adult. Besides, there isn't much going on. We won't have any guests until Valentine's Day weekend, so as long as you are back by then we are good."

Tess snorted loudly. *"Yeah, I'll be back by then. I may not have seen my family in twenty years, but I still can't take them in large doses for very long. Hang on."*

Chase heard muted conversation in the background and figured Tess was talking to someone in her family. *"Hey listen, that was my mom. We are getting ready to sit down for dinner. Can I call you back later?"*

"No, don't do that. I'm fine. Spend your time there with them. I'll be here when you get back."

"Okay, cool. I'll call you when I figure out when I'm coming back and give you the flight info." Tess was quiet for several seconds. *"Chase?"*

"Yes?" Chase heard the tentativeness in her voice.

"Thank you...for being such a great friend."

Chase smiled, warmth effusing her body. "You're welcome." She felt herself starting to get emotional, her happiness for Tess hitting her. "Now go eat. I'll talk to you next week."

"Okay. Later kid." Tess pushed end on the phone. She smiled a real smile, the first one in several months. At that moment, she knew everything would be all right.

Chapter 19

Jude stared at the cursor flashing on her computer. She glanced at the clock and did a double take. She had been staring at the computer for almost thirty minutes and still hadn't managed to start writing. She was supposed to be preparing a will, but her mind kept wandering.

She grimaced when she thought about last night. Another failed attempt to *seal the deal*, as she called it, thanks to Chase. She'd had a date with Jessica Stone, a fellow attorney who specialized in adoption cases for a firm in Portland. They shared the same idea as far as women were concerned. They were like disposable cameras, use them once and throw it away. Add to that, Jessica was gorgeous. A natural redhead, she made femme look good. Any other time and Jude would have no problem having a night of sex with this woman, but not last night, or any night for that matter. Not since Chase came into her life.

Every time she had tried to kiss Jessica, it was Chase's face she saw, Chase's full lips that called to her primal need. Finally after several failed attempts and several awkward minutes of conversation, Jude had excused herself. She got to her car and a stream of expletives flew out of her mouth. Slamming her fist against her desk, she cursed loudly.

She glanced up when Beth knocked lightly on the door and stepped into her office. "Everything okay in here? I haven't heard you yell that loud since the Bernards."

"Argh!" Jude growled at just the mention of the Bernards. A couple she had worked with several years before who revised their will seven times before eventually getting divorced and negating the need for a joint will. "Yeah, that's twelve months I'll never get back. I'm okay though, just having one of those days, you know? I can't seem to focus." She didn't tell Beth that she could focus, it was just on the wrong thing, or person.

Beth shook her head. "Yeah, I know. I'm PMSing and Todd and I are fighting. I'm having a really hard time concentrating myself."

"Huh, Todd." Jude stared at Beth, her eyebrow raised. "When are you going to come over to the dark side and give us a chance?"

Beth winked and hit Jude back with a saucy reply. "I'm too afraid to come over to the dark side. You'd get one taste of me…" she waited while Jude leered at her and shook her finger at her. "Bad girl. You'd get a little taste of me and be addicted and I don't want to be the woman you break the rules for. Besides, my dad always told me don't get your meat where you get your bread, or I guess in this case, don't get your pie where you get your bread."

Jude groaned. "Ugh Beth, that was bad, even for you." She turned to the blank screen and sighed. "I've got to get out of this funk."

"Yes you do. You're depressing me. When was the last time you got laid?"

"Too long." Jude snorted loudly. "I think I've forgotten what it's like."

"What do you mean?" Beth flopped into a chair across from Jude, looking confused. "I thought you had a date with some hot attorney last night. What happened to that?"

"Yeah, what happened?" Jude rolled her eyes and sat back in her chair. "I'm still trying to figure that out. Did you ever get something stuck in your head and you just can't get rid of it?"

"What's her name?" Beth smiled cryptically. "I'm assuming you are talking about a woman. I highly doubt some*thing* could have you all wigged out."

"There's no one." Jude shook her head, unable to answer Beth's question honestly, because it meant bearing parts of her soul she wasn't even sure she was ready to acknowledge. "I just don't feel…like myself lately."

Beth shrugged. "Maybe that's a good thing." She caught Jude's surprised look. "Don't get me wrong, I like who you are. You are a great person, but maybe you are ready for a change. Maybe you're evolving into the next phase of your life."

Jude laughed and shook her head. "Nah, I'm pretty happy right where I am. Today's just an off day." Her mind wandered back to Chase. She pictured her beautiful brown eyes, watching her with barely concealed longing. Her beautiful mouth begging to be kissed. Her perfect, round breasts that…Jude's breath caught in her throat and she felt her face flush with embarrassment. She glanced at Beth and saw the amused look in her eyes. "What?"

"*What?*" Beth laughed. "What *is* that the look on your face is enough to get me hot and bothered. I think it's time you start talking."

"I just don't know what's going on." Jude rubbed her face and ran her hands through her hair. "Okay, let's say hypothetically speaking I may be attracted to someone I probably shouldn't be attracted to. Every time I am with her I want to rip her clothes off."

"So what's stopping you? The Jude I know goes after what she wants and doesn't take no for an answer."

"It's complicated." Jude picked absentmindedly at the corner of her notebook. "This one is different. She's unlike anyone I've ever met. She's smart, beautiful, funny…she gets under my skin. I physically want her more than I have ever wanted any woman."

Beth rolled her eyes. "So I'm asking again…what's stopping you? Is she interested in you?"

"I think so." Jude smiled shyly. "If the looks she gives me are any indication. It's just that…"

"It's just that what?" Beth regarded Jude thoughtfully. "You want her, she wants you. I don't see the problem."

Jude huffed loudly. "The problem is…she's not exactly the one night stand type."

"Yeah, I still don't get your rules." She shrugged. "I mean what are rules made for if not to break them?"

"Nope. I made the rules for a reason. I won't break them. Even if I gave in and took what I wanted, I think I would hurt her in the process, and part of the rule is take what I want as long as the other person is on board and there is no chance of anyone getting hurt."

Beth raised her eyebrow. "Well aren't you just a softie at heart? All along I was thinking that you just run with it no matter the cost." She smirked at Jude. "Love 'em and leave 'em. That's the Stafford way."

"Stop it!!" Jude tried to glare at Beth, but she couldn't stifle her smile. "You don't really think that…do you? That I'm some heartless bitch that discards women left and right? They all know what they are getting into with me. I'm totally up front with any woman I sleep with."

"Yeah, why do you think I've stayed straight all these years? I just can't handle the heartbreak hooking up with you would bring me."

Jude looked chagrined. "Seriously? Do I really come across that way? Cause I would never hurt you…"

Beth was trying hard to keep from laughing. She couldn't remember a time when her boss was ever concerned about anyone's feelings, except her own. Whoever the mystery girl was had obviously done a number on her. She had always thought she could read people pretty well, and right now, despite what Jude was saying about not breaking the rules for anyone, she had a pretty good idea that Jude may not have much of a choice. Even Jude wasn't powerful enough to make her heart stop feeling. And if Beth knew her boss at all, it was going to be a bumpy ride. Beth snickered into her hand. "Simmer down. I'm just messing with you."

Jude glared at Beth. "Bitch. That's it, you're fired."

Beth laughed out loud. "Oh please. Do you know how many times you've fired me since I started here? More than I can count on one hand." She got up and started towards the door. "Why don't you get out of here…you're no good to me today."

"What?" Jude pretended to be offended. "I'm perfectly fine."

"Yeah, cause it normally takes you all morning to even start preparing a will." She rolled her eyes for effect. "Seriously though, why don't you take off for the day? We don't have any appointments and nothing we absolutely have to do." She put her hand on the door and opened it, watching Jude's reaction.

"And do what?" She shook her head. "I don't see how I can be any more effective outside these walls."

"I don't know. Maybe call your *friend* and see if she wants to hook up." Beth winked at Jude and walked out before she could respond.

"Very funny." Jude held her middle finger up to the door and smiled. It never failed, if anyone was going to call her out, it was Beth. And Beth was one of the few people she would allow to take that liberty. She thought about her suggestion to call her *friend.* She wondered what Chase was up to right now. *Right, like you just started thinking about her. More like you can't stop thinking about her. Son of a bitch!*

Suddenly, a thought started in the recesses of her mind and worked its way to the forefront, sounding less and less crazy the more she dwelled on it. She needed to go to Portland anyway, why not have some company? Plus, it just might get her out of her funk.

She picked up the phone, waited for the dial tone and punched in the number. When Chase answered, Jude's heart flip—flopped. Just the sound of her voice was enough to send Jude into a tailspin. She took a deep breath and tried to level her voice out. "Hey, it's Jude."

"Hey, what's up?" Chase shook her head. She knew that Jude couldn't have known she was thinking about her and hoping she would call her. The fact that Jude was on the phone now had to be mere coincidence, but it still rattled Chase. She had never been a believer in the paranormal, but now she wondered if she hadn't wanted something so bad, she actually willed it into being.

"I was hoping I would catch you and Tess." *Well you actually, but let's not split hairs.*

"Well, you caught me. Tess is still in Connecticut with her family. What's up?"

"Are you serious?" Jude couldn't keep the disbelief out of her voice. "So things are going pretty well then. That's great! Well I guess that sorta changes the reason I called."

"I can tell her you called…next time she checks in." Chase tried to keep the sadness out of her voice. *"Hopefully, it's not too important."*

"Well no, it was no big deal really. I just have to run into Portland to drop some paperwork off and I thought you ladies might like to join me. Help take Tess's mind of everything. Like I said, it's no big deal. This way I can just run down there and get back up here earlier."

"If you are okay with just me, I don't have anything else to do. If that's not okay though, I understand." Chase's voice quivered and she hoped Jude hadn't heard it over the phone. *"I'll tell Tess you called."*

"Chase, wait! Are you sure? I'll treat you to dinner in exchange for the company." Jude held her breath waiting for Chase's response. She crossed her fingers.

"If you're sure it's okay, I'm game."

"Please, I'd like the company. It will give us a chance to get to know each other…since we are going to be friends." Jude had trouble uttering the last part of that sentence. Even with their decision to remain friends only, there was still that little issue of attraction. One she was fighting an uphill battle against. *Jude, we can do this. It's one afternoon.* "How soon can you go?"

"Anytime. I just have to throw some clothes on. I just got out of a hot bath."

Jude's grip tightened on the phone. *Oh fuck!* "You're..." Jude swallowed, her eyes suddenly out of focus. "...naked?" She no sooner said the words than she pictured Chase, naked in front of her, begging for her touch.

"Yeah, not so much really. I'm wearing your favorite slinky robe." Chase smiled. If Jude wanted to play this game, she was up for it. What could a little flirting hurt? They had both made it clear it would go no further.

Jude felt heat building in her body, all rushing towards her already aroused center. Thinking about the robe didn't help, it just made Jude think about what forbidden pleasures were hidden underneath. She glanced at her watch. Maybe she would have a little time to take care of herself before they left for Portland. Right now, her clit was throbbing so hard, she knew it wouldn't take much. She decided to resort to humor to cover the influx of emotions she was feeling. "You don't need to change on my account. Maybe we could use your legs to our advantage. Free dinner, maybe?"

Chase laughed out loud. *"Only if you plan on starving. These legs wouldn't get you a cup of coffee."*

Jude rolled her eyes and resisted the urge to reply. She had seen those legs, and they would probably buy the restaurant. "So what do you say we meet in like an hour?"

"That sounds good. Do you want me to come to the office?"

"No, why don't you meet me at my house? It's about halfway between here and your place. Then you can leave your car at the house, where no one will mess with it."

"Sure. Just tell me how to get there."

Jude gave Chase detailed directions to her home, her code to get inside the fence and her cell phone number. "So I'll see you in an hour. Just dress casually."

"Sounds good...and Jude? Thanks for the invite."

"My pleasure." Jude hung up and smiled. She realized that she actually meant the words. And she was looking forward to spending time with her, even if it was *just friends*.

Chapter 20

Chase found Jude's house with little trouble given the excellent details Jude provided. She pulled up to the gate, punched in the code and when the gate opened, started up the long driveway that wound between towering pine trees. When she got her first view of the home, her jaw dropped. Chase wasn't sure what exactly she expected, but this exceeded any expectations she may have had.

She was sure that if it had not been designed by Frank Lloyd Wright, it had to have been on of his students. The home resembled one she had seen in Buffalo as a child and many she had seen only in print. It looked like a series of geometric blocks built together to create a home. She parked the car in the driveway in front of the house. There were two large urns flanking the massive staircase leading up to the porch. Windows covered every inch of the house. It was magnificent and it was Jude.

Chase was about to ring the bell when Jude opened the door. Chase's breath caught in her throat as Jude greeted her with a dazzling smile. She was wearing a navy turtle neck that made her emerald green eyes almost blue. It hugged her perfect breasts and fit tightly enough that Chase could make out a narrow waistline and a very flat stomach. She had faded blue jeans that hugged her hips, and accented her long legs. By the time Chase's gaze swept the entire length of Jude's body and back up again, she was ready to pass out. She gulped in several large breaths and begged her knees not to collapse under her.

"Hi! You didn't have any trouble finding it, did you?" Jude stepped aside and invited Chase in.

"Not at all. Your directions were great." She took her coat off and laid it in Jude's waiting arm "This place is amazing. Is it a Wright home?"

Jude smiled warmly. "Good eye. And the answer to that is yes and no. It's Wright inspired, Stafford designed."

Chase looked confused. "You?"

"Yes." Jude's face was beaming. "I minored in architecture at Tulane. I've always been fascinated by architecture and after we studied Frank Lloyd Wright, I knew that I wanted to live in a home like he had designed. There aren't any here, so I did the next best thing. I designed and built my own."

Chase was mesmerized by the home. The clean lines and incorporation of glass allowed light to stream through the open floorplan. "It's Prairie Style?" The sentence was more a question than a statement.

"Yes." Jude's smiled widened. "I'm impressed. Most people can guess that it resembles a Wright home, but only a few can pick the style."

Chase blushed. "I have to admit I may have had the upper hand. I was born in Buffalo and one of his most famous Prairie Style homes was there."

"The Martin house." Jude eyes lit up and her hands moved excitedly as she continued. "I visited that one and the Westcott house in Ohio several times when I was designing mine. For the most part, I stayed true to the Prairie Style Design…with one exception." She started walking to the back of the house. "Check this out."

Chase forced herself to stop staring at the well—appropriated great room. Everything in the home fit Jude, from the leather couch and chairs to the artisan fireplace that took up most of the wall opposite the entry way.

"Did you ever see Fallingwater?" Jude was referring to one of Lloyd's more famous homes, designed to be as much a part of the nature around as any home could be. The home was built over a waterfall that could be heard from all over the house, but only seen from the top terrace. "I didn't have a waterfall on the property, but I did have a great view of the ocean." She slid a large glass door open and stepped outside.

Chase followed Jude out onto a large stone terrace and her jaw dropped. Jude had designed the home so that the terrace sat directly over the bay and the view was truly awe--inspiring. Chase closed her eyes and inhaled the salty air. She felt the strong wind race across her face. "Oh my God. It's beautiful! I've never seen anything like this before. Jude, this is amazing. You are…amazing. You have an amazing talent."

"So all in all, I guess you think I'm pretty amazing." Jude's voice was more intimate than Chase could bear. They had agreed to just be friends, but Jude was making it hard for Chase to keep her resolve. Jude caught the slight flush in Chase's cheeks and laughed. "I'm glad you like it. This is honestly the masterpiece of my otherwise mundane life."

Chase was about to contradict Jude's statement when she winked at her. Chase laughed. "Oh, you're kidding. I thought for a second you were serious, and all I could think was how unboring your life is."

Jude chuckled. "I'm sure it's much more glamorous in theory than in actuality." She waved away Chase's objection. "Let me show you the rest of the house and then we can get going." Jude led Chase back inside and showed her the remainder of the house, including a modern kitchen with a large open feel. Off one side of the kitchen was an entrance to a long walkway that was covered by a pergola. At the opposite end was a large sunroom that also looked out over the ocean. Chase was beside herself. Not only was Jude an incredibly attractive and sexy woman, she was also extremely talented. Chase groaned softly. *I really am screwed!*

"What did you say?" Jude had stopped walking and turned to face her.

"Oh, me? Nothing." Chase smiled. "Thanks for the tour. Your home is beautiful!"

"Thank you. I'm glad I could show you." Suddenly Jude cocked her head and looked at Chase thoughtfully. "You know what? You're the first woman I have ever invited home." Jude suddenly pictured them lying naked in her bed, breasts pressed together, their hips undulating together, stroking her hard clit against Chase's, bringing them both to a furious climax. She felt wetness flood her panties. Jude's face flushed and she fought to keep from shuddering in front of Chase. She cleared her throat and handed Chase her coat. "I guess, we, ahh, better get going."

Chase hadn't missed Jude's eyes darken and the flush in her cheeks. She would never know, but she hoped she was the reason for the look. She pulled her coat on and smiled. "Sounds good. Lead the way."

She followed Jude through a hallway and down a narrow stairway. Jude stopped at the bottom and pulled her black leather coat off a hanger on the wall, put it on and wrapped her white scarf around her neck. The effect on Chase was the same as the first time she had seen her in that coat. It took her breath away. She took several deeps breaths and tried to prepare herself for the car ride to Portland.

Jude walked towards a black Jaguar X-Type. She opened the passenger door for Chase, waited till she got in then shut the door and walked around to the driver's side. She saw Chase eyeing the BMW. "I figured we would take this...since it's not snowy."

Chase ran her hand over the grey leather seat. She raised her eyebrows appreciatively. "Nice."

Jude turned on the ignition and the engine roared to life. "You okay with some tunes?" Chase nodded and Jude hit a button on the dash. The new CD from Ladyhawke filled the car. She smiled at Chase. "You'll have to forgive me, my tastes run a little off the beaten track. I can change it if you want."

Chase shook her head. "No, this is fine." She studied Jude as she maneuvered the car out of the garage and up a narrow drive out to the main road. Chase looked over her shoulder at the house. "It really is amazing."

Jude shrugged, but her eyes danced. "I'm really glad you like it." She paused at the end of the drive, checked for traffic and eased the car out onto the road. She looked at Chase and smiled. "So, you ready for me to take you on an adventure?"

"Yes." Chase smiled cryptically. "More ready than you know."

Chapter 21

The hour drive to Portland flew by. Chase did her best to remain cool and collected being in such close proximity to Jude. From Jude's calm exterior, it was impossible for Chase to know that her heart had been beating double time since the moment Chase had shown up at her home.

Several times Chase had put her hand on the console only to pull it back when it grazed Jude's hand. She had to pull it back because every time she touched her, she felt electricity shoot through her body. She was in constant amazement that her body still reacted to Jude with such ferocity. Each time that she jerked her hand back she would glance furtively at Jude to see if she was feeling the same reaction. Other than a slight blush in her cheeks, she showed no signs that Chase's touch had any more effect on her than a stranger.

Moments later, Chase absentmindedly put her hand on the console and brushed Jude's. When she went to pull it away, Jude surprised her by capturing it in hers. She laced her fingers through Chase's and Chase felt her palm graze Jude's. Warmth radiated through her body and a slight moan escaped her lips. Jude caressed the top of her hand lightly, never taking her eyes off the road. Chase breathed a sigh of relief, sure that if Jude had bestowed her perfect smile on her, she would have melted. Jude offered no explanation, no justification for toeing the thin line that separated friends and lovers, she was content to simply feel.

Jude had chosen to take Route One since it was still early so she could point out some of the sights. She pointed out the *Hesper* and *Luther Little,* two four—masted cargo schooners in Wiscasset. They drove past Bath Iron Works, a famous shipyard on the Kennebec River in Bath. Jude told Chase that Harriet Beecher Stowe had written *Uncle Tom's Cabin* while she lived in Brunswick.

"And if you ever wondered, Freeport is the home of L.L. Bean. There are also some outlets down here, if you ever wanted to fight the summer season crowds and shop."

Chase laughed. "No thank you! I'm not much of a shopper to begin with, and you can forget crowds."

"Me neither. But when my mother comes to visit, she insists I take her there. Why she can't shop at home is beyond me." Jude was still holding Chase's hand and she gave it a gentle squeeze. "I guess you and I are alike in more than one way."

Jude merged onto I-295 just past Freeport and she picked up speed. "There isn't too much to see on Route One between here and Portland, so we'll just take the highway."

The last stretch of the trip was uneventful. Jude had to take her hand away when the traffic picked up. Chase missed the warmth and security and the flutter in her stomach from just touching Jude. Jude drove like she did everything else, fast and with sharp precision and before Chase knew it, they were in the parking lot of the offices of Jameson, Brady, Franklin and Crowe, Attorneys—at—Law. "I won't be a second. I'll leave the engine running though." She jumped out of the car, pulled her briefcase out of the backseat and disappeared inside the building. Two minutes later, she got back in the car. She caught Chase's surprised look and smiled. "I told you it wouldn't take long. So what are you up for?"

Chase shrugged. "I don't know. I've only seen the Portland airport, I don't even know what there is to do."

Jude laughed softly. "Oh yeah, I keep forgetting you haven't really had a chance to see much of our fair state. Do you like art? The Farnsworth Museum is here...we could go there. We can shop...not that either of us wants to do that. I guess first, are you hungry?"

"Wow!" Chase raised her eyebrow and stared at Jude. "I think you said that all without taking a breath. Impressive."

"Sorry." Jude smiled ruefully. "I seem to have two speeds. Fast and faster."

"That's okay. I'm a good balance. Most of the time, I'm slow and slower. Together we'll be just average."

Jude smiled wickedly. "Oh sweetie, we'd be anything but average together."

Chase felt the heat rise in her face. Her stomach flip--flopped, her body telling her that the two of them together would be more like spectacular. She swallowed and tried to push images of Jude kissing her to the far recesses of her mind. "I'm not starving…*at least not for food…*but I could eat a snack or something."

"I have a great idea." Jude put the car in drive and turned out of the parking lot. "There is a great little place in the East End on Munjoy Hill. It's very fittingly called Hilltop Coffee Shop. It's a little eclectic, but the coffee and scones are out of this world."

Jude maneuvered her way through early afternoon traffic and within minutes they were stopped in front of the coffee shop. "You wanna come in or do you trust me?"

"I don't know…should I? Or should I worry you will take advantage of me?" Chase smiled coyly.

Jude smirked. "If I do take advantage of you, I promise it will be completely worth your while."

"I'm from Missouri honey, you're gonna have to show me." Chase replied saucily.

Jude's gaze traveled over Chase and stopped boldly on her breasts, before lifting her eyes to rest on her lips. Chase saw her eyes darken with desire and she shuddered. The effect on Chase was the same as if Jude's lips were really on hers and at that moment if Jude had tried to kiss her, she would not, could not have resisted her.

Jude prided herself in getting that reaction from women by merely looking at them, but seeing Chase react like that was like a drug. Her mind was reeling and her breath was ragged. Chase was practically giving herself to Jude. She only had to lean across the seat and capture Chase's mouth against hers. She felt herself being pulled closer and closer by some unseen magnetism. She was powerless to put distance between them.

Suddenly a car horn blared in the distance and broke the spell. She jerked away from Chase and blinked rapidly. "I'm…I'm sorry, where was I?"

Chase licked her lips nervously, her brain unable to will her mouth to utter any coherent thought. "You…were…coffee."

"Oh yeah, coffee. I'll be right back." She fled from the car and sought shelter from Chase, from herself, from her feelings in the safety of the small coffee shop. She stole glances at Chase as she waited for their order. Chase caught her staring and waggled her fingers. Jude smiled shyly, thinking Chase was the sweetest thing she'd ever seen.

"Miss? Miss?" The woman behind the register said loudly. "You're order is up." She smiled at her, when she realized what had captured Jude's attention. "She's cute. You're a lucky woman."

Jude blushed slightly, embarrassed at being caught. "Yeah, she is. But we're not together."

The woman winked mischievously. "If you aren't now, you will be soon. If you looked at me the way you are looking at her…and vice versa…you could have me right now."

This caused Jude to blush outright. She quickly reached for the coffee and bag of scones. She smiled at the woman. "Ahh thanks. I better get back out there."

"You do that. And if doesn't work out, why don't you come back and see me? I am sure we could have some fun!" She laughed loudly as Jude backed out of the store, unsure if she was being serious or just messing with her.

"Yeah, okay." Jude pushed open the door and fled to her car. She flopped in the driver's seat and handed Chase a cup and the bag she was carrying. "Carmel Macchiato and blueberry scones. That okay?"

"Perfect." She nodded her head towards the coffee shop. "Looks like you picked up a new admirer."

Jude shrugged. "Well actually, she was telling me that if I were smart I would stop messing around with coffee and take you to bed. She said it was obvious that the look of hunger on your face wasn't for coffee." She stifled a laugh, and buried her smile in her drink, ignoring Chase's look of shock.

Chapter 22

Jude glanced at her watch. It was quarter till four. "I guess it is later than I thought. Maybe we will skip the museum this trip. I don't want to keep a respectable girl like you out late. Wouldn't want you to turn into a pumpkin."

Chase snorted loudly. "Respectable? You obviously don't know me that well."

"Not yet...but I'm getting closer every day." Jude met Chase's gaze and held it. Her eyes searched Chase's face slowly. With effort, she tore her eyes from Chase's lips and faced forward, putting the car in reverse and backing out of her parking spot. "Tell you what...I do have one stop I want to make and then we can grab some dinner. Although, if there is something here you have been dying to do, we can bump that up on the to—do list."

"I've been dying to see Portland Head Light, but given that it is..." Chase stole a glance at the Jaguar's instrument panel, "...thirty-five degrees outside, I think I can wait till it's a bit warmer. So lead on, captain. Your wish is my command."

Jude raised her eyebrow and stared at Chase. "Anything?"

"Anything." Chase smirked. "Although we would be limited to only non—bedroom activites...since you did turn me down."

Jude smiled ruefully. She cracked her knuckles nervously. "Believe me, that was not as easy a choice as you may think it was. And you are so damn cute, it's seriously testing my resolve in that area. Why do you have to get cuter every time I see you?"

"I'm not trying to be cute." Chase pretended to scowl, but a smile still twinkled in her eyes. "I'll try to be uglier. I could pick my nose or something." She stuck her finger to her nose and pretended to pick it.

Jude giggled. "Nope, not working. You're just being silly, and that makes you even more irresistibly adorable."

Chase felt the heat rise to her cheeks and she smiled sweetly. "Good, irresistible was really what I was going for. It's good to know I haven't lost my touch completely."

"No, I'd say your touch is working just fine." Jude said with a shrug. "You're just not supposed to be using your *touch* on me."

Chase smirked. "Oh really? Cause I'm pretty sure if I were using my *touch* on you, you'd definitely enjoy it."

Jude felt heat surge through her body. Chase's words felt like a caress and she swallowed nervously. Her body had never responded to another woman the way she did to Chase and she jumped inwardly at the thought. This was new, uncharted territory for her and she was unsure how to navigate through it. Somehow sanity and reason managed to win the battle over reckless abandon and Jude steered the conversation back to safer ground. "Okay, to Bull Moose we go."

"Bull Moose?" Chase asked, quickly following Jude's lead back into platonic banter.

"Bull Moose Music. It's this great music store downtown. They carry pretty much everything. There are a couple new titles I want to get on wax and I can always find them there." She laughed at Chase's quizzical expression. "Wax is just an old school record. I collect them. I usually have them on CD too, that way I don't mess up the record."

Chase stifled a laugh. "You collect records? Got any Civil War relics too? Me, I've got some old vases from the Ming Dynasty."

Jude rolled her eyes and looked askance at Chase. "Ha, ha! Very funny. It may surprise you to know that records are making quite a resurgence lately. Of course, I have been collecting them since I was a kid, now it just happens to be cool." Jude pulled into a parking lot and shut off the engine. "You may want to grab your coat. The entrance is around the front of the building and the wind coming off the ocean blows through the alley and you will seriously freeze your ass off."

Jude reached into the backseat to grab their coats. When she turned to give Chase her coat, she froze. She saw Chase's eyes locked on her breasts. Her eyes were dark and hungry and her lips were parted slightly, silently begging to be kissed. Jude felt Chase capturing her nipple between her lips and she shuddered. The warning bells rang loudly in her head and she shoved Chase's coat towards her with more force than she had intended to.

Chase shook her head, abruptly torn from her reverie. She muttered a thank you and forced herself to look straight ahead as she struggled into her coat, wrapped her scarf around her neck and pulled on her gloves. "Okay, I'm ready. Take me to the wax museum."

Jude rolled her eyes again. "You just keep getting funnier. Just wait, I have a feeling you are in for a surprise." She got out of the car and ran around to the passenger side to open the door for Chase. She put her hand out and gently pulled Chase from the car. Even through their gloves, the contact sent electricity surging through her body. She struggled to breathe and could tell from Chase's sudden stillness that she was feeling the same palpable energy. She dropped her hand and stepped away from her. She hit the lock button and waited till Chase fell in step next to her. More to herself than to Chase, she asked aloud. "What are you doing to me?"

"Huh?" Chase heard muffled words, but she couldn't make them out over the wind whipping around them. "Did you say something?"

"Me?" Jude shook her head. "No, I didn't say anything."

"Oh? Okay." Chase was suddenly forlorn and she hoped Jude didn't sense her disappointment. They walked quickly through the alley, turned left and when Jude started to descend a flight of stairs, Chase hesitated.

"Come on, silly. It's in the basement." She smiled wryly. "Why do you think it's an underground music store?"

Chase shook her head. "No, it's not that. I smell pizza."

"Oh yeah, there's a pizza place right up the street. The smell has a habit of settling in here. That beats musty, old basement smell any day." She continued down the stairs and held the door open for Chase. The landing was smaller so when Chase walked by her, her body brushed against Jude. Jude held her breath and willed her heart not to beat out of her chest. She caught Chase's amused glance and smiled. She stepped in behind Chase and let the door close after her.

Chase's eyes swept over the large room and the racks and racks of CDs, albums, cassettes and other paraphernalia. She glanced sideways at Jude and smiled, all too aware of the feelings her proximity were stirring in her. Jude's cheeks and nose were rosy from the cold and Chase struggled to find something unattractive about her. Unable to do so, she slowly stepped away from Jude. "I'm gonna start over here."

Eager to put some space between them as well, Jude nodded to the other side of the store. "That's my side. I'll catch up to you in a little bit." She strode away quickly and soon found herself leafing through the latest alternative releases. She had just finished the A's when she sensed someone standing beside her. She glanced sideways and smiled at the young woman beside her. "Jules, what's up?"

"Nada." She said shrugging her shoulders. "Just working." She gestured towards Chase and raised an eyebrow inquisitively. "Friend of yours?"

Jude followed her gaze and pinpointed Chase across the room. "Yeah, we're friends..."

Jules snorted. "Friends, huh? Then I guess you won't mind if I ask her out."

Jude glared at her. "I don't think she's your type...or should I say, I don't think you're her type."

"Hell, yeah, she's my type. She's hot and she's got a pulse. And what do you mean I'm not her type? I can hold my own next to you. If I remember correctly, I was good enough for you once. And I won't be working in a record store forever, you know."

Jude blushed, remembering the time she and Jules had hooked up in one of the back rooms at the Bull Moose. "Simmer down, Jules. I'm not saying anything about you personally. I'm just saying she doesn't ahh, lean our way, if you know what I mean."

"Bullshit! I saw the way she looked at you, and she looks at you *alot* when she knows you aren't looking. That woman is hungry for some one hundred percent certified grade gay meat, baby!"

Jude groaned. "You are not right." She glanced up and met Chase's eyes. Chase blushed when she realized she had been caught staring, but Jude smiled and nodded almost imperceptibly. No words passed between them, but both of them knew what the other was thinking. The corner of Chase's mouth curved upward then she looked away quickly.

"Friends, huh?" Jules said sarcastically. Even I can tell from a distance, I don't stand a chance with her. It's obvious you've gotten to her."

"Me?" Jude feigned innocence. "No way. We're just friends, take my word for it."

"Sure." Jules winked mischievously and ran her thumb across Jude's chin. She caught Jude's confused look. "I was just wiping the drool off." She skirted around Jude and hurried away, avoiding the punch Jude had sent her way. Tossing her head over her shoulder, she smiled. "Catch ya later."

Jude shook her head and smiled. "Bitch."

Sometime later, Jude was interrupted by soft laughter. She saw Chase eyeing the stack of records she had cradled in her arm, and the CDs in her hand. She joined in the laughter. "The sad thing is I'm only to the T's."

Chase took the CDs from her and started to look through them. "*Empire of the Sun, Girl Talk, Keane, Florence & The Machine, Raining Jane*...I haven't heard of any of these. You are really weird."

Jude burst out laughing. "More than you know." She looked back down and scrunched up her face.

Chase laughed. "You baby. Go ahead, you can look through the rest." She stuck out her hands. "Want me to hold those?"

Jude handed them to her and smiled. "You don't mind?"

"No." Chase said, shaking her head. "Not at all. Besides, it should help you look faster and I am starving. I seem to remember some promise about feeding me."

Jude looked chagrined. "Oh, yeah, dinner. I got a little sidetracked. Five more minutes, I promise." Her eyes pleaded with Chase.

"How can I say no to that face?" She stood quietly beside Jude and waited as she looked through the remainder of the section and handed her two more CDs in the process.

Finally, Jude looked up and smiled. "Ready?"

Chase's stomach growled in answer. She jumped when Jude played her palm against her abdomen. The same languid hunger registered in Jude's eyes and she held her hand there a beat longer.

Jude cleared her throat loudly. "I guess that's a yes."

Chapter 23

"Are you okay with Irish food?" Jude asked Chase as she pulled along side a car, then expertly parallel parked behind it. "I guess I should have asked before I assumed this place was okay."

"Normally, I would say don't be such a man and just think you can make choices for me, but you are lucky this time. I love Irish food!"

Jude smiled. "Hey if the suit and tie fits...right?"

"Uh—uh. I've seen you in a suit, you look nothing like a man. You are one hell of a sexy woman, Jude, and don't think for a second that a suit makes you otherwise."

"See, there you go being cute and sweet again."

Chase smiled ruefully. "Oh yeah, I forgot, that's not allowed. Motion to strike the last comment from the record."

Jude laughed out loud then held Chase's gaze. "Do you have any idea how sexy a woman with a dry sense of humor is?"

"No, but you could tell me if you want. I do especially well with tactile learning. I'm the hands on type." Chase smiled wickedly, opened her door and exited the car leaving Jude staring at her mouth agape.

When Jude finally caught up to Chase, she pulled the door open to the Ri Ra Irish Pub and followed her in, wishing that Chase's perfectly rounded backside was not hidden by her coat. She smiled at the hostess and requested a seat on the restaurant's second floor. The bar was noisy, even for a weekday and she preferred the quiet so they could still talk.

After the waitress had taken their order for Guinness and Irish Potato cakes, Chase rested her elbows on the table and put her chin on her folded hands. She watched Jude, her hands moving adroitly as she unfolded her napkin and placed her silverware beside her on the table. She felt her stomach jump and realized her mind had helplessly drifted to thoughts of those hands roving all over her naked body.

She shook her head and took a drink of her ice water to try and clear her head. Jude looked up, caught her staring and smiled. Chase had the good grace to appear embarrassed, but in actuality, it was becoming harder and harder to not stare at Jude. She was heart—achingly beautiful. She was like a piece of fine art, Chase could look all she wanted, but she could never touch, or possess her. Not the way Jude had gotten inside and possessed a part of her. Chase wondered if the force pulling her towards Jude would ever lessen and she would be able to break the invisible bond. She suspected it would take something greater than Chase herself to do that.

Chase smiled, determined to have fun and not dwell on what she couldn't have. "So, who is Jude Stafford? Tell me about yourself."

Jude waited while the waitress set two pints of Guinness in front of them. She thanked her, took a long sip and smiled at Chase. When she spoke, she sounded like a game show announcer. *"Who do we have tonight Charlie? Well Pat, tonight's contestants include Jude Stafford, a thirty—five year old estate attorney from Boothbay, Maine. When she's not preparing wills and settling estates, she divides her time between Maine and Boston. An avid Red Sox fan and season ticket holder, she enjoys going to all their home games. She has no pets, isn't married, is quite the catch in the Portland lesbian community and hopes to one day open her own lesbian bar."*

Chase waved her hand in the air, pleading with Jude to stop. She was cracking up and trying desperately not to spit her beer out. Somehow, she choked it down without losing any and narrowed her eyes at Jude, who was laughing at her. "That's not funny."

"Really? Cause the beer coming out your nose tells me otherwise."

"Well if you weren't being so damn funny, I wouldn't be blowing Guinness out my nose. You're lucky I didn't get it on you."

"Mmm, yes lucky. Although I probably would have made you lick it off." Jude smirked wickedly.

Chase sat up abruptly and grabbed her mug. "Then by all means, proceed. This may be my only chance to lick anything off of you." She replied saucily. She gulped her beer hoping to hide the color creeping into her cheeks.

Jude blushed, and rather than steer away from the rough water, she plunged straight ahead. "Well, maybe if you play your cards right, I'll give you another chance." She watched Chase pull her purse from the chair next to her, and start rifling through it. She watched her, a confused expression on her face. "What are you doing?"

Chase didn't look up from her purse. "I'm looking for my cards. I'm not sure how long it will take to play them right." She continued digging, ignoring Jude's shocked expression. "Well dammit! I can't find them. Too bad for you." She winked, tempering her words.

Jude smirked. "Don't worry, we can always stop and get some on the way home. I don't know what game you play, but a little strip poker could get you close to the right cards."

"I'm game. Let's just skip dinner and go straight to dessert." Chase said, her eyes twinkling.

Jude gulped. Behind the twinkle, there was naked desire in Chase's eyes. Suddenly the just friends thing was taking a turn. A sharp turn down a slippery slope that Jude knew she couldn't avoid falling down. She had to rein it in fast…before she pushed them both over the steep precipice. "I'm afraid I am too hungry to partake in any extracurricular activities. I think my stomach is eating itself."

Chase recognized the swift change in conversation and was helpless to do anything about it. She sighed softly and smiled at Jude. "So you want to open your own lesbian bar."

"It's crazy. But we don't really have anything close in Boothbay. There's a place in Bangor and several in Portland, but who wants to drive that far. I want to open a modern, upscale bar. I'll cater to a more settled, affluent crowd, not the loud techno, strobe light kind of place."

"Oh you mean like a more boring place." Chase rolled her eyes. "Sounds like a lot of fun. Count me in."

"I'm immune to your sarcasm. Besides, it's a lesbian bar, not exactly your kind of bar, if I recall correctly."

Chase reached across the table and covered Jude's hand with hers. She caressed her knuckles with her thumb, all the while holding Jude's eyes captive. "If I gave you the impression it wasn't my type, forgive me. I'll try to be more forward from now on." She held her gaze a moment longer, than pulled her hand away and took a sip of her water, glad that Jude couldn't see her pulse in the dim restaurant.

Jude gasped, the contact almost more than she could bear. She had done a fair job so far today, feigning bravado in her efforts to resist Chase. But if Chase did what she promised to do and was more forward, Jude knew she was royally fucked.

Jude was spared having to address Chase's admission by their waitress. She returned with their potato cakes and asked if they were ready to order.

Jude said yes then held her menu up and regarded Chase thoughtfully. "Do you mind?"

Chase snickered. "Not at all, sir." She lost it when Jude hit her with a glare. "I'm kidding. I trust you."

Jude glanced at the menu then turned to the waitress. "I'll have the Bistro Steak, medium—rare, with a side of roasted mushrooms. And she will have the Kilbeggan Salmon."

Chase stifled a laugh. The salmon was what she was planning on having, it just surprised her that Jude had nailed the exact item from an entire menu.

"Anything else?" The waitress asked as she jotted the items down then looked at Chase quizzically.

"That's what I was going to order, but I'd like to add a side of Colcannon too." Chase caught Jude's smirk out of the corner of her eye and she winked. After the waitress left the table, she faced Jude who was watching her smugly. "Okay, so you guessed pretty well. I suppose you just got lucky."

"Oh honey, I haven't gotten lucky yet." The smirk turned to a look of longing, and Chase watched her green eyes go dark with desire.

"Hey, you made that choice." Chase shrugged nonchalantly. She pulled her eyes from Jude and pretended to check out the restaurant. "Neat place."

Jude looked around. "Yeah, it's pretty cool. It's actually a restored pub that was salvaged and shipped over here from Ireland…well actually a couple different pubs. We'll have to come back sometime when it's still light out. The views are amazing!"

Chase felt her heart jump when Jude said *we* will have to come back, acknowledging that there would be future trips together. She was going to say something about it, but didn't want to scare Jude. They had been toeing the line between friendship and lovers all day and Chase didn't want to risk either one pulling away completely out of fear.

"Seriously, tell me about yourself. Why did you become an attorney?" Chase asked casually.

Jude sighed softly. "Well, it started out as rebellion actually. My mother and father divorced when I was pretty young, and my mother was always saying how much she didn't want my sisters and I to turn out like him. You know to someone who is going through the rebellious child of a divorced parent syndrome, those words just added fuel to the fire. Of course, by the time I found out what a jerk my father really was I had already made the decision to go to law school. So rather than change that, I just decided to go into a different area of practice. Anything to be different from him."

"Which is estate law." Chase smiled. "What does your father practice?"

Jude snorted. "He is a criminal defense attorney. And I bet if you ask him, he will tell you he doesn't practice anything…he's perfect. Pun intended."

Chase raised her eyebrow. "It doesn't sound like you think very highly of your father."

"I don't. At least I haven't in a very long time. When I was younger, I thought he hung the moon. The older I got, the more I realized he wasn't someone I wanted as a role model. That and the fact that he has no respect for women, me included."

Chase scrunched her forehead up. "What do you mean?"

Jude smiled enigmatically. "Let's just say he has an issue with my being gay. Damn hypocrite is what he is. Treats woman like possessions and then balks at me because I am not attracted to men. Well let me tell you, if he is the shining example of options for straight women, I'd go gay for that reason alone."

Chase snickered. "Yes, because your love 'em and leave 'em idea in relation to women is sooo much better."

Jude feigned indignation. "Hey, I'll have you know I totally respect women, I adore them." She caught Chase shaking her head and mmm—hmmming sarcastically. "Oh, stop it. I have nothing but the utmost respect for a woman when I am involved with her…the *one* time. She knows in advance it's not going to be more than a one time thing."

"And you think total disclosure raises your view of women from objectification to respect? You think that because you tell a woman up front that you are a one night stand kind of girl that it makes it okay to disregard her personality and existence as an individual?" Chase saw the anger flashing in Jude's eyes and knew she should stop, but she was tired of her cavalier view of love and relationships, and she forged ahead. "You don't see the woman she is or appreciate her for anything more than her physical and sexual appeal. You've reduced a woman to nothing more than an instrument for your pleasure. How is that better than what your father does?"

The words stung Jude more than they should have, and she knew it was because there was truth beneath them. Maybe she had been jaded by her past and the heartbreak she had experienced, but that wasn't Chase's business and she had no right questioning her behavior towards women. Jude took several deep breaths, calming herself before she replied to the harsh words Chase had spoken. She didn't want to damage the tender friendship they were struggling to maintain, despite the obviously mounting attraction both women felt, she thoroughly enjoyed Chase's company. Besides, she wasn't really mad at Chase, what she said was true. She was mad at herself for allowing someone to get to her like Chase did.

Chase watched the emotions on Jude's face and her heart sunk. She hadn't meant to be so mean, Jude just got to her in ways that no one else had and it was like a fire burning beneath her skin. Immensely remorseful, she interrupted Jude before she could respond. "I'm so sorry. Please forgive me. I shouldn't have said that about you. I didn't mean it…I don't really think that about you."

Jude put her hand up to stop Chase. "Don't apologize. It's true. I won't make excuses for my behavior, it is what it is. I've never been knowingly mean or unkind to a woman. I would never intentionally hurt anyone…you have to know that." Her eyes implored Chase to believe her. "That's why you and I would never work. I know myself and I know I couldn't give you what you want and that would hurt you in the long run. It would kill me to hurt you, Chase."

Chase saw nothing but aching honestly in her eyes and it broke heart. "How do you know? I'm not asking for a commitment. Hell, I don't even know what I'm asking for. All I know is I'm attracted to you…very attracted, and I think you are attracted to me. Are we seriously going to keep hiding behind the guise of friendship?"

"I have to. I don't know how to be any other way, and at this point in my life, I have no aspirations to be anything but the person I am today. Chase, you are an amazing woman and I enjoy spending time with you…as friends, but that's all it can ever be."

"Why does it sound like you are trying to convince yourself of that fact and not me?" Chase held Jude's gaze, her eyes piercing into the depths of her soul. Jude tried to pull away, look anywhere else but into eyes dark with longing. She knew if she let herself she could get lost in those eyes forever. Chase leaned towards her, her voice dropped to a whisper. "Tell me you don't want me and I won't bring it up again."

Jude tried desperately to catch her breath. She felt the overwhelming enormity of the statement hit her square in the chest and knock the wind out of her. She watched the emotions play across Chase's face and struggled to utter the two words it would take to end the torture. *I don't...but I really do!*

"Bistro Steak, medium—rare." Both women looked up, surprised by their waitress. She set the steak in front of Jude then put the salmon in front of Chase. "Enjoy. Let me know if I can get you anything else." She winked at Chase and didn't bother to hide a little smirk as she walked away.

Jude stared at her steak. Suddenly eating was the furthest thing from her mind. She didn't know what to say to Chase. Either way she answered, she would cause her some pain. If she said that she wasn't attracted to her, at the very least it would hurt her pride. If she said she was attracted to her, and acted on the primal urges she felt then ran the other way, that would hurt Chase emotionally. Either way, they would both lose. "Chase, listen…"

Chase put her hand up to stop Jude. "Let's just enjoy dinner and each other's company. I declare a moratorium on all things relationship." Chase said paraphrasing the latest *Alanis Morisette* song. "I just want to sit with my friend, find out what is behind the mystery that is Jude and maybe let you get to know me some. Deal?"

Jude let out a breath and her face broke into a relieved smile. "Deal."

"By the way, my salmon is really good. You wanna try it?" Chase held her fork out towards Jude, who took the bite from her and moaned.

"Mmm, that is delicious. Steak?' She started to cut a small bite when Chase stopped her.

"No, thank you. I will steal a fry though." She reached across the table and stole a french fry, drowning it in ketchup before stuffing the whole thing in her mouth. "Fries are my weakness."

"And here I thought I was your weakness." Jude winked.

"Uh—uh…you're my addiction." Chase smiled then started laughing when Jude choked on the bite of steak in her mouth.

"Breathe. I'm kidding. Man, if only it was as easy getting you into bed as it is to get you flustered." She winked at Jude mischievously.

"Chase Berkley, you are one evil woman. Just remember paybacks are hell."

Chase laughed out loud. "Oh yeah, bring it. You want a piece of me?"

Jude shook her head. "I want the whole thing." Her green eyes pierced through the dim light of the restaurant and sent electricity racing through Chase's body. It was her turn to be flustered. Somehow the agreement to not talk about a relationship made it the only thing either one of them could talk about.

Chase cleared her throat loudly. "Wow, this salmon is really good. And the colcannon...best I've ever had. Great pick on the restaurant."

"My choice of company is even better than my food choice." Jude's eyes held nothing but sincerity in them. "Thank you for coming with me."

"Thank you for inviting me. It beat staying at home alone all afternoon. Plus, I get a free meal." Chase winked at Jude. She decided to continue steering the conversation away from them. "So you have two sisters...anymore siblings besides that?"

"No, that's it. Jenna and Jessica, both older than me. Then there's me, the baby, the last great white hope." Chase saw a flash of pain in Jude's eyes, but it disappeared almost as quickly as it appeared.

"Great white hope...like the movie?" Chase raised her eyebrow and stared at Jude.

"Nah, just my father's last chance of having a boy. He was devastated when he got three girls. What about you...any siblings?"

"Nope, just me. The spoiled brat." Chase shrugged her shoulders as if to say too bad, what you see is what you get.

"Spoiled? Somehow I highly doubt that. If you are, you have done a great job hiding it from me. And believe me, I would know. That is the common thread that runs through my father's long line of wives and girlfriends. It's not something you can hide, Chase, at least not from me."

"Oh really. You think you know me pretty well, huh?" Chase countered.

"I got the salmon, didn't I?" Jude said smugly, a challenge in her eyes. "I think I know you pretty well."

Chase shook her head. "Not that well, but I could give you the opportunity to know me *very* well...if you want."

Jude felt the heat rising in her cheeks. "I want to so much it hurts, which is exactly why I can't."

"Can't or won't?" Chase asked.

"Does it make a difference?" Jude searched Chase's face. "The outcome is still the same. Chase, I know you think you want me, but you don't know me. You and I are in two very different places right now. I will admit there is something between us that I can't control, but I can control what I do about it."

Chase smiled. "I know and I should be fine with things staying the way they are. From what I know about you, I would say you don't let too many people get close enough to be your friend. That makes me feel special. I agree we can't control what we feel. I will try to control the impulse to act on it. I can't promise there won't be times I slip though. Sometimes I just look at you and I want you to dive inside me and consume me."

Jude reached across the table and covered Chase's hand. When she spoke again, her voice was low and shaky. "I know the feeling. You are so incredibly sweet and smart and sexy. You make it almost impossible not to take the plunge. You'll have to forgive me if I slip too."

"Jude Stafford, I think I could forgive you almost anything." With that, Chase pulled her hand away, unable to think straight. She couldn't take the heat from Jude's hand and the dark green eyes that were regarding her with the intensity of a thousand suns. At that moment, she would have given anything to get lost in those eyes.

Chapter 24

Jude fastened her seatbelt and pulled the car away from the curb. Somewhere in the course of the day, Chase had gone from a want to a need. A force threatening to reach inside her and strip her soul bare if she allowed it entry. She wasn't sure how she would be able to continue keeping Chase at arms length, ignoring the desire that was welling inside her. It was a need so deep inside her that they were one soul. "Fuck!"

Chase jumped, surprised by Jude's sudden outburst. "What fuck? What's wrong?"

"It's nothing." Jude shook her head. "I'm sorry, I didn't mean to scare you."

Chase put her hand on Jude's arm and she felt her tense. "You sure you don't want to talk about it?"

"Yeah, I mean no, I'm sure I don't want to talk about it." She pulled her arm away and rested it on the gear shift. "Let's talk about you instead. What were you like growing up? Did you play any sports? Get good grades? Drive your parents crazy?"

"Hmm, I was kind of a tomboy. I played soccer. Got straight A's. And I was the worst one of their kids as far as driving them crazy."

"The worst of the kids?" Jude laughed. "You were the *only* kid."

Chase laughed, amused with herself. "Yeah, I know. But I was still the worst."

Jude snorted. "Somehow I highly doubt that. I can't see Miss Goodie Two Shoes doing anything remotely bad."

Chase swatted Jude's arm lightly. "Hey, I can be bad...just give me a chance, I'll show you just how *bad* I can be."

Jude's breath caught in her throat and she struggled to push images of Chase writhing naked underneath her to the back of her mind. "Maybe now, but I'm sure as a child, you were probably a model of propriety, never misbehaved."

"Mmm, if you only knew…" Chase replied cryptically. "What are you laughing at? What's so funny?" Chase asked when she heard Jude laughing softly next to her.

"I just had this picture in my head of you wearing peg—rolled jeans, with matching shirts and socks and your hair in a pony tail on the side of your head. I imagine you were a really cute kid."

Chase laughed. "You have me pegged…no pun intended, although you forgot the Eastland shoes with the laces rolled on the side instead of tied. I was Samantha from *Who's The Boss?*"

Jude burst out laughing. "A total prep. I like it."

"What about you? What were you like growing up?" Chase asked, resting her hand comfortably against Jude's.

"Well if you were Sam from *Who's The Boss*, I was John Bender from *The Breakfast Club*...a rebellious, bad—ass. I can't tell you the number of times I was in detention."

"John Bender, huh? I bet you looked pretty cute in leather." Chase laughed. "Did you wear the gloves too?" Chase slid her hand over Jude's as she asked the question.

"Of course." Jude managed to choke out the words, the feel of Chase's hand resting on hers made it difficult to speak. She inched it away and started messing with the radio. "More so when I got my license and my first bike, a 1990 Triumph Trident. I worked every summer from sixth grade on at a local landscaping place to save money for a bike. I fell in love with my Triumph the moment I saw her. Man I was sixteen years old and I thought I ruled the world. I could get almost any chick I wanted with that bike. The same goes for the Triumph Rocket I just bought. Girls and bikes."

"Hmm, guess you've always been a player." Chase crossed her arms and looked straight ahead, feeling a pang of sadness pierce her heart. "Good thing you aren't after me or I would think you were using the Jag to get me into bed."

Jude winced at the words. She had always been okay with her choices and how she lived her life, but now something had changed. Chase had managed to get inside her head and knowing that Chase felt like she was shallow and insensitive hurt her feelings. At thirty—five, a woman she had just met was challenging everything she thought was important and making her wonder why it suddenly wasn't enough anymore. Jude felt empty and hollow inside, and that thought scared her more than she was prepared for. *Dammit! Suck it up, you wimp. Your life is perfectly fine the way it is. It was before Chase and it will be long after she is gone.* "Chase, listen…"

"Jude, you don't have to explain. It's none of my business. You like women…you don't like commitment. That's your choice. I may not agree with it, but I really don't have a say now do I?" She paused, trying to formulate her next words carefully. "What you do with your personal life is your business. While it disappoints me that you are so narrow—minded and hardened against love, I can't do anything about it. I played the hand I was dealt, obviously it wasn't the winning hand. I'll deal with that the best way I know how. I'm not sure this whole friend thing was such a good idea."

Jude slowed and pulled into the narrow drive that led to her house. She didn't respond until she had pulled the car into the garage and cut the engine. She turned to Chase and when she spoke her voice was low and shaky. "Please don't say that. I know I haven't made it easy. I've crossed the line with you and that was unfair. You're just so damn sexy I can't help it." Jude smiled crookedly, hoping that it would ease some of the tension that was mounting between them.

Chase smiled ruefully. "I think it might be best if we didn't see each other for awhile. I need some time and space to sort through the things I am feeling." She saw Jude's face drop and she felt a sharp stab of pain hit her in the stomach. "I'm sorry. I really like spending time with you, and that makes it even harder. I keep thinking that if I hang around long enough you will realize that there is a chance we could have something great. Today made me realize just how hard it is to be with you, but not *with* you. I don't think I'm up for the challenge right now."

Jude turned sideways in her seat and laid her head against the head rest. She studied Chase for several moments before she spoke again. "The pragmatist in me knows you are right. When you play with fire, you are bound to get burned. But the idealist in me wishes things could just stay the way they are." She caught the look Chase gave her and looked chagrined. "I know, that's not fair to you. Maybe one day, we could try this friend thing again. I really like you. I haven't met anyone that gets under my skin like you do. It's refreshing."

Chase shook her head and smiled. "I know. I feel the same way. Maybe one day we can try, just not right now." She put her hand on the door and opened it, sliding out and closing it in one fluid motion.

Jude jumped out and walked to the front of the car, waiting for Chase to join her. "Thanks for coming with me today. It was nice to have the company."

"You're welcome. Thank you for dinner. I owe you...sometime." Chase waited till Jude started up the steps leading from the garage then started walking several steps behind her. When they reached the front door, Jude stopped with her hand on the doorknob. She smiled, but her eyes were sad. "So maybe I'll see you around."

"Maybe...I don't know. Tess will back soon and I know she will want to see you. Maybe we can all do dinner or something at the house. That should be safe. I don't want her to know you and I are having any issues."

Jude stepped forward and put her hand on Chase's arm. "Issues? Is that what we are calling it?"

Chase shrugged and pulled her arm away. "What else is there to call it? There's something between us. Every time I look at you I want to rip your clothes off and make mad passionate love with you, but you won't let it happen. And you look at me like you could devour me. What's *not* happening between us is crazy. I can't think of any other way to say it than having issues."

Jude shuddered involuntarily. She cocked her eyebrow and stared at Chase. "Devour huh? Good word, very appropriate." She leaned towards Chase, her eyes smoky.

Chase could see the pulse beating erratically in her neck. She ached to touch her there, press her lips softly at the base of neck. She closed her eyes and imagined her tongue raking across Jude's body. She swayed at the thought and felt Jude's hands wrap around her to steady her. She allowed Jude to pull her against her body and wrap her arms tightly around her. She pressed her cheek against Jude's neck and drank in her scent. The feel of Jude's hands rubbing soft circles on her back made her head swim. She pressed her lips softly against Jude's neck and Jude froze, her hands suddenly still on Chase's back.

Jude's stomach flip—flopped at the touch of Chase's lips. She gently pushed Chase away from her, catching the stunned look in her eyes. "I...I'm sorry. I shouldn't have done that."

Chase shook her head, a frown momentarily touching her face, replaced quickly by a sad smile. "It's okay. It's just another one of our *issues.*" She put her hand on the door and opened it quickly.

"Goodbye Jude." She walked out and pulled the door shut quickly, not hearing Jude's soft reply or seeing the sad eyes that followed her to the car.

Jude swung the door open, surprise registering in her eyes. She watched Chase come back up the steps towards the door. "Forget something?"

Chase strode confidently across the expanse of the porch, an enigmatic look on her face. She stopped directly in front of Jude, her gaze piercing. "I'm sorry…"

Before Jude could reply, Chase slid her hand around Jude's neck and pulled her head down. The moment their lips met, Jude shivered and gasped. Chase's lips felt warm and soft. She moved her lips softly over Jude's, the slight pressure sending sparks shooting through her body. Too stunned to move, Jude stood rigid, her arms tight against her body, her fists clenched against her.

Chase increased the pressure softly, her tongue teasing Jude's lips, seeking entry. Jude moaned, her lips parting and Chase's tongue darted in. When Chase felt her tongue brush Jude's, her knees quivered, and she put her arms around Jude to steady herself. Her heart was pounding, her body truly alive for the first time. She was home. This was where she was supposed to be. She felt the heat surging through her body as Jude's tongue danced with hers. After what seemed like an eternity, she wrenched her lips away from Jude's and took a step back. Her gaze roved over Jude, every fiber aching to hold her. "I just wanted you to know what you were missing." She spun on her heel and walked across the porch and down to her car, leaving Jude staring after her, mouth agape, unable to utter a word.

Chapter 25

Jude shivered, the cold finally breaking through the haze. Stepping inside, she shut the door quickly. She closed her eyes and leaned against the door, sighing heavily. She was still a little shocked at what had just transpired. The kiss had left her reeling, unable to focus. Looking back, she realized she must have looked like a complete fool. She stood there, feet rooted, her arms planted firmly against her sides, unmoving. She had never had that reaction with a woman before. She'd never been catapulted into a state of complete and total oblivion, and the mere thought of Chase's lips against hers, threatened to dismantle her again.

Shaking her head, she heaved herself off the door and padded to the kitchen. She pulled a Heineken out of the fridge, twisted the top off and took a long swig. *This is nuts. I am seriously losing my freakin' mind.* Shaking her head, she realized that she had let Chase walk away…just like that. No fight, no asking her to stay. *I should call her. No, no you shouldn't call her you idiot. You should leave well enough alone.* She growled at the voices in her head.

She was not used to the moral struggle she was fighting with herself. Normally, if there was a woman she wanted, she just went after her, no questions asked. Not Chase, no Chase was different. She was more than a physical want, she was a need and that was the main reason Jude hadn't thrown caution to the wind and just jumped in head first. *What if she is different? What if she's not Myra?* Jude pinched the bridge of her nose and answered her own question out loud. "What if she is worse than Myra? I got over that pain, I don't know if I could get over Chase." *How do you know if you don't try? You should at least call her. She kissed you, and you loved it, remember?* "Argh! I know, I know, all right. Okay, well this is fabulous. Not only are you talking to yourself Jude, you're carrying on a fucking conversation."

She looked up at the ceiling and swore. "Fine! I'll call her." She started looking for her cell phone, the Heineken building her bravado. When she couldn't find it in the house, she realized she must have left it in the Jag. She stormed into the garage, pulled open the door. She didn't see her phone. Suddenly, a smile played at the corners of her mouth. "Ahh, Chase." Jude leaned in and picked up the glove that was lying on the floorboard.

#

Chase turned on the porch light and opened the door slowly. She stared at Jude, no emotion on her face. "Yes?"

Jude cocked her head, the corners of her mouth upturned in a lop—sided grin. "Aren't you going to invite me in?"

"I hadn't planned on it." Chase said testily, but she stepped aside and allowed Jude to come in. She stood in the foyer, robe wrapped tightly around her, waiting for Jude to speak. "What do you want?"

"I, uh, I came to return this." Jude held up a glove, as if explaining her late and rather unexpected appearance. "Figured you might need it."

Chase rolled her eyes and took the glove, but Jude held on, not letting it go immediately. She saw the look in Chase's eyes and decided not to push. She let go and awkwardly shoved her hands in her pockets. "It's been pretty cold lately."

"I think it could have waited. It's not like I don't have other pairs of gloves." Chase leaned against the wall, her hands behind her. The movement pulled on her robe and Jude could see the vee of her breasts peeking out from beneath the robe. She gasped and tore her gaze away, but not before Chase caught her and fixed her with a inquisitive stare. "Besides it's late and it's probably not a good idea for you to be here."

"Chase, I'm sorry…" Jude took several tentative steps towards Chase.

Chase shook her head slowly. "Can we not do this? I'm tired, I just don't have the energy to face this again."

Jude cupped Chase's face in her palm and caressed her cheek with her thumb. She felt Chase flinch, saw desire flicker across her face. She rubbed her thumb lightly across Chase's lips, remembering the soft feel of them against her.

"Jude, I don't think you should…" Chase stopped suddenly. Jude's emerald eyes were dark with desire.

"You kissed me tonight and I don't think I did a very good job holding up my end of the kiss." She stepped closer, her thumb still resting lightly on Chase's mouth. "I wouldn't want you to feel let down."

Jude closed the distance between them and before Chase could stop her, Jude's lips replaced her thumb. She brushed her lips over Chase's, catching her bottom lip and sucking it gently. She ran her tongue gently over her mouth, content to wait for Chase to allow her entry. She heard Chase moan and when her lips parted, Jude's tongue darted inside her mouth, her tongue brushing against hers softly.

Chase melted into Jude, her body fitting perfectly against hers. She felt her head spinning, the heat of Jude's kiss sending tremors through her body.

Jude slid her hand behind Chase's head and angled it so she could delve deeper inside her, the kiss binding them together. Jude could feel Chase's pulse against her palm and she smiled inwardly. Her heart wasn't the only one beating wildly. She slid her palm along Chase's neck and chest, needing to fill Chase's skin against hers.

Chase gasped when Jude's palm brushed the top of her breast. She wrapped her arms around Jude's neck and held her tightly, craving her touch. When she felt Jude's hand caressing her below the edge of her robe, her body arched higher. "Yes! Yes!"

Jude swallowed her pleas, crushing her mouth against Chase's, her tongue plunging hungrily into Chase's mouth. Her palm caressed Chase's chest, and she felt her jump when she grazed her nipple softly. She felt it harden to a taut peak at her touch and the feeling surged through her like flames, licking her aroused center. She felt her knees weaken and she struggled to lock her legs so they didn't buckle beneath her. She raked her palm across Chase's nipple again, catching it between her thumb and forefinger. She heard Chase moan against her and she squeezed it softly, rolling it between her fingers.

Chase's body reacted involuntarily to Jude's touch. She couldn't have willed the heat away. She couldn't stop kissing Jude. Her tongue sought Jude's hungrily, matching her stroke for stroke, their tongues an extension of their souls. She felt years of doubt and insecurity falling away, replaced by feelings of warmth. The first kiss wasn't a fluke, what she felt with Jude was real, more incredible than she could ever have imagined. She suddenly knew how it felt for her life to be right, for her to be in the exact place she was supposed to be.

Jude felt Chase's hips undulating against her and desire pooled between her legs. She pulled her hand from Chase's breast. She skimmed it along the outside of her breast, cupping it gently, then releasing it and continued exploring Chase's body. She felt Chase's narrow waist where it curved into her hips and could tell she wasn't wearing panties. "Oh god."

Chase's breathing was ragged. She hadn't wanted the kiss to end and when Jude pulled away, she felt cold.

"We have to slow down, or I'm finished. I can't stop myself...you're like a drug to me." She laid her forehead against Chase's and closed her eyes.

Chase put her finger underneath Jude's chin and tilted her head up, meeting Jude's dark eyes with her own unmasked ardor. "No one is asking you to stop."

Jude took a deep breath and exhaled loudly. "This isn't a good idea. It's not what you need. It can't be more..."

Chase put her finger on Jude's lips to silence her. "Every time I look at you, I am completely undone." She smiled tentatively. "Tonight, I don't want to think about whether it's a good idea or not. I don't want to think about tomorrow or what happens after this. I just want you."

"Are you sure? It's not too late to..." Jude spoke softly, trying to maintain some control.

"I need you to make love to me more than I've ever needed anything." Chase took a step towards the stairs and held her hand out towards Jude, her eyes regarding her expectantly.

Jude hesitated, wrestling with one last effort to be gallant and do the right thing.

"Please." Chase's voice was quivering, a testament to her desire.

Jude felt the final barrier collapse and she placed her hand in Chase's and followed her up the steps.

Chase led Jude into her bedroom. She stopped just short of the bed and looked at her, her eyes silently questioning her. Chase had initiated the kiss, but beyond that she wasn't sure what to do.

Jude took Chase's hand and brushed her lips over her knuckles softly. She held her gaze and whispered softly the words that Chase needed to hear. "Shhh, it's okay. We can take it as slow as you want."

Chase's breath caught in her throat and she blushed. "I need you to teach me. I don't know…"

Jude put her finger over Chase's lips to stop her. "Don't worry honey, you'll know what to do."

Chase warmed at the gentle endearment and she pushed the thought that Jude probably used that on anyone to the far recesses of her mind. Jude's eyes boring into her were making her searing hot and she needed to feel Jude against her. She opened the robe and pulled Jude's hand to her breast. She heard Jude swallow and her breath come in short gasps. "I want you to touch me all over."

Jude shook her head slowly, her hand starting a slow exploration of Chase's breast. Her eyes, dark with hunger, stayed focused on Chase's face. "Watch me. I want to see your eyes when I touch you." She lifted her other hand and cupped her other breast softly, brushing lazily over her soft nipple, smiling at the surprised gasp that left Chase's lips. "You're very soft, and you have a beautiful body."

Chase watched Jude lean closer to her and graze her lips against hers. The urgency that was there earlier had been replaced by a slow, sensual burning somewhere deep in her soul. She parted her lips and waited for their tongues to meet. When she felt the warm softness of Jude's tongue brushing against her she felt her body surrender, melting into Jude. She kissed her back with all the longing she felt, hoping to somehow show Jude just what she felt for her.

Jude increased the pressure, the need to feel Chase growing inside her. She slid her palm along the underside of her breast and caressed her abdomen softly. She knew she needed to go slow, letting Chase set the pace that was comfortable for her. She pulled her mouth away from Chase's and feathered kisses along her neck and chest, stopping just above her breast. She cupped her breast and pulled it towards her, taking her nipple in her mouth gently. She sucked it then ran her tongue over the taut peak. When she caught it between her teeth, she heard Chase gasp. She nipped it gently, and felt Chase arching against her.

Chase felt her world spinning. Her nipples were so hard and sensitive and Jude's mouth on them was like sweet torture, sending electric shocks through her body. They converged between her legs, and Chase felt heat spreading quickly. She was more turned on by Jude than she had ever been before. She wasn't sure she would be able to take what came next. If Jude continued what she was doing, she knew she would come soon.

Jude sensed she was close and wrenched her mouth away. She planted quick kisses on her lips and smiled. "Your nipples are so perfect. And you are so responsive."

Chase smiled shyly. She wasn't sure how to answer. She had never talked dirty during sex or foreplay and she didn't want to say the wrong thing. She bit her lip and said quickly. "If you keep touching me like that, I'm going to have an orgasm."

Jude chuckled softly. "That's the idea, sweetheart."

Chase felt herself melt a little more. For now, she was Jude's sweetheart. She wouldn't think about tomorrow. She looked into Jude's eyes and smiled tentatively. "I want you to make love to me...please."

Jude felt herself blush. This sweet, innocent, beautiful woman was asking her to make love to her...to be her first and that touched Jude somewhere deep inside. She kissed Chase softly then turned towards the bed. She pulled her turtleneck off and started to unbutton her jeans.

Chase put her hand on Jude's and stopped her. "Let me." Her eyes paused on Jude's small, perfect breasts and she felt her heartbeat quicken. She had seen breasts before, but none like Jude's. They were round and perfect. Chase wanted her mouth on Jude's nipples. She raised her hand hesitantly then stopped.

Jude caught Chase's hand and pulled it to her quickly. She put it on her breast and moved it in slow circles around her already taut nipple. "I want you to touch me."

Chase felt the taut peak against her palm and it made her heady. She loved the control she had over Jude's body and it made her want more. She pulled her hand away and started to unbutton Jude's jeans. She undid the zipper and pulled the flaps apart. She saw the tops of Jude's black briefs, dark against her smooth stomach. She inched her jeans over her hips and slid them down her legs. Her eyes took in Jude's body hungrily, finally resting on the vee between her legs. Suddenly, her confidence faltered. "I don't know what to do."

Jude slid the robe off Chase's shoulders and let it fall in a puddle at her feet. She stepped closer and wrapped her arms around her, their breasts pressed together firmly. She pulled Chase's head against her cheek and held her there, her breath warm against her neck. She broke the connection slightly and took Chase's right hand in hers and guided it inside her waistband. She held it against her. "Touch me. I want you to feel what you do to me."

Chase felt the soft curls and her instincts took over. She slid her hand down and felt the heat coming from Jude's body. She knew her own body by heart, but nothing prepared her for what came next. Her fingers slid into warm wetness and she gasped for air. She did this, she made Jude wet with arousal. She felt the velvet folds slick against her fingers, and she ran her fingers along the outside, covering Jude's sex with moisture.

Jude's neck arched back at the first touch. It was soft and gentle, an innocence she hadn't experienced in a long time. She felt herself pulsating against Chase's fingers, aching for her touch. She moaned and bit her lip. "Go inside me...please."

Chase circled Jude's clit then she reached lower and plunged her fingers inside her. She felt Jude's muscles contract around her and her heart jumped. She could feel Jude raising and lowering herself on her fingers, and her courage grew. She withdrew her fingers only to plunge them back inside her even deeper. She met Jude's rhythm with eagerness. Her thumb rubbed circles around Jude's clit and she heard Jude moan.

Jude knew she was close to coming all over Chase, and she forced herself to slow down. She couldn't let herself come before she had pleasured Chase. She tried to pull away, but Chase through an arm around her and held her tightly. "Chase, please. You're going to make me come."

"Let me Jude. Just let go for once. I want this, I want to make you come." Chase's voice was soft but urgent. Her fingers were plunging deeper and faster, she increased the pressure on Jude's clit. She cupped Jude's chin and pulled her face up. "Look at me. I want to watch you." Jude's eyes were almost black with desire and she held Chase's gaze. Chase sensed she was close and she pressed harder against Jude. She felt Jude's body stiffen and she held her as the first waves of her orgasm hit.

Jude struggled to keep her eyes open, but the fight was getting impossible. She knew Chase wanted, needed to see her. It was part of her growth. She clamped her jaw shut and tried to hold it. Finally giving into the primal need, she threw her head back and let it wash over her. Wave after wave of electricity surged through her, spasms hitting her body like tidal waves. "Oh god, Chase!" When the final wave hit her, her body relaxed involuntarily. Her knees, weak from exertion buckled and she threw her arms around Chase for support. Her mind was hit by a sudden influx of emotion and a symbolic crash thundered in her ears. Her emotional wall had just cracked wide open.

When Jude's heartbeat had finally slowed to a more normal pace she held Chase at arms length. "Wow! Are you sure this is your first time?"

Chase blushed, pleased with the compliment since despite Jude's very eager reaction to her touches, she still worried that it wasn't up to par. That she had disappointed Jude in some way. "Mmm, thank you. Nothing in my life could have prepared me for the feeling of touching you for the first time. Making you so wet…that was amazing." She closed her eyes and moaned.

"Watch it Berkley, you're going to get me hot and bothered again." Jude gasped when Chase moved her fingers that were still buried deep in the warm recesses of her sex. She nearly jumped out of her skin when Chase rubbed her thumb lightly over her still sensitive clit.

"That's the idea sweetheart." Chase said saucily.

Her response was cut short when Jude stilled her hand and pulled her mouth against hers, her tongue hungrily seeking entry. Jude's tongue plunged in savagely and her hand found Chase's breast again. She rolled her taut peak between her thumb and forefinger and groaned when she felt it grow harder. She stepped out of the puddle of clothes on the floor and nudged Chase towards the bed.

Chase's head swam, Jude's tongue was assailing her and the fierceness of it turned her on even more. She squirmed to get closer to Jude's body, wanting to feel all of Jude pressed against her. The back of her knees hit the bed and suddenly Jude's arm was around her, swiftly guiding her to the mattress. She felt Jude pull away rather than joining her on the bed. Her eyes searched Jude's questioningly.

Jude shook her head solemnly, but her eyes teased Chase. "I want to look at you."

Chase's normal reaction would have been to try to cover herself or turn off the light, but she felt powerless to hide what Jude's eyes were hungrily craving. She felt Jude's gaze rake across her body and it sent shivers down her spine.

"God, you're gorgeous." Jude said more to herself than to Chase. She ran her palm along Chase's shin her thumb rubbing lightly along her calf, lost in incoherent murmurs. She slid along Chase's knee and looked up surprised when she jumped.

"I'm a little ticklish." Chase said shyly.

"Then perhaps I should change my tactics. I want you to be able to relax." Jude winked wickedly. She moved her hand away from Chase's knee and kissed her softly. She tried not to look at Chase's sex, wet with desire. She knew if she looked, she would not be able to resist touching her there. Instead she concentrated on her soft skin. Jude ran her tongue along Chase's inner thigh and she felt her hips jump in excitement.

"Jude. You're killing me. I need you to touch me...now." Chase was breathless with need, her voice anxious to the point of pleading.

"Patience my dear. Anything good is worth waiting for." Jude stopped before she reached the apex and inhaled Chase's sweet scent. She ached to taste her. Needing to prolong this experience, she wrenched her mouth away from the tempting hollow between her legs and ran her tongue along her hips. She gently kissed Chase along her abdomen and chuckled softly when Chase tried to squirm away. She kissed her breast than pulled her nipple into her mouth and sucked it gently, feeling it grow with each expert stroke of her tongue. She felt Chase moving beneath her and knew she was close. She gently nipped her nipple between her teeth and Chase moaned loudly.

Chase squirmed against Jude, trying to bring their bodies together. She needed to assuage the pressure building between her legs soon. Jude's mouth on her breast was going to make her come and she didn't want to...not without Jude inside her. She felt Jude pull away and capture her mouth with hers. Their tongues danced around each other's, building the fire that burned inside her. Just when she thought she could take no more, she felt Jude's fingers sliding through the soft triangle of hair.

Jude's fingers found Chase's sex and slid inside her slowly. She held them there long enough to feel Chase's muscles tighten around her, then she pulled them out only to plunge them deeper inside her. She felt Chase arch her hips to pull her in deeper and she pulled them away, prolonging the torture. She watched Chase, her eyes dark with desire, pleading for her touch. Slowly, she scooted down the bed, her eyes never leaving Chase's face. She began a slow rhythm with her fingers, her thumb pushing Chase closer to the edge. Her eyes dropped and she looked at Chase's sex, her silky folds wet with arousal and her clit hard and pulsating. The sight ripped through Jude like wildfire and she groaned loudly. She lowered her head and her tongue stroked Chase's clit softly. Suddenly a need so primal and foreign surged through her body and she could no longer wait to taste her.

Chase felt Jude's tongue on her and she nearly came. One soft stroke on her clit and she almost lost it. She felt Jude's fingers leave her. When Jude's tongue pushed inside her, she gasped out loud. "Oh fuck Jude. That's so good." She felt Jude lick up and down the inner folds, then plunge deep inside her again. This is it, this is what she waited for her whole life. She could feel the urgency building inside her and her hips raised off the bed urging Jude deeper and deeper.

Jude was heady with the taste of Chase. She felt alive and whole for the first time. She ran her thumb in circles around Chase's clit, marveling at the unbidden response. She felt a new surge of wetness and knew Chase was at the brink. She wrapped her arm around Chase's leg to hold her against her mouth and increased the pressure of her other thumb on her clit. Chase's hips arched in a rhythmic cadence, the two of them connected in a symbiotic dance. Suddenly, she felt Chase's body tense against her.

The orgasm crashed over Chase and she reeled as wave after wave of intense pleasure rippled through her. She opened her mouth to scream but all that came out were incoherent moans and gasps for air. She felt herself crest, and fall, then crest a second and third time. Jude's mouth raking over her and inside her, bringing her to a point of absolute completeness. Her body reveled in the perfect union with another soul. Her orgasm an extension of her immense need for Jude.

When the waves finally ebbed and stilled, Jude kissed her softly and rested her head on Chase, listening to her faint heartbeat. Her arms wrapped tightly around her, trying to hold onto the moment and etch it in her mind. When she felt Chase twitch with sleep, she crawled up beside her and gathered her in her arms, content to hold her while they slept.

Chapter 26

Jude awoke with a start, momentarily confused by the warm body that was tucked against her. Chase was spooned against Jude, her firm, shapely bottom nestled in the curve of Jude's hips. Jude's hand rested possessively on Chase's breast, her mind suddenly replaying flashes of last night's lovemaking. Visions that made Jude's stomach flip—flop dangerously. She listened to Chase's even breathing, achingly aware that she was in danger of breaking her own rules—rules she lived by so she didn't end up with another broken heart.

Jude sighed softly, amazed at how easily Chase had gotten to her. *Oh yeah, great job following the rules, dumbass!* First, she had sworn she wouldn't sleep with Chase, yet here she was, lying next to her. *And getting turned on again. Argh!!* Second, she had stayed the night. *What was the rule for that, Jude? Oh yeah, never, ever stay the night. Never allow it to be personal. It's just sex...well, at least it was just sex until Chase.* All of Jude's ruminations were making her restless. Her hand had begun to caress Chase's breast, and when she felt Chase's nipple harden beneath her hand and heard her moan, Jude jumped. *Oh shit! Don't wake up, please don't wake up.* Third, she would never let herself fall in love again. She would never allow herself to be hurt again. The first two rules were blown, but she would be damned if she broke the third and most important rule. *That's one rule I promise I won't break...no matter what it costs me.*

Jude tried to pull her hand away without disturbing Chase. She slid her arm over Chase without touching her and slowly inched her way out of bed. She breathed a sigh of relief when her feet hit the floor and she stood silently beside the bed. She grabbed her clothes off the floor, where they had been haphazardly discarded last night. She tiptoed to the door and stopped, her shoulder resting on the doorframe. She watched Chase sleeping, so sweet in repose. Her hair framed her angelic face, a wisp of it draped across her lips. Jude's heart jumped, her stomach dancing wildly, remembering what those lips had done to her last night.

Jude blinked rapidly and shook her head, trying desperately to keep her mind from running with that thought. If she allowed herself to think that way, she knew she would crawl back in bed with Chase and tease her awake with her...*no, no stop it! Not gonna happen.* Jude watched her a moment longer, then walked noiselessly to the bathroom.

She didn't see Chase's eyes open, hoping to catch a final glimpse of her. Eyes that reflected the sadness Chase felt in her heart. Last night, the only thing she wanted was to feel Jude, to know what it felt like to have her make love to her. Today, she felt empty. Jude didn't have to stay to tell her this was her one time, Chase knew. No matter how wonderful last night had been, dawn brought heartbreaking truth with it And the truth was, Chase was in love with someone she would never have. She felt a tear trickle down her cheek and land softly on the pillow.

Jude dressed quickly then looked at her reflection in the mirror. She ran a hand through her hair, trying to get it to lie down in the back. She finally gave up. She frowned at her reflection...messed up hair, rosy cheeks, eyes sparkling. Normally, she would be happy with the look of someone so sated, but today the face looking back bothered her tremendously. *I look the same, how come I feel like a totally different person?*

Jude walked silently down stairs, pulled her coat on and slipped out the front door. She shivered as she got into the car and turned the engine over. She punched the button to turn on her heated seats. She put the car in drive and with one final glance at the house, she quickly drove away from Serendipity and from Chase.

Chase heard the engine turn over and resisted the urge to go to the window and watch Jude drive away. Instead, she rolled onto her back and stared at the ceiling, trying desperately to drive Jude's image out of her mind. Her efforts to do so only made it worse, and before long she gave up trying to fight it. She closed her eyes, and immediately felt Jude's hands on her body. She curled onto her side, and fell into a restless sleep, her dreams plagued by visions of Jude.

Jude pulled into the garage. Mentally exhausted, she drug herself to the bathroom. She cranked the shower on high and stripped. She looked at her naked body in the mirror, focusing on the marks of last night's love affair. Faint teeth marks on her collar bone and over her left breast made her smile sadly. She stepped into the open shower and let the scalding water hit her body, praying it would burn away the feelings she was fighting.

Chapter 27

Chase pulled into the passenger pick—up lane at United Airlines and scanned the people streaming out the door. Her face broke into a wide grin when she spotted Tess's wild blond hair. She jumped out of the car and ran to meet her, throwing her arms around her and catching her in a giant bear hug.

Tess laughed and hugged her back. "Well I guess I don't have to ask if you missed me." She stood back and gave Chase a once over. "You don't look any worse for the wear, although something is different. I can't put my finger on it right now, but there's something amiss."

Chase shook her head and grabbed Tess's bag. "Nothing different, just glad to have you back. It gets lonely in that big old house."

"Well then I have good news for you." Tess hung her dress bag in the back seat and got in the passenger seat. "I don't know if you checked the schedule or not, but we are getting our first company of the year next weekend."

Chase eased the car into traffic. "I know Valentine's Day."

"Yep." Tess smiled cautiously. "I don't know if I am more excited or nervous. All I know is my stomach is churning like crazy. This will be our first time running the inn together. I've never done it without Avery." Her voice quivered slightly when she said Avery's name. "I'm glad you're here. I don't think I could do it alone."

"Me too." Chase squeezed Tess's hand. "I miss her too. I can't believe it's been almost four months."

"Me neither." Tess blinked rapidly, fighting tears. "I did have a break through though. I'm not crying myself to sleep every night anymore. It's still hard, and I miss her everyday, but at least I am starting to function again."

"So the trip was good for you?" Chase asked quietly.

Tess shook her head and smiled. "Yeah, I think so. Do you know I'm an Aunt Tess?"

"Wow…that's awesome!" Chase said excitedly.

"I know. It's kind of crazy. Both my sisters have girls. Well teenagers really! I don't know who was more surprised…me or them. They are great girls. Both of them are cheerleaders…" Tess made a face. "I know…cheerleaders. I would question whether they are related to me at all, but they are both on the honor roll at school, so at least they got a little of the brains too. I promised both of them I would facebook, so we could keep in touch."

"Oh Tess, that's wonderful! Those girls couldn't ask for a better aunt." Chase paused then continued slowly. "So how about the rest of the family? Everything go okay with them?"

Tess's smile broadened. "Well you know I stayed with them the rest of my trip and honestly, I was worried at first, but everything turned out okay. I found out my dad had a heart attack about six months ago. Apparently, he's a changed man now. I guess he realized how important family is. He instituted a weekly family dinner, he's always going to the girl's cheerleading competitions. He takes my mom on dates all the time. He knows life is fleeting and he wants to make sure he gets as much time with them as possible. I wish he would have realized that twenty years ago." Chase saw a look of sadness wash over Tess's face then it disappeared as quickly as it appeared. "But at the same time, if he had then my life wouldn't have gone in the direction it did and I would never have met the love of my life…or you for that matter. I probably would have had some boring, safe life in Connecticut. No matter how much time we lost, I wouldn't change the few years I had with Avery for anything. What about you? Do anything or anyone fun while I was away?"

Chase pictured Jude's naked body and she nearly choked. "No, of course not. You were only gone a couple of weeks. And besides, there aren't a whole lot of eligible *anyones* in this town." She hoped Tess couldn't see the red that was creeping up her neck. She was more flushed with arousal at the mental images of Jude than she was embarrassed, but either way, explaining the recent events would be somewhat difficult. "I did go down to Portland for the day. That's a neat town."

Tess watched the color in Chase's face go from tinges of pink to bright red and smothered a giggle. "Oh yeah? Did you drive down there by yourself?"

Chase cleared her throat loudly. "Uhm, no, not exactly."

"Not exactly? Well who exactly did you go with?" Seeing Chase's discomfort was becoming more and more amusing by the minute.

Chase continued to stammer, unable to utter a sentence succinctly. "I, ahh, well we, I mean, I went with, oh hell, I went with Jude, okay? Happy now?" She looked at Tess with a completely frustrated look on her face. When she realized Tess was enjoying this little interrogation, she glared at her. "Bitch! Are you sure you can't go back to Connecticut indefinitely?"

Tess burst out laughing. "I'm just messing with you. I talked to Jude a few days ago. She called to see what my schedule was and she mentioned that you kept her company when she went to drop some paperwork off." Tess paused for a moment, then cocked her head and stared at Chase. "Hmmm."

Chase shot an exasperated look. "What hmmm?"

Tess shook her head nonchalantly. "Oh nothing." She paused for effect, letting the silent question hang in the air. "It's just you seem different and Jude was kind of weird on the phone. If I didn't know better, I'd say something happened between the two of you."

Chase's ears turned bright red, her face on fire. She started coughing loudly.

Tess banged on her back with the palm of her hand. "Breathe, that's it, just breathe." She waited for Chase to stop coughing then smiled at her coyly. "Was it something I said?"

Chase's eyes narrowed and she glared at Tess. "Grrrrr!"

Tess stifled another laugh and wisely let the matter drop. Obviously, Chase was not ready to talk about whatever it was that had transpired between she and Jude. And Tess knew better than to push. If and when Chase was ready to talk, she would be there, ready to listen.

Moments later, Chase let out a sigh and faced Tess. "So tell me about our guests."

"I don't know much other than their names and that it's their fiftieth wedding anniversary. Beyond that, we find out when they come. Fifty years with the woman he loves. Lucky guy!" Tess smiled wistfully. "Anyway, they are arriving the thirteenth, which is a Friday and staying through Sunday. They wanted to stay in the Lily Room a.k.a. the Whitman Room. Apparently, they stayed at the old inn on their honeymoon and he wants to surprise her on their anniversary by bringing her back here."

"How romantic! I can't wait to meet them." Chase replied emphatically.

"Neither can I. He sounded like such a sweet old man when I spoke to him on the phone. Didn't even make the reservations online…called here to make them. Probably doesn't even own a computer." Tess chuckled softly. "I think we will, I mean you will cook and I will offer moral support, a wonderful Valentine's day dinner. Avery found the old register and menus from the original inn when she renovated the place. I bet we could find what was served on Valentine's Day fifty years ago and make that."

Chase laughed softly. "Why Tess, I didn't realize you were such a softie!"

Tess shook her head from side to side. "I didn't used to be. One of the benefits of falling in love with Avery, she is a romantic at heart, and I guess it just rubbed off on me."

"I'm beginning to think that Avery and this place cast a spell on me too!" She didn't elaborate and Tess didn't push. She was content to ride in amiable silence, her thoughts on her past, her now and surprisingly, her future.

Chapter 28

"…and I knew the first time I saw Ginny, she was the woman I wanted to spend the rest of my life with." Robert Weller looked at his wife Virginia with love and adoration.

"He may have known I was the one, but don't let him fool you, my dears. He didn't win me over quite so easily." Virginia Weller's clear blue eyes danced. "Robbie was such a prankster when I first met him. I couldn't decide if he liked me or just liked tormenting me."

Tess leaned forward in her chair and gestured to their coffee mugs. "Can I get anyone a refill? I hear a story in there somewhere."

The Weller's declined, and when Tess returned with full mugs for she and Chase, Virginia started their story from the beginning. "I met Robbie the summer I turned nineteen. Our families had traveled from inland to the shore for the summer. That was back in the fifties when families still traveled on extended vacations together. We stayed here, back when it was still called the Flower by the Sea Inn."

Tess smiled. "Oh yes, that is why you called the Whitman Room the Lily Room."

"Oh yes, and the other rooms all had floral names too. The Tulip Room, The Rose Room, and I believe The Lily Room. And now I believe they are all named after authors."

Tess nodded. "You are correct. All the rooms are named after authors that were alive during the Victorian era. That was Avery's idea, since the house is an old Victorian."

Robbie chuckled. "Quite fitting…especially the Whitman Room. He and Elizabeth Barrett Browning are Ginny's favorite authors. She's quite the romantic."

"Don't let Robbie fool you…" Virginia winked mischievously. "…if anyone is romantic, it's him." She stopped and smiled at Robert, love evident in her eyes. "Now where was I? Oh yes, our families had come here for the summer. We were staying here and

Robbie's family was staying just down the road. We didn't know his family at all, other than by reputation, and let me tell you, Robbie had quite the reputation."

Robert covered Virginia's hand with his and smiled. Turning to Chase and Tess, he chuckled ruefully. "I thought I was quite the catch back then. I was twenty—two years old, just graduated from the University of Maine and this was my last summer with the boys before I started teaching. I had good prospects, and if I do say so myself, I was quite a handsome devil. I had women swooning all over me."

"Oh he was a devil all right. I wanted to clobber him with my umbrella the first time I saw him." Virginia's eyes were wistful, remembering back over fifty years.

Chase smiled warmly. "I'm sure he was quite taken with your beauty as well, Virginia."

"Please, it's Ginny. You can't tell it, but I was quite the looker when I was younger. Raven hair, and bright blue eyes. I had quite a few beaus in my early days…although none as forthcoming as Robbie."

"I think I speak for both Chase and I when I say you still are quite the looker. If I was thirty years older…" Tess winked at Virginia.

Virginia chuckled softly. "You're quite the flatterer Tess. You do an old woman's heart good."

"And an old man." Robert interjected. "Why imagine how proud I was to be with Ginny…especially after that summer."

Chase looked intrigued. "Yes, that summer. What did happen?"

Virginia smiled. "It was the weekend of the annual Lobster Fest. I believe it was late July, so we had already been there almost two months. I was engaged at the time, but William couldn't join us for the summer, so I didn't see much of him at all. He finally managed to get away from the store. You see he managed his father's store and was always busy. Finally, the weekend of the Lobster Fest he drove up to surprise me. William and I were at the Lobster Fest with my family enjoying lunch when Robbie, quite literally, fell into my lap."

Robert looked at the girls sheepishly. "I couldn't think of any other way to get Ginny's attention. I had seen her before, but couldn't work up the nerve to introduce myself. Then I saw her with her fella and I realized if I didn't jump…" Robert pumped his fist for emphasis. "...at the opportunity, I would miss my chance. And I had already decided she was the girl for me."

Chase and Tess watched the couple with rapt attention. "What did you do?"

Robert chuckled. "I decided right there it was time to make my move, so I..."

Virginia interrupted, finishing his story. "I'll tell you what he did. He, and his tray of lobster and pie, mind you blueberry pie, fell into my lap. One minute I was eating lunch and enjoying William's company and the next minute, I'm looking down at Robbie, bumbling through an apology. My skirt was ruined."

"It was quite an apology too." Robert laughed. "Here I was throwing caution to the wind to get her attention, and she is giving me what for." He winked at Chase and Tess. "And let me tell you, she is a beauty when she is mad, eyes blazing. Little did she know that I had done it on purpose just to meet her. Tripped and threw myself on top of her just to get her attention."

"I found that out much later, when he knew it was safe to tell me." She squeezed his hand softly. "The next day he sent me a note with money to replace the skirt and a question...will you marry me? Of course, I said no. For the next month, he would come visit me every day, whether William was there or not, and he would bring me some little present, a bar of chocolate, flowers, just little things. Each one came with a note...will you marry me? He was quite persistent."

Robert smiled. "I was. There was no way I was going to let her get away...engaged or not. William was a nice enough chap, but not the right man for my Ginny. There is only one man for her, and that was me, whether she realized it or not that summer."

Virginia continued. "Somehow Robbie managed to get our home address, so even after we left the coast, I would receive letters in the mail from him. I probably shouldn't have corresponded with him as much as I did, since I was engaged, but there was something about him. He was a dashingly handsome, dark devil. But he had a good heart, and as I got to know him better, I realized he was sincere in his feelings for me. He certainly tested my resolve."

"That I did." Robert smiled proudly. "I was going to fight for her until I won her over."

"On Christmas Eve, I received a package. When I opened it up, I was stunned. Robbie had written one last letter telling me that he loved me and wanted to spend the rest of his life with me. However, he didn't want to hang onto empty hopes, and if I turned him down this last time, he would stop asking me and let me get on with my life. At the end of the letter he had tied an engagement ring and wrote will you marry me?" Virginia's voice quivered and her eyes misted up briefly.

Robbie leaned over and kissed her on the cheek. "When I wrote that letter, somehow I knew it wouldn't be the last one. I just knew that Ginny and I would end up together. Don't get me wrong, I was as nervous as I can remember, especially when she didn't respond right away."

Chase and Tess leaned forward in their chairs, their gaze locked on Virginia. "Well, what happened?"

"I can tell you I fretted over it for weeks. I came close to mailing the ring back several times, but when it came down to it, I just couldn't. I had never really been able to picture a future with William, but Robbie, I saw us together in everything. I even imagined what our children would look like." She paused and took a sip of her now cold coffee. "Finally two weeks before Valentine's Day in 1959, I sat down with William and we had a long talk, then I mailed a letter back to Robbie with one word."

Robert's face broke into a smile. "Yes. It was the most wonderful word I had ever heard. And I wasn't going to give her a chance to back out. That Saturday I drove to her house and I proposed properly. I had talked to her father that summer and told him my plans, and he looked at me and I remember the words exactly, 'Son, that's plum crazy, but if you can win over my Virginia, stubborn as she is, you have my blessing.'"

Virginia smiled. "My father never really liked William. They just didn't connect. But he and Robbie did, they were both the intellectual type and could chat nonstop. So it's no wonder my father would give my Robbie his blessing."

"So then what happened?" Tess inquired. "Today is your fiftieth anniversary, so you must have been married on Valentine's Day."

"Oh we were, with a little finagling." Robert winked mischievously. "Ginny's father helped with the arrangements. It had taken me months to court her and finally win her hand, I wasn't waiting months for a wedding. Valentine's Day seemed like the perfect day."

"After the ceremony, Robbie drove us here for our honeymoon and we stayed in the Lily Room. He said he had to bring me back to the place he first saw me and fell in love."

Chase swiped at her eyes. "That is so romantic. And now you're back here fifty years later."

Virginia smiled. "Yes, we finally are. That weekend was the last time we made it here. Robbie took a teaching job that fall in New York. Between that and raising a family, we just never made it back. But he was always the romantic, nonetheless. Do you know for every anniversary he would send me lilies with a note that said will you marry me?"

Robbie smiled warmly. "She made me the happiest man alive. I learned a valuable lesson the summer I met her. If you love someone, don't ever give up. You fight for them. Even if something is meant to be, it doesn't always happen on its own. Sometimes you have to help it along some." His gaze settled on Chase, his warm eyes regarding her thoughtfully as if he were talking to her directly. "Always remember that if you love, I mean really love someone, you fight for them. Don't live your life with regrets. The smartest thing I ever did was falling into Ginny's lap."

Chapter 29

Chase groaned and shielded her eyes from the bright light arching across her face. She cursed at Tess for opening the curtain.

"Do you know what today is?" Tess asked excitedly.

Chase rolled over and covered her head with the pillow. "Whatever day it is you are freaking insane!" She lifted her head and squinted, trying to make out the numbers on the clock. "Argh! It's 7:30...in the morning."

"It's Avery's birthday. We have to celebrate."

Chase mentally calculated the days in her head. Yes, it was March 3rd already. *Did I just hear Tess say we have to celebrate or am I dreaming this whole thing?* "Ahh, Tess?" Chase asked cautiously.

Tess slapped her butt playfully. "No, I haven't lost my mind. But she would have wanted us to get out and celebrate her life, not be miserable and sulk around the house all day thinking about her being gone." She jumped off the bed, and jerked the covers back. "Come on! We have to start now. This is an all day celebration."

Chase groaned loudly, and when she realized that Tess wasn't going to let her sleep longer, she rolled onto her back, pulled herself up and threw her legs over the side of the bed. She rested her elbows on her knees and flopped her head in her palms. She hadn't slept very well the past month. Recurring dreams of Jude plagued her throughout the night. Constantly restless and in a heightened emotional state, she was barely getting a few hours of sleep each night. When Tess asked why she was so tired and depressed, she brushed it off as winter doldrums.

Chase ran her hands through her hair and sat up straight, stretching her arms high above her head. She glared at Tess, who was tapping her foot impatiently. "I'm coming, okay." She followed Tess downstairs to the kitchen and gratefully accepted the mug of steaming coffee Tess placed in her hands.

"It's blueberry crumble…Avery's favorite." Tess said proudly. "Be careful, though it's really hot."

Chase slipped the hot liquid slowly, welcoming the reviving effects of the caffeine. "So now that you have me awake, what's the plan?" She asked wryly.

Tess smiled sweetly. "Well first, you make me blueberry pancakes?"

Chase nearly spit her coffee out. "What?!"

"Avery always made them for me." Tess countered.

"Avery? Avery always made them? Even though it was *her* birthday?" Chase asked incredulously.

"Well duh." Tess's voice implied that she thought the question was ridiculous. "I can't cook…even pancakes. But I do make one hell of a great cup of coffee."

"I'll give you that one." Chase sighed loudly. "Fine, I'll make you pancakes, but you are helping. Grab the griddle out of the pantry and get it hot while I mix everything up. Oh yeah, and pull the blueberry syrup and Redi—Whip out of the fridge too. If we are doing these in honor of Avery, we're gonna do them right!"

#

Chase pushed back from the table and groaned. She looked across at Tess and tried her best to look pathetic. Avery's birthday celebration centered around food, and Chase couldn't remember when she had eaten that much food. They had just finished a large Greek pizza at the Portland House of Pizza. Lunch had been twin two pound lobsters from Cook's Lobster House on Bailey Island, one of the few lobster houses open year round. To top it all off, before they had left Boothbay, Tess stopped at the Fudge Factory and bought three different kinds of fudge, swearing up and down, they were all Avery's favorites. "I don't think I can move a muscle I'm so full."

"Don't worry, you can dance it off tonight." Tess said cheerfully.

"Aww Tess, I don't know. I know it's tradition, but it's a gay bar. I'll feel so out of place." The wheels in Chase's mind turned frantically. Avery's birthday always ended up at Styxx, her favorite gay and lesbian bar in Portland. Chase was sure she would feel awkward and out of place.

Tess smiled reassuringly. "Don't worry. It's Tuesday, so it won't be super busy. Besides, there's a lot of straight people that go there too. You'll be fine."

Chase rolled her eyes. "You do know I am *only* doing this for Avery."

Tess reached across the table and clasped Chase's hands in hers and smiled, her eyes watering. "Thank you for today. Thanks for being here for me. I needed this."

Chase smiled warmly. "I know honey, I'm glad I could be here for you." She pulled her hand away and swiped at her own eyes, Tess's emotions wreaking havoc on her own tired, frayed nerves. "Come on, you cry baby. Let's get outta here before you get me all choked up too. You know I hate to cry in public."

Tess stood up and pulled her coat on. She caught Chase's gaze and smiled. "I know you already know but…I love you, man." She looped her arm through Chase's, forever bound to her. Two women brought together under the worst of circumstances, both leaning on the other for the strength to move forward.

Chapter 30

Jude's hand stopped halfway to her mouth, the glass never making it to her lips. Her mouth dropped in shock before she managed to get herself under control. She watched Chase walk into the bar with Tess right behind her. She felt her stomach jump into her throat and the heat rise in her cheeks. She hadn't seen or spoken to Chase since that night…the night that haunted her dreams and filled her waking moments. She watched them walk to a table near the back of the room and sit down. Neither one of them had seen her and she wrestled with sneaking out and avoiding any kind of scene and going to their table and sitting down. The desire to be near Chase won out, and moments later she was weaving between tables trying not to spill the drinks in her hands. When she set them down with a loud plunk, Tess turned to her and her face broke into a smile.

"Jude!" Tess said enthusiastically as she jumped up and gave her a big hug. "What a pleasant surprise."

Jude put her arms around Tess and squeezed her hard. "I'm glad you're back. I missed you!" She loosened her grip and held Tess at arms length. She held Tess's gaze and smiled. "You look good…happier than I've seen in a while."

Tess's smile widened. "I am, things are going good." She raised an eyebrow and stared at Jude. "You, on the other hand, look like shit."

Jude laughed wryly. "On second thought, I don't think I missed you at all." She sat down on a stool and turned to Chase, her eyes searching Chase's face for some sign of welcome, a smile playing at the corner of her mouth. "Hi."

Chase dipped her head, slightly embarrassed. She had wondered how she would feel when she finally saw Jude again. Warmth effused her body and she smiled shyly. "Hi yourself."

For a moment, everyone in the bar but Chase disappeared from Jude's vision, her eyes drinking in Chase's face. Tonight Jude thought she was the most beautiful woman she had ever seen. She brushed a lock of hair out of Chase's face and her thumb grazed her cheek. She pulled her hand away, the heat from the simple touch too much to bear. Memories flashed in her mind, and Jude was assaulted by a sharp pang in her heart. She felt like someone had just shredded her last wall of resistance.

Chase jumped when Jude's thumb grazed her cheek, her stomach clinching with desire. She saw naked emotion in Jude's eyes, quickly replaced by a look of fear. She couldn't be sure, but in that brief moment, she thought she saw something more than desire in Jude's eyes, a look that sent heat rushing through Chase's body, pooling between her legs. Chase jumped when she heard Tess clear her throat, the spell between them broken. She looked at Tess, guilt evident on her face. "What?"

Tess smiled mischievously. "Ahh, hello. I'm still here."

Jude looked embarrassed at being caught in such an intimate moment. "Sorry, spaced there for a bit. So tell me about Connecticut? We haven't really had a chance to talk about it."

"Sure, spaced out…uh-huh." She smiled sarcastically. "It was good. I stayed with my family, for the first time…"

Chase heard Tess's talking, but her mind was elsewhere. She watched Jude's narrow fingers resting lazily on her glass. She shivered when she remembered those fingers on her body, stroking her expertly, bringing her to climax again and again.

"Chase?" Tess said Chase's name again, louder this time.

Chase jumped when she heard a giggle. "What?"

Tess gestured with her head towards Jude. "Ahh, I was just saying that I didn't know how you made it by yourself for two weeks and Jude said again how nice it was to have company when she went to Portland."

Chase's eyes flicked to Jude and she saw her smirk. She felt the heat rise to her face and she grabbed her glass and took a drink, trying to hide her blush of embarrassment. "Oh yes, it was a long two weeks, but the trip helped, ahh, break up the monotony."

Tess stifled a laugh. "I'm sure it did." She watched the looks that passed between her two friends and she smiled. *I wonder how long it will take them to realize they are falling in love with each other. More importantly, will they stop fighting fate and take a chance at happiness?* Tess wasn't sure, but she did know from experience, the longer they fought it, the harder they would be to live with.

Jude, eager to break free from the spell that Chase was casting over her, lifted her glass and shot Tess an inquisitive glance. "So what brings you two lovely ladies out tonight?"

"Avery." Both women responded at the same time. They dissolved into laughter. Tess stopped laughing long enough to explain to Jude that they were celebrating Avery's birthday. She recounted the day's events. When the story got around to the bar, Jude smiled and raised her glass higher.

"Then I say let's toast to Avery." She clinked her glass against theirs and threw the last remnants of the glass back. She watched them drain their glasses as well and winked. "Looks like it's time for another round."

Chase watched her walk away, her eyes following the graceful movements as Jude weaved her way through the small crowd of tables. She had taken her suit jacket off and her black dress pants hugged her body in all the right places. Chase felt blood surge through her veins, her stomach flip—flopping wildly.

"Want a picture...it will last longer." Tess asked sarcastically.

Chase wrenched her eyes off of Jude and mumbled an apology.

"What's going on between you two anyway?" Tess's eyes pierced through Chase. "And don't try to tell me nothing."

Chase sighed wearily. "I slept with her." She raised her eyes expectantly.

Tess nearly spit out the piece of ice she was sucking on. "What! I knew something happened, but I never suspected that." She shook her head. "Huh...huh...huh."

Chase cringed. "I know, I still can't believe it myself."

"So how was it? Being your first time and all." Tess was smiling now, her eyes dancing mischievously.

"Amazing." Chase's eyes sparkled. "Well it was beyond amazing. I never knew it could be like that...so wonderful and so right. I understand completely how Avery must have felt. Jude makes me feel things I never knew were possible. I have all these emotions running through my head, making me crazy. Sometimes I don't even recognize myself, but it's okay, it still feels like it's me, only better. Like I am finally in the exact place I was meant to be and everything fits perfectly. Does that make sense?"

"Of course it does honey, I could have told you that." Tess glanced towards the bar, making sure Jude was still there. "How does she feel about it?"

Chase's eyes clouded over. "I don't know, this is the first time I have talked to Jude since that night." She shrugged. "But I'm sure she doesn't feel the same as me. I'm just another notch in her belt."

Tess turned towards the bar and watched Jude coming back to the table, her eyes locked on Chase. She turned back to Chase and smiled. "I'm not so sure about that."

"I am, she and I…" Chase broke off when Tess cleared her throat loudly and nodded her head sideways, her eyes telegraphing a silent warning. She looked up just as Jude got back to the table.

"You two look serious. Did I miss something?" Jude inquired.

Tess laughed. "Not at all. We were just discussing our existence and the role that fate plays in our place in the universe."

"Good thing I brought more drinks. That conversation is entirely too serious for me." Jude smiled crookedly and swept a lock of hair off her forehead.

Tess laughed. "What? You don't think that fate brought us all three together at this precise place, in this precise moment?"

"Hardly." Jude sipped her drink. "This was coincidence. We make our own fate. I don't believe we are part of some grand master plan, our path pre—defined, leaving us no choice but to merely trip along the road that was chosen for us."

"Fair enough." Tess's voice suggested she was not in agreement at all. "So you think you have control of every aspect of your life?"

"Outside forces aside…yes." Jude answered cautiously. She knew Tess had a sharp wit, and she was a little nervous about the direction of the conversation.

"So you agree there are things that are out of your control?"

"I will admit that there are people and situations that I have no control over. But that's not fate, it's something or someone that is outside of my direct circle and therefore, beyond my control." Jude paused, thinking about her next sentence. "But my life, the circumstances that directly affect me, I can control those. I choose which direction my life takes."

Tess's eyes narrowed thoughtfully. "In that line of thinking then you believe you can control your thoughts, emotions and feelings as well."

Jude opened her mouth to answer then shut it quickly. Something told her she was about to get tripped up. "Yes." She said slowly, hoping to sound confident.

"Hmm," Tess cocked her head and stared at Jude. "I guess that means you can control whether you fall in love or not."

Jude's gaze flicked to Chase, and her confidence faltered. She met Chase's eyes and felt an invisible force sucker punch her in the stomach. She suddenly knew that she could not control that, no matter how much she wanted too. She looked at Tess, and immediately knew Tess could see right through her. She didn't know if Chase had told Tess about them, but it didn't matter. She knew Tess could see everything in her eyes. She felt panic set in and knew she was dangerously close to the point of no return. She sat up straighter in her chair, her head tilted up slightly, a tactic she had learned to use when she wanted to let people know she meant business. "Yes I can."

Tess met Jude's gaze head on, not affected by her commanding demeanor. She shook her head. "Honey, you know I love you and think the world of you, but right now you are either the most stubborn or the most blind person I have ever met. I'm having a hard time deciding." Her laugh belied the harshness of the words.

Jude was taken aback by her directness, but she had to admit Tess was right. She threw the rest of her drink back and set her glass on the table. "If you will excuse me, I see something I can control. Enjoy the rest of the celebration." She slid off the stool and walked away, leaving Tess shaking her head.

"Sometimes I wonder if she will ever learn."

Chase watched Jude walk towards a tall blonde who had just come in the front door and she was immediately jealous. She fought down the urge to go scratch the woman's eyes out, trying to focus on the reason they were here…Avery's birthday. "Forget about it…that's Jude."

"Jude's a smart woman, but she is stupid when it comes to love." Tess shook her head. "She'd settle for being unhappy just to prove some point."

"What point?" Chase tore her gaze from Jude and looked at Tess. "That she's a consummate player and she happens to like sex. It's her prerogative."

"That's not who she is. She running from her past and hiding behind the 'I'm a one night stand kind of girl', thinking she is protecting herself from another broken heart." Tess shook her head. "I've got news for her, one day she is going to wake up and regret being too scared to let herself live."

Suddenly, everything was starting to make sense to Chase. She leaned her elbow on the table and rested her chin in her palm. "Who broke her heart?"

"I'm sorry, I shouldn't have said that. It wasn't my place to talk about Jude's personal life." Tess looked chagrined. "That's something she will have to share with you one day…if she wants to. But I will say this one thing. Normally, I try to keep my opinion to myself, but you two are my friends and I hate to see you miss out on something wonderful. If you care one bit about Jude and it wasn't just sex for you, do something about it. Don't let her get away."

Chase glanced at Jude. She was sitting at the bar, the mystery blond tucked between her legs. She felt a pang in her heart and she winced. "What if it's not my choice? What if she doesn't want me like I want her?" She sneered, obviously disgusted that the mystery woman had her hands all over Jude, and she was making no effort to stop it. "She looks pretty happy where she is."

Tess smiled. "Take it from me, looks can be deceiving. Anyone looking in on Avery and I would have thought we hated each other."

"But this is different. Besides how can we fight, when we haven't spoken more than two words to each other in weeks." Chase put her head in her hands and growled. "Why do I let her get to me?"

Tess tossled Chase's hair and laughed at the pathetic look on her face. "Cause you love her, darlin'." She raised her eyebrows in Jude's direction. "I'm going to the restroom, why don't you go have a little heart—to—heart with her…before things get out of control." Tess slid off her stool and walked to the bathroom, leaving Chase to debate the wisdom of telling Jude how she felt.

Chase watched Jude out of the corner of her eye, her jealousy firing her courage. *Oh hell, what do I have to lose? Oh yeah, my heart and my pride.* She stood up and threw the rest of her drink back, praying for some courage. She shook her hands at her side and blew out a breath. *All right, let's do this!*

She strode quickly to the bar and stopped beside Jude, clearing her throat loudly. Jude's eyes flashed surprise, before they clouded over and her face was masked with feigned annoyance.

Chase squared her shoulders, her chin jutting out defiantly. "Can I talk to you…" She glared at the woman wrapped around Jude. "…alone?"

"I'm a little busy at the moment." She tossed her head towards the blonde.

Chase bristled at her dismissal. She felt anger building inside her. She shut her eyes and took several deep breaths before she spoke again. "Leave her…we need to talk."

The blonde, who up till this point, had wisely kept her mouth shut, turned to Chase. "Obviously honey, she's not inter…"

Jude put a hand up to silence her. "I'll handle this." Turning to Chase, she pasted an insincere smile on her face. "There's nothing to talk about. I told you it was a one time thing. You knew that going into it. This is why I don't get involved, Chase. Too much drama. Now if you will excuse me, you had your one time."

Chase wasn't sure what came over her, but her hand flew on its own. She grabbed a glass off the bar and flung the contents on Jude. She spun on her heel and ran outside. She was walking towards the car when a hand grabbed her arm and spun her around roughly. She stared into Jude's dark eyes, anger flashing in them.

She was about to protest when Jude's lips covered hers fiercely. She tried to push away, but Jude held her tight, her lips punishing her. She felt Jude's tongue brushing her lips, seeking entry. Her anger started to mix with arousal as Jude continued her onslaught. Giving in to her, Chase parted her lips and felt Jude's tongue plunge angrily into her mouth. This turned her on even more.

She eagerly returned Jude's kiss, knowing this was what she wanted, longed for. Jude's grip loosened and she softened the kiss, her tongue dancing languidly with hers. She moaned, her defenses shot to hell at Jude's touch. Her mind flashed back several minutes and she felt her anger returning. She pushed Jude away roughly.

She glared at Jude, her voice sharp with anger. "What the hell was that for?"

Jude answered her question with matched anger. "What the hell was this for?" She tugged on her shirt. She was furious. She had been trying to get Chase out of her head, and in the process hurt her more than she wanted to and that angered her. She knew she was better than that, but Chase got inside her and made her act crazy. She was furious at herself for not being immune to Chase.

Chase's shoulders slumped forward. "That was for...hurting me."

Jude heard the quiver in her voice and saw the tears brimming in her eyes. Her anger dissipated. Chase's words sliced through her, leaving rough, jagged edges on her heart. "Chase, I'm sorry..."

Chase shook her head. "I'm sorry. I was foolish to think that you felt the same about me." She felt, rather than heard Jude start to interrupt, and she put her hand up to stop her. "The first time I met you, I knew that you would change my life. I just didn't know it would hurt this bad."

Jude wanted to gather Chase in her arms and kiss her pain away, but she sensed that the chasm her carelessness had created between them was too wide to cross. She suddenly felt more alone than she had ever felt. "I never meant to hurt you."

Chase wiped her eyes. "It's my fault. My head knew the rules, too bad my heart ignored them." Her eyes searched Jude's face and she shook her head sadly. "I couldn't help falling in love with you." She smiled wryly. "If this is what love feels like, I can see why you avoid it."

Jude took a step towards her, needing to hold her, wanting to heal the pain. She felt Chase pull away physically and emotionally.

Chase swallowed the lump in her throat and pasted a brave smile on her face. "Go back inside Jude. Don't worry about me. I'll be fine...tomorrow. You've made it easy to move on, and I assure you, you haven't gotten inside me enough that I can't get over you." She pivoted, and walked away from Jude, never looking back.

Jude's heart plunged. She felt sick to her stomach. She had taken a sweet, wonderful woman and hurt her more than she could have imagined possible. At that moment, Jude realized she hated the person she had become.

Chapter 31

Connie Carson looked at the haggard woman standing at her front door, bags in hand, smiling sheepishly. "Hi Mom."

"Chase!" Connie pulled her into her arms and hugged her tightly. "What a surprise! Is everything okay? Why didn't you call and tell us you were coming? I could have had your father pick you up at the airport." She disengaged Chase and stepped aside.

Chase walked inside and set her bags down. "I wanted to surprise you. I hope it's okay."

"Of course it's okay honey." Connie gave her daughter a once over and raised her eyebrow quizzically. "Rough flight?"

"Yeah I guess you could say that." Chase sighed and flopped wearily into a chair. "Rough flight, rough couple of months, you name it…it's been rough."

Concern was evident in Connie's eyes. "Oh honey, I know it's been hard lately. What with Avery and your job and well, with Derek leaving you for a…" She rolled her eyes sarcastically. "…a man, I don't know how you have been holding up. You should have come here sooner."

Chase shook her head. "I couldn't, too much going on with the house and with Tess."

"What's going on with Tess?" Connie's eyes narrowed almost imperceptibly. "You're not carrying on with that woman, are you?"

"Mom, not now. *That woman,* as you so eloquently put it, is my friend. She's had it worse than me, and what she needs is our support, not your condemnation."

"I'm sorry Chase." She smiled cautiously. "It's just that I'm your mother, and I worry about you, don't you know that? I only want what's best for you."

"Even if it means having something you didn't agree with?" She paused, picking at a piece of lint on the couch. When she met her mother's eyes, the uncertainty in them shocked her. She smiled to allay her fears. "Mom, don't worry, it's nothing like that. Really, Tess and I are *just* friends." *Tess and I are friends, but how shocked would little Ms. Goodie Two Shoes be if she knew that her daughter had fallen in love with a woman.*

Connie visibly relaxed. "I mean I like Tess, she sounds like a wonderful woman and I am sure she was good to Avery. It's just that that isn't you, honey. That lifestyle isn't for my baby girl."

Chase pinched the bridge of her nose and sighed softly. "Can we just drop it? I came here to relax and visit my favorite two people, not be harangued to the brink of insanity." Her tone held a hint of laughter, and her mother laughed softly.

"Touche!" Connie bounced off the couch, still spry at fifty—eight, and walked towards the kitchen. "Are you hungry dear? Your father will be so excited to see you. We weren't planning on seeing you again until we went back to Indy. I'll just call him…no wait, we'll surprise him too. Wait till he tells you…"

Chase's mind drifted to yesterday's conversation with Tess. Her encounter with Jude still stung like an open wound and somehow she thought escaping, *running away*, was the best way to drive Jude from her mind.

"How long will you be gone?" Tess fingered the bedspread distractedly.

Chase shoved the pillow into its case and punched the ends together to fluff it up. "I don't know. A couple of weeks maybe. I guess as long as my parents can stand me."

"Or you can stand them." Tess snickered.

"Exactly. I guess I'll be back in time to wrap everything up with the will." She pulled her side of the bedspread up and straightened it over the pillows. Turning to the throw pillows on the floor, she laughed cynically.

"What's so funny?" Tess asked her.

"It's ironic, don't you think? This whole situation."

Tess looked confused. "How do you mean?"

"All of us, you, me, Avery, Jude, brought together by this house. You find the love of your life and she's gone. I meet Jude, and she's, well who knows what she is. But she's gone. It's a whole lot of heartbreak. So much for Serendipity." Chase scoffed loudly.

"Aww, honey, you can't look at it that way." Tess hugged a pillow against her. "You're looking at the negative side of this when you should be looking at all the wonderful things that have happened here. Look at me, I spent my whole adult life trying to replace my family, and I met Avery. I had the best, *absolute best* years of my life with the most wonderful woman I had ever met. Yes, she was taken away from me, but loving her was the best thing to ever happen in my life. And you, how do you know what will happen? Your story isn't over. It's just beginning. You found yourself here too. We both did. We may have loved and lost, but we found something valuable and real in the whole process, we found ourselves. And nothing can take that away. I'd say that is true Serendipity."

"Damn it Monahan!" Chase swiped her eyes. "Why do you always have to be so sappy and make me cry? Why can't you just let me sulk in peace?"

Tess laughed out loud. "Paybacks honey. You didn't let me sulk. You were there when I needed a friend, and I will always be that for you." Her eyes searched Chase's face slowly. "I'm sorry about things with Jude. That's a hell of a way to come out of the closet."

Chase snorted. "Almost knocked me flat on my ass back in the closet."

"Are you sure this is the way you want to handle it…running away?"

"Ouch! You certainly know how to make me sound like a scaredy cat." Chase pretended to wince. "I don't know if it's the right way, but it's the only way I know how to handle it. That's my M.O., run as fast as hell in the opposite direction."

"…and pray that they can't run faster than you." Tess dodged the pillow that Chase flung at her.

"Funny Monahan, real funny." Chase responded wryly.

Chase looked up as her mother came back into the living room. "The best thing to do is get your mind off everything and I have the perfect idea."

Twenty minutes later, she and her mother sat in chairs at Lee's House of Nails, five minutes into a pedicure. "See honey, I told you this was perfect."

Chase sighed contentedly. "Yes, mom, you were right. This is perfect." She closed her eyes and rested her head against the back of the chair. Not surprisingly, the first thing she thought of was Jude.

She wondered what she was doing right now in Boothbay. Was she at the office? Was she out with someone? Did Jude think of her as much as she thought of Jude? *Not likely, unless it was thinking about what a fool she was.* Chase remembered the saying about fool me once, shame on you, fool me twice, shame on me. She would not let herself be fooled a second time. It wasn't like Jude had fooled her really, she had been totally up front the entire time. Chase just chose to ignore it. *Okay, so shame on me.*

Her self-recrimination gave way to thoughts of sadness. She had really mucked this one up. It hadn't ever struck her before now that she might be gay, and that she would fall in love with someone totally unavailable. She stole a glance at her mom and winced. Now, not only was she unlucky in love, but unless her mom changed her opinion, she was going to be the cast aside daughter as well. That wasn't a prospect she was too keen on exploring…at least not right now. She figured she better find someone that loved her back before she sprang that one on her mom.

"What was that dear?" Her mother's eyes popped open and she was watching Chase curiously. "Did you just growl?"

"Me, growl?" She tried to hide her embarrassment. "No, that was more like a contented groan."

Connie smiled. "They are the best aren't they? They don't speak English very well, but oh, the massages. That's one language I understand perfectly."

Chase smiled back at her. "Agreed." She leaned in and lowered her voice. "Although, I think they speak perfectly good English." Her suspicions were confirmed when the young woman sitting at her feet winked, the corners of her mouth curling up slightly.

Chase shook her head, she loved her mother, but she was incredibly naïve sometimes. She hoped one day her views on just about everything would broaden considerably.

Chapter 32

James Berkley glanced at his daughter with a worried look. Unusually reticent, she was staring out the window, her fingers tapping rhythmically on the car door.

"Something you want to talk about honey? You seem a little out of sorts lately."

Chase jumped at the sound of her father's voice. "I'm sorry. I guess I just have a lot on my mind."

"I assumed as much. Not that your mother and I aren't enjoying your visit, but it was rather sudden." His heart went out to his daughter when she turned to him and he saw the lost look in her eyes. "You know you were always able to talk to me about things before. Maybe if you laid it on your old man, we might be able to sort some things out."

Chase's eyes held her father's and she smiled. She and her father had always been close. She was his little girl and always would be even though she was thirty-three and had been out on her own for years. Her father had always been the more even—keeled of her parents. His more relaxed personality drew Chase to him, especially when she was fighting with some inner demon and needed an unbiased opinion.

She took a deep breath. "Do you remember in high school when Travis Reed said he wanted to take me to the prom?" She waited for his nod and continued. "I was all excited. I had already purchased my dress and shoes, and then two days before the prom Travis called to say he wasn't taking me."

"He was taking Lori Weiss instead." James chimed in.

"You remembered that?" Chase's voice registered surprise. "I was devastated. I had just been rejected. I felt like such a fool."

James squeezed her hand. "I was so mad at him. I wanted to go to his house and give him a piece of my mind."

Chase laughed softly. "I know. I would have been mortified though. The way you handled it was better and I had the most handsome, distinguished date for the prom."

"Stop it, you're just flattering an old man." He smiled, warmed by the thought that his presence at Chase's prom had meant as much to her as it had him, especially when she should have been at the age when no girl wanted to be caught dead with her father. "So is that what all the uncertainty is about…a man? I'm not too old to go after someone for breaking my little girl's heart."

"Not exactly." Chase sat up in her seat, squaring her shoulders. Determined to get her feelings out in the open, she forged ahead. "It's about a woman." She turned quickly, anxious to see his reaction.

When he offered no censure, she continued, her confidence building the more she talked. "Her name is Jude. She's the lawyer handling Avery's estate." Chase told him everything from her reaction to Jude the first time they met, to the disastrous last time she saw her. She left out the more intimate details of the relationship, concentrating instead on her feelings for Jude and her emotions about the whole thing. "You know I have never been attracted to a woman before, and wouldn't have thought of myself as gay, but something about all of it feels right." When she finished, she was short of breath. More from the excitement of finally getting it all out, than her hurry to tell the story.

"The first thing I will say is that Jude is as big an idiot as Travis was." He smiled sideways at Chase. "Any person that wouldn't want to be with my daughter is daft. With that said, I have to admit I am relieved. I worried that it was something horrible that was bothering you."

Chase stared agape at her father, disbelief written all over her face. "You aren't shocked, or worse grossed out that I'm gay?"

He chuckled softly and shook his head. "Do you know what my favorite picture of you is?" When Chase shook her head no, he continued. "The picture of you in a backpack on my shoulders. You were wearing a white and blue sunhat with the biggest smile on your face. You were about a year old and you loved to go out with your old man."

Chase smacked him playfully and pretended to scorn him. "Stop it! You're not an old man."

"Oh I know that." James grabbed Chase's hand and squeezed it. "What I'm trying to say is you're my baby girl and *no matter* what, you will always be."

"Even if it means me being with a woman and having to accept her too?" Chase spoke hesitantly, knowing this was ground that they had not had to tread on before.

"Chase, your mother and I raised you to be a responsible adult. With that means respecting your choices, knowing that we taught you how to make good ones. I trust that no matter what path you choose, you've done it because it's what is right to you. I love you and support you no matter where your life takes you and whom you choose to live it with."

Chase hadn't known what to expect when she started the conversation with her father, but what she felt was all the love and warmth a father could possibly give his child.

James rubbed his chin thoughtfully. "Have you told your mother about Jude?"

Chase shook her head slowly. "No, not yet."

"I think you better let me talk to her about it. You know how opinionated she can be and it may be better if you let me discuss it with her first. I know she will be fine, it may just take her a little longer to warm up to the idea." He caught Chase's worried look and smiled reassuringly. "Don't worry honey, your mom loves you very much. It will all be fine, I promise you."

Chase leaned over and hugged her father's arm tightly. "Thanks dad. I love you."

James patted her head with his other hand. "I love you too honey."

#

Several days later, Chase sat in the sunroom drinking coffee. She watched her mother moving around in the kitchen. They hadn't talked, but Chase could sense a subtle difference in the way that her mother interacted with her. She seemed a little wary of her, more distant somehow. She figured that her father must have shared their discussion with her.

Connie poured herself a fresh cup of coffee and stepped into the sunroom tentatively. She wasn't sure why she was nervous. This was her daughter, she wasn't any different than she was yesterday, she was just gay. She shook her head. She loved her daughter unconditionally and that meant that even if Chase was attracted to women, she had to accept that. She may not agree with it, but love meant accepting even when you didn't see eye to eye on things. She sat down awkwardly and waited for Chase to look at her.

"So I guess Dad talked to you." It was issued more as a statement than a question, since Chase knew the answer. "I know that you have a problem with people being gay, but I'm begging you to please just accept that this is who I am."

Connie looked at her daughter, her eyes pleading with her. *Please try to understand, I'm trying. This is a shock to me, but I'm making an effort.* "I guess it isn't so much that I have a problem with you being gay, it's just all I know are the stereotypes that are out there."

"Mom, it isn't about the stereotypes that are out there, this is about me and who I am." Chase tried not to sound so defensive. She knew her mother was trying to reconcile the daughter she had known for thirty—three years with the woman in front of her. "I'm sorry, I didn't mean to snap."

Connie held her hand up to stop Chase. "I know honey. I'm just worried about you. I know that people are more accepting these days, but I also know that there are still a lot of people, me included, that just don't understand it. Those people aren't as accepting, and I don't want anything bad to ever happen to you or for you to be treated badly because of who you love."

Chase smiled. "I know you worry about me, but you have to let me live my life too. You can't always protect me…as much as you want too. Yes, it may be a difficult life, and I know I will meet some narrow—minded people that will try to hurt me out of spite, but I'm an adult now. I can deal with that."

"I just wanted you to know that I love you and I only balk out of concern for you. I know I seem narrow—minded sometimes, but it's fueled by love." Connie sighed softly. She knew that no matter what concerns she had, Chase would be just fine. She was a smart woman and she didn't make rash decisions. She also knew that Chase was a strong enough woman to embrace the wonderful singularities that made her who she was. "So tell me about your…ahh…what do I call her? Your girlfriend Jude?"

Chase laughed wryly. Her mother had a way with words that was for sure. "Unfortunately, she isn't my girlfriend."

"Well why not? What's wrong with her?" Connie was indignant. "I don't think she is good enough for you if she doesn't want to be your...girlfriend."

"Oh mom, if it were only that easy. It's...ahh...complicated." Chase felt a little anxious. They had cleared the air and Connie seemed to be opening up to the fact that her daughter was gay, but Chase wasn't so sure she was comfortable discussing Jude with her mother.

"Nonsense, what's complicated about it? She loves you and she wants to be with you or she doesn't and you move on." Connie's voice raised emphatically. "And if she doesn't, she's a damn fool!"

Chase couldn't help but laugh. Her mother had done a one—eighty and was giving her advice on the women in her life. *Will wonders never cease?*

Chapter 33

Jude stomped into the office and slung her coat over the coat rack in the corner. "Fuck!" She swore as she bent over to pick it up off the floor. She hung it over another hook and yanked it down, making sure it was in place and wouldn't fall again. She heard Beth snicker and she turned and fixed her with a glare that was sure to stop any further laughter. Beth just laughed harder.

She walked past Beth's desk with her hand held out, her middle finger sticking up prominently. She stopped abruptly when Beth called her name and turned to her with a now what look on her face.

"Coffee?" Beth asked as sweetly as possible.

The tone did little to diffuse Jude's surly demeanor. "Black." Thinking better of her attitude, she returned Beth's fake smile with one of her own. "Please."

"And you have a visitor." Beth announced.

Jude turned to make sure the door to her office was shut then she leaned towards Beth. "At nine o'clock in the morning? Tell me you are joking."

"Uh-uh. Some of us actually manage to function on a normal schedule….unlike yourself. Nine o'clock isn't exactly early." Beth smiled, amused at the bedraggled woman standing tall, trying her best to intimidate her. "Suck it up, buttercup. I'll bring you a hot cup of coffee and it will all be all right."

Jude rolled her eyes and walked away. She stopped at the door and tried to plaster a smile on her face, an insincere one at best. She turned the doorknob and opened the door slowly, dreading whoever was behind the door. Her face broke into a grin when she saw the wild blonde hair. "What's up!"

Tess watched her walk around her desk, sling her briefcase on the desk and flop into the chair. "You look like shit."

"It's great to see you too." Jude replied sarcastically. "And to what do I owe the honor of this visit? We aren't finalizing everything for another two weeks."

Tess smiled. "I'm sorry, I shouldn't have hit you with that." She cocked her head and stared at Jude. "But you do look like shit."

"Gee thanks. I'm really glad you could come here and give me crap first thing in the morning."

Tess rolled her eyes. "Someone has to give you crap. What are you doing to yourself? You look terrible. You have bags under your eyes, you look wasted, not to mention you smell like a fifth of vodka." She watched Jude's eyes flash. "What's going on with you?"

"Nothing." She fumbled with the corner of a notepad, tearing little pieces off the edge. She glanced up and met Tess's hard gaze. "Absolutely nothing is going on. I went out last night."

Tess wrinkled up her nose. "Yeah you smell like it." Her eyes softened. "You look like you've been going out a lot. Beth says you haven't been in the office before eleven for the last two weeks."

"Beth has a big mouth." She glanced at her watch. "Besides it's only quarter after nine. Well before eleven in my book."

"Seriously? What's going on with you? You're working late, partying later and haven't been to work before lunch for days."

Jude's head jerked up. "What are you, spying on me? Dude, seriously."

"Not exactly. Beth said…"

Jude cut her off abruptly. "Well she needs to learn to keep her big mouth shut. I'm thirty—five, own my own law firm, and last time I checked, totally independent. I don't recall needing you or Beth to keep tabs on me, and I certainly don't need permission to live the way I do." She said the words more viciously than she meant, but she was still pissed at herself and unfortunately Tess was in the line of fire.

Tess didn't even blink. "Hey don't be a bitch to me just because you let her get away."

Jude's eyes narrowed. "Let who get away?"

Tess shook her head and took a deep breath. "Don't play stupid with me. You know exactly who I am talking about."

Jude's face dropped. "You know about it?"

"Of course I know about it. I may have been born on a Thursday, but it wasn't yesterday. What I don't know is how you can deny what you are feeling for Chase. She is crazy about you, and if I'm not mistaken, I would say you are pretty hung up on her."

"It's that obvious?" Jude said softly. "You know that nothing can come of this."

"Why the hell not!" Tess leaned forward in her chair, eyes flashing. "This isn't college and she isn't Myra."

Jude's shoulders slumped. When she met Tess's gaze, her eyes were sad. "I wish I could believe that. It's just not that easy."

Tess stood up and grabbed her coat. "Come on. I think this conversation is going to require more than office coffee."

Ten minutes later they pulled into the parking lot at Townsend Avenue Coffee House. Tess pulled Jude inside and ordered them both the House Blend and slices of fresh coffee cake. "I think you could use a little sugar today. Might sweeten you up a bit."

Jude knew Tess was teasing her, trying to cheer her up and she couldn't keep the corners of her mouth from curling up. "Why do you put up with me?"

"Cause I tried driving you out to the country and leaving you in a field, but you found your way back." Tess grinned wickedly. "You know I love you honey…despite your personality."

Jude followed Tess into the parlor, where they sat down in two cushioned arm chairs. She sipped her coffee. Hesitant to return to a painful conversation about Chase, she attempted to steer the conversation towards the weather. "Hell of a nor'easter that moved through here this week."

"No way, chica. We aren't talking about the weather, we are talking about you and Chase and about you potentially making the biggest mistake of your life."

Jude winced as a sharp pain knifed through her heart. She was sure that she had already made the biggest mistake of her life by hurting Chase. She was also sure that even if she decided she wanted to pursue a relationship with her, it was too late for that. "I think that has already happened."

Tess smiled cryptically at Jude. "I wouldn't be so sure about that. Do you know why Chase means so much to me?"

Jude shrugged. "She's Avery's best friend, I guess."

"No, because she's my best friend. Avery being taken from me was the hardest thing I have ever had to endure. I could have fallen apart. But I didn't. Know why?"

"Chase?" The way Jude said her name spoke volumes. Anyone that knew Jude at all could tell she cared for Chase more than she was willing to admit.

"She didn't let me fall apart. She was there for me through all of it, and she still is today. As a matter of fact, I know she will be here for me for the rest of our lives." Tess paused and took a bite of her coffee cake, washing it down with a swig of coffee. "Mmm, this is way better than the swill you have at your place."

"Ouch. Tell me how you really feel." Jude replied, making a mental note to replace whatever generic coffee she did have with some from Townsend Avenue. "How can you be so sure about Chase? What's to say she won't decide one day this is too much to handle and just leave?"

Tess raised an eyebrow. "Do you honestly believe that?" When Jude didn't reply, she answered the question for her. "She won't. I know that because I know Chase. She doesn't let people in very easily, but once she does, she takes hold of the person and keeps them right here." She put her hand on her heart as she said that. "She is one of the most loyal women I know and if a relationship ends, it's because the other person pulled away, not Chase. That's how I know she will always be here for me...or anyone else, for that matter." Tess's gaze locked on Jude, and it was obvious she was referring to her.

Jude looked at Tess, disbelief in her eyes. "Even if I wanted to pursue anything with her, I ruined any chance of a relationship with Chase."

Tess waited to respond until the waitress had refilled their mugs with fresh coffee. "I think we need to back up a bit before a guilty verdict. Maybe if we look at this from a more objective angle, it might help you realize that matters of the heart aren't cut and dry. There's no black and white in emotions, there are no guarantees, and I think you need to know that before you make up your mind. You're a smart woman, Jude, but sometimes you can be so naïve."

"Okay, seriously, I can get this kind of abuse from Beth." Jude's bottom lip jutted out slightly. "You're supposed to be my friend."

"That's exactly why I am here today, because I am your friend and you are miserable. And I'm not saying this to cheer you up, but she is miserable too. I hate to stand by and watch two people I care about fight happiness tooth and nail. You are hard—headed and stubborn and if you don't realize what you heart is trying to tell your brain, you are going to regret it." Tess paused a second, her eyes boring into Jude. "Let me ask you a question. Are you happy?"

"Of cou…" Jude stopped abruptly. She had been conditioned to say yes automatically, but something made her question the validity of that answer. Was she happy? Surely she had things in her life that made her happy. "Sometimes."

"When? What makes you happy?" Tess pushed her to think, to base her answer on concrete evidence.

Her brain ran through images in her head, associating feelings with each picture. The majority of them evoked no feeling of joy or contentment, only feelings of indifference. She saw her motorcycles and the feeling started to change, she saw Tess and the corners of her lips curled slightly, her nephews and she smiled more. When Chase's image locked in place warmth spread through her body and she found herself grinning sheepishly. "You do. My nephews do, I love spending time with them."

"What else? Is there anything or anyone that makes you happier than you have ever been?" Tess's words drilled into her. She could continue to deny what was blatantly obvious or she could take Tess's lead and admit that Chase made her happy, happy in a way she hadn't known with anyone else. She bit her lip nervously, and silently berated herself for letting someone break through her walls. But at that moment a thought struck her right in the gut and left her reeling. She deserved happiness just as much as the next person and she had denied herself that for so long because she was afraid to be hurt again. She hadn't allowed herself to live, really live since college. All the things that she had accomplished meant nothing. She had just been going through the motions like a robot on auto—pilot. One relationship that had ended badly left her cynical and void of emotion. She had meaningless encounters trying to fill the emptiness and all it did was make it bigger. And one person had managed to break through her defenses and now filled every bit of her, heart and soul. Her breath was ragged, raw emotions had left her open and defenseless. She met Tess's expectant gaze and answered in a voice that wasn't her own. "Chase. Chase makes me happier than I've ever been."

"And that scares you." Tess said softly.

Jude shook her head up and down. "Hell yes, that scares me."

"Why?" Tess's eyes held hers captive.

Jude couldn't escape. She couldn't deny admitting her infallibility. "What if she doesn't want me anymore? What if I hurt her so bad that there is no way she'll let me back in?" Her head dropped. "What if she let's me in and for a moment everything is wonderful...and then she decides this isn't what she wants and rips my world out from under me?"

Tess answered Jude's questions with one of her own. "What is it about Chase that makes you happy?"

Jude's face softened, and some of the worry left her face. "Everything. She's smart, funny, beautiful, sexy as all get out, she makes me laugh, she pushes my buttons and gets under my skin. Sometimes I think she says things just to frustrate me, and all I want to do is kiss her feisty mouth. She is the first person I have wanted to go to sleep with and wake up lying next to."

Tess was silent and Jude could tell her mind was working. "So which feeling is greater...the happiness or the fear?"

Jude felt her heart jump. "The happiness."

"Then you need to do something about it. Don't let your fears of rejection or hurt outweigh the happiness you both deserve. You need to tell yourself it's okay to be happy, and to try to make someone else feel the same. Don't rob yourself or Chase of something wonderful because you are using the past as your measuring stick. You can't base every relationship on Myra or you will be miserable and alone the rest of your life. I know that you are afraid, so was I, but if I had it to do all over, I would have made the same choice...even knowing the future. The reward is worth the risk, I promise you."

"So what do I do now?" Jude's voice was a mixture of hope and sadness.

"You fight for what you want. As hard as you were fighting to keep Chase at arm's length, you fight even harder to get her back. To paraphrase *The Beatles* you found her, now go get her."

Jude rolled her eyes at the reference to the song bearing her name. "What if she doesn't want me anymore?"

"Only time will tell. But the Jude I know doesn't leave without a fight. You finally found someone worth fighting for, let her know that. And if in the end, it doesn't work out, at least you finally let yourself love. But if she does love you even half as much as I think she does, everything you do will just prove what your heart has been telling you for the last few months."

"I know…and Tess?" Jude said quickly.

"I know, you're welcome for being wise beyond my years and showing you the error of your ways." Tess smirked.

Jude laughed. "Ahh yeah, you're the all—powerful Oz. But no seriously, thanks for the advice…I was just hoping you would save poor defenseless cats and dogs and not break out into a high pitched, off key version of Hey Jude."

Jude jumped back quickly, avoiding the punch Tess threw at her.

#

Chase looked at the caller ID on her phone and nearly choked. Jude Stafford. She couldn't imagine why Jude would be calling her…unless something was wrong with Tess. She quickly accepted the call and answered anxiously. "Jude, what is it? Is something wrong with Tess?"

There was a slight pause at the end and a slight chuckle. *"Uhm, no Tess is fine."*

Chase's worry was quickly replaced by anger. "Then why are you calling?"

"I wanted to hear your voice." Jude said softly.

Chase's heart clenched. Two weeks ago she would have given anything to hear those words, before the night at the bar. Now, it was too late. Jude had made her choice, and hurt her irreparably in the process. "You shouldn't have called."

"Chase, I know I hurt you and I am the last person you probably want to hear from, but I would really like it if we could talk when you get back." Jude's voice was shaky and she had to take several deep breaths to calm down. *"Please."*

One word and Chase felt her resolve start to crumble. *Stay strong!* Picturing Jude wasn't helping either, imagining her mouth all over her body…*No! No! No!* She took a deep breath. "There isn't anything that you and I need to talk about. Once everything with the will is signed, we can both go our separate ways and put this behind us. I'm sure you will agree that is the best way to end things." She was about to pull the phone away and hit end, when she heard Jude say her name.

"Chase? I know I made a huge mistake with you. I am so sorry for hurting you. I just can't stop thinking about you. I don't want this to end before we've given it a chance."

"Jude, please stop." Chase's voice was stronger now, an air of authority. She remembered the pain that Jude had caused and it made her stronger and more determined to resist Jude. "There isn't anything that we need to give a chance. There is just a series of mistakes that won't be repeated." She suddenly felt the need to be spiteful. "Besides, this isn't worth breaking the rules."

Jude opened her mouth to reply when she heard a loud click. Chase had hung up. *Well, this is going to be harder than I thought.*

"Arrgghhhh!" Chase threw her hands and yelled to no one in particular. She looked at her phone and started talking to it. "Why do you have to make this so hard? Can't you just keep being a bitch? It was so much easier to be mad at you." She threw the phone on the bed, and started pacing. She felt like a caged animal again. Why did Jude have to get to her like that every time? Chase had to do something. She couldn't stand still any longer with Jude's words pounding in her ears.

Jim raised an eyebrow and stared at Chase. She was on all fours, scrubbing the kitchen floor. "Ahh, Chase, what are you doing?"

She looked up, surprise in her eyes. "Oh, me, I was, ahh, cleaning the floors."

"You do know your mother has a mop for that." There was a hint of laughter in his eyes. "I hate to even think about whose toothbrush that is."

She stared dumbly at the brush in her hand then smiled innocently at her father. "I got it out of the toothbrush holder on your side of the bathroom. That's okay, right?"

Jim growled and booted her playfully in the rump. "So what spurred this rather unorthodox cleaning fit?"

"Jude called." Chase stood up slowly, and pressed a hand on her lower back. "Oh, that's a little sore."

"Your Jude?"

"She's not my Jude." Chase huffed loudly.

"Well? What did she want?"

"She wanted to apologize for everything and see if we could maybe talk about us when I get back…to which I promptly said no." Chase flipped the faucet on and rinsed the toothbrush off. She held it up to her father. "Back in your bathroom?"

He growled playfully. "In the trash, if you please." He studied Chase's face for a moment. "I'm confused though. Don't you like Jude?"

"Not anymore." Chase answered defiantly.

"Chase? Don't be hasty. You can't tell me you just forgot everything you felt for her overnight."

"No, of course I didn't but I'm trying to." She caught her father giving her a look and pretended to pout. "Hey whose side are you on anyway?"

"Aww honey, you know I'm on yours. I just thought this was what you wanted. It sounds like she's finally come to her senses. You're not going to at least hear what she has to say?"

Chase shook her head slowly. "I don't think so. You're right, I haven't forgotten how I feel about Jude. That's why this is so hard. I feel like someone is sticking a knife in my heart every time I think about her. She made it quite clear in the beginning that she was not into relationships. That's the real Jude, not this one that is calling me and being entirely too sweet to me."

Jim rubbed his chin, a sign that he was about to say something he thought was very profound. Chase tried to hide a smirk when he spoke. "Do you know that I had to ask your mother out thirteen times, *thirteen,* before she agreed to go out with me? That means she turned me down twelve times. That's a lot of rejection for one man, and if I wasn't so allured by having to chase your mother, and so nutty about her, I may have given up. Then the thirteenth time she said yes. Obviously, I wore her down with my charm."

Chase rolled her yes. "Obviously."

"Anyway, you know the rest of the story." Jim finished matter of factly.

"Yeah, but our situation is a little more complex."

"Nonsense. The situation isn't complex, it's the people that make it difficult. It's the feelings and emotions involved that cloud things. The bottom line is that I didn't give up and your mother agreed to go out with me. Imagine what I would have missed out on if I didn't pursue your mother. Obviously Jude cares enough for you to not give up."

"Dad, I know you think it's simple, but those feelings you were talking about are mine and right now they are hurt. I feel raw inside, and I don't think I can bare my soul again." Chase pounded her fist on the counter. "Argh! Why couldn't she have just left me alone?"

Jim put his arm around his daughter and squeezed gently. "My guess is she cares a great deal for you and she is finally realizing it…and hoping it's not too late."

Chase couldn't reply. She knew her father wanted what was best for her, she just didn't think Jude was it. She just hugged her father and then turned to go to her bedroom.

Suddenly her father yelled after her. "It's kind of funny though. First Jude won't let you get close to her at all and resists your advances, and now it would seem, she is all about the *chase.*" He winked at her and left the room laughing.

Chase groaned loudly. "That was bad." But she found herself chuckling and knew her father had accomplished the one thing he wanted…to make her smile.

Chapter 34

Chase hugged her mother, then turned and hugged her father. He pulled her to him and hugged her fiercely. She felt love, and warmth, and most importantly strength flowing from his body into hers. She knew that this impromptu visit was just the thing she needed to begin to mend her wounds and try to move on. "Thanks Dad. I love you."

"I love you too, Chase." He pushed her away from him and held her at arms' length. "Whatever happens, just remember you are a strong woman and you will get through whatever life throws at you."

"Thanks Dad...Mom for everything. This was a wonderful visit." Chase smiled, picking up her carry—on bag. "I'll see you in a few months."

Connie leaned in and gave Chase a quick peck on the cheek. "And if you need to escape again, your room is always available."

Chase smiled, the relationship with her mother was back on track after a few bumpy days. "I know, but I think I need to face life head on. No more running away for me."

Jim smiled broadly. "That's my girl. Have a safe flight, honey. We love you!"

Chase walked inside, then turned and waved one last time. *Well back to reality.*

#

Tess watched Chase unpack her bag, sorting through and dividing the clean and dirty clothes. She was so glad to have Chase back with her. The last three weeks had been incredibly lonely. She filled some of her time with calls home to speak with her parents. Since her visit home, the calls were more frequent, and the majority of the time, she and her family played catch up on their lives. Her parents had stopped apologizing every time they called for losing the past twenty years, which was fine with Tess. She had forgiven them a long time ago and didn't need them to bear the burden of guilt any longer. After the first two or three times, she had very kindly, but bluntly, told them to stop feeling guilty. The important thing was they were back in each other's lives and they weren't wasting any more time. Other than that, Tess had kept herself busy reading, shopping in Portland and giving Jude a hard time. She chuckled out loud as she thought of her conversation with Jude.

Chase looked up when she heard Tess laughing. "Care to share the secret? What's so funny?"

"Ah, nothing. I'm just glad to have you back." Tess said quickly, redness rising in her cheeks. "I missed you."

"And that made you laugh?" Chase looked at Tess suspiciously. "Why do I not believe that for a second?"

"I don't know…maybe you're a naturally suspicious person." Tess winked at her mischievously.

"Very funny, Monahan. I happen to be very trusting…too trusting I'm afraid." Her voice dropped. "Gets me hurt sometimes."

"Yeah, about that…I ran into Jude last week." Tess spoke slowly, knowing the topic would not be one that Chase welcomed talking about. "Apparently, the last few weeks have been rough on her too."

"Tess, I don't want to talk about it. I can't, the wounds are still too deep. As a matter of fact…" Chase paused and grabbed a piece of paper off her dresser. "…I need you to do something for me."

Tess took the paper from Chase and started to read it. She looked up confused. "A power of attorney form?"

"Yes, I can't go and be around Jude. She called me last week and the pain of hearing her voice was almost too much. I can't see her, I don't think I could keep it together." She met Tess's gaze, her eyes pleading for her to understand. "This way I don't have to go. You can sign everything for me. We just have to get our signatures notarized. Tess, I really need you to do this for me."

Tess smiled, her heart breaking for Chase. She was torn between telling Chase that Jude was in love with her and honoring Chase's request. She loved them both and she knew they were equally miserable. "I'll do this for you…if it means that much."

"It does. I need to get past this point as quickly as possible. Figuring out I was gay was hard enough. But then you add falling in love with the most unavailable lesbian out there, and you're talking mental and emotional breakdown. Talking to her and seeing her would only add to the jumbled mess I already have up here." Chase knocked on her head for emphasis. "Besides I don't want Jude to feel obligated to play nice just because she feels guilty. It was one night, I'll mend."

"But Jude may not." Tess said cautiously. "I know you don't want to hear this, but Jude is pretty messed up right now. I think you got to her more than she ever expected or wanted to let you. Jude may seem tough, she's built up this wall to protect her heart and now you've broken through that and it scared her." She saw Chase about to object and she continued quickly. "If she is trying to make amends for her actions and wanting to pursue a relationship with you, it isn't because she feels guilty, it's because she genuinely cares for you. Before you shut her out completely, you may want to ask yourself if moving on and not giving this a chance is worth losing someone that could be the love of your life? Sometimes you have to take risks without knowing if there is a reward at the end."

Chase swallowed a lump in her throat. She was not the type of person to make rash decisions. She couldn't help falling in love with Jude, but sleeping with her was not something she would have done before. Even now, her heart still ached for Jude, but she was past the days of reckless abandon and her sense of survival had kicked in. "Whatever Jude is feeling is based on some misguided sense of obligation. I was a *virgin* so to speak and as tough as she is, I am sure she feels like she has some responsibility to me. As my first, she has some mistaken sense of duty to take my hand and lead me through the coming out process, unable to let me navigate the journey myself. I don't want that. I don't need her pity or whatever you want to call it. I've lived and I've learned my whole life, and I may have stumbled along the way, but I picked myself up and kept looking forward. Giving Jude a chance would be asking her to be something she's not, and we would both lose ourselves in the process. I think it's better this way. We both go our own separate ways, not owing the other one anything."

"I have to respectfully disagree. I know Jude and I've never seen her this way about any woman. Chase, she's been other someone's first time too, and it didn't mean anything. She was running just as much as you were from a past that haunted her. And just as much as you are looking to start the next phase of your life, so is she. I think you both want it to be something you do together. The only difference is Jude is saying it out loud and you…you are fighting against it." Tess knew that Chase didn't believe that Jude really felt obligated or guilty, she was just trying to not get hurt…again. "I know you get tired of me comparing every situation to mine and Avery's, but that's what I know. There were times before we got together that I wanted to leave. The last month or so before we finally admitted we were in love with each other was hell. I almost left so many times. Every time we fought it was like a knife in my heart. But I stayed. I stayed because I had faith that things could be better and that no matter how much it hurt right then, the thought of not having Avery in my life hurt more. Yes it was a risk, and I could have ended up with nothing, but I took it nonetheless." Tess saw Chase's chin jutting out defensively. "I know that Jude hasn't made it easy. She's been holding you at arm's length this entire time. Even when you put your heart on the line, she kept her distance. Jude wouldn't give herself to you damaged. She doesn't do anything halfway, it's all or nothing. You have to trust that if she offers you her heart, it's because she loves you completely and wants to be with you." She sighed softly. "With that being said, I can't force you to do something you don't want to as much as I disagree. I'll sign the POA and take care of everything."

"Thank you." Chase's shoulders slumped. She knew she should be relieved. This was what she wanted. Instead she felt empty.

Chapter 35

Jude tapped her pen nervously on the desk. She glanced at her watch. 1:20. Any minute now, Chase would be walking through that door. Her stomach flip—flopped just thinking about her. She was nervous and exhilarated all at one time. It had been almost a month since she saw her and the last time they had spoken, it was disastrous. She hoped that face—to—face would be better. There would be other people there, but Jude was intent on getting Chase to talk to her, if not give her a few minutes alone.

She looked around the well—appointed office and sighed. Six months ago this had been her life…work and random hookups with strangers. But then she met Chase Berkley and none of that mattered anymore. All that mattered was righting the wrongs that she had committed and proving to Chase that she was in love with her. Not much of a believer in a higher power, she looked heavenward and smiled wryly. *Please, please don't let it be too late.*

An incessant beeping broke through her reverie and brought her back to reality. It took her a moment to realize it was her phone. She hit the button for the speakerphone. "Yes?"

Beth was using the professional voice she reserved for clients. *"Your 1:30 is here."*

"Thanks. I'll be right out." Jude hit the button to disconnect and took a deep breath. Anxiousness was making her stomach nauseous. Never before had she experienced such elation at the prospect of seeing someone, coupled with such agonizing dread. She walked over to a mirror on the wall, pulling her suit jacket on as she walked. She gazed at her reflection in the mirror and was surprised to see the sunken, hollow eyes, dark smudges beneath them. *Jude, you royally fucked this one up.*

Shaking off an ominous feeling, she tucked her hair behind her ears and took a deep breath, willing herself to walk out there and face Chase. When Jude walked into the lobby, she saw Tess and the Carson's. *I guess Chase is driving separately. That could be good.*

She strode purposely toward the Carson's, her right hand extended. "Joe, Barb…it's good to see you again."

Joe grasped Jude's hand in his and shook it firmly. "Jude…it's always nice to see you."

Barb hugged Jude and placed a quick peck on her cheek. "Goodness Jude, when was the last time you slept? You look a little tired."

Jude laughed, but it sounded hollow even to her ears. "Damn the advent of DVR. I can't seem to get any sleep these days for all the TV I am watching." *Sure, that sounded believable, right?* "It's good to see you too, Barb."

Jude turned to Tess and hugged her fiercely. The past few months had brought them even closer together, and right now Jude was thankful to have Tess, if only to keep her in line. "Hey stranger, long time, no see."

Tess chuckled. "Yeah, what's it been…about two weeks?" She held Jude against her, her heart going out to her. Jude honestly looked lost, and Tess was sure when she found out Chase wasn't coming, it would send her into a tailspin.

Jude stepped back and smiled at everyone. "Can I get anyone anything? Water? Coffee? Tea? I have this great new roobios tea that Beth picked up. It's pretty good. Kind of a spicy, orange flavor." When everyone had politely declined, she led them into her office. She had everything set out on the large table in her office and she waited till everyone had taken their seats, then she sat down across from them. She fiddled with a stack of papers in front of her. "I guess we'll wait for Chase before we get started."

Barb looked at Joe, slight discomfort evident on her face. Jude tried to decipher the look and when she couldn't, she turned to Tess. Tess shook her head almost imperceptibly from side—to—side, her eyes sending Jude a silent message. When she spoke her voice was tinged with regret. "Chase isn't coming." She opened a folder and pulled out several sheets of paper, handing it to Jude in an effort to explain.

Jude took the papers and started reading them. They were financial power—of—attorney papers. Chase had made Tess her representative, giving her full legal power to sign any paperwork with regards to the execution of Avery's will. Chase wasn't coming.

She didn't want to see her. The thought hit her like a hot poker, her stomach lurching. Had she not been in her office, surrounded by people, she would have vomited. Mentally, she tried to shake the fog that had overtaken her. It wouldn't do her any good to let people see her like this, vulnerable and broken. She took a deep breath and said in a shaky voice. "Well everything looks like it's in order, I guess we'll get started…"

#

Jude stared at the POA, a drink in her hand. After everything was signed, she had pulled Tess aside and whispered desperately. "She hates me doesn't she?"

Tess shook her head sadly. "She doesn't hate you. She's hurt, Jude. What she is going through is unlike anything she's has had to face before. Just be patient and give her some time."

"It hurts so much Tess. More than I ever thought I could hurt." Jude ran a hand through her hair, doing nothing to hide the despondent look on her face. "How much time?"

Tess put her hand on Jude's arm and looked squarely in her eyes. "If you love her, as much time as she needs."

Jude threw the rest of her drink back and set the glass down. She was suddenly aware of one compelling thought, a singular decision that grew from the depths of her despair. It took root and filled her mind, feelings of calm spreading quickly through her body as it blossomed. She would give Chase all the time she needed, but she would be damned if she was going to sit idly by and wait for it to happen. Jude was a fighter and she planned to fight to the death. "Look out, Chase. You aren't going to know what hit you."

Chapter 36

Chase glared at the envelope, then tossed it in the trash and went back to making lunch.

Tess stared at her incredulously. "Aren't you even going to read it?"

"No." Chase turned and popped a carrot in Tess's mouth.

"Trying to shut me up?" Tess mumbled.

Chase's eyes sparkled mischievously. "Yes. Is it working?"

"Uh—uh." Tess said, shaking her head. "Aren't you even curious about what she has to say?"

Chase shook her head no, but not before Tess saw the truth in her eyes.

"Have you read any of them?" Tess asked softly. "All these months, have you thrown them all away?"

"I read the first few, and then I stopped. I got over her a long time ago. I wish she would do the same and leave me alone."

"Are you really over her?" Tess watched Chase, measuring her reaction. "You've buried yourself in this house, taking care of me and every guest that comes through here, making sure *we* are happy. But you never stop to take care of yourself."

"I do too." Chase answered indignantly.

Tess raised an eyebrow and searched Chase's face. "Do you? I have watched you fly around here for months trying to figure out what makes everyone else happy and bending over backwards to do it."

Chase put the knife down and crossed her arms over her chest defensively. "That's my job. That's what keeps people coming back here, and that's what we want right?"

"It's business Chase. Of course we want repeat customers. But if you aren't happy then all this place will be is a job. No matter how great Serendipity is, it can't take the place of your life and love and happiness."

"I am happy. I love it here, I love you." Chase walked to the fridge and took out a bottle of salad dressing and shook it up. "Just because I'm not falling all over Jude…again, doesn't mean I'm unhappy or that something is missing in my life. I like where I am right now. I like this life that I have. I don't want to be with someone just so I won't be alone. I want to be with a woman because I'm in love with her and she is desperately in love with me."

Tess chuckled. "Honey, I'd say Jude fits both of those categories."

Chase rolled her eyes. "I highly doubt that she is madly in love with me, and I am certainly not in love with her."

Tess cocked and eyebrow and stared at Chase. "Aren't you?"

"No!" Chase said indignantly. She turned around and hid her face from Tess's scrutiny. After a moment, she turned back around. "What makes you think I am still in love with her?"

Tess shrugged. "Oh, I don't know. Maybe that you wait for the flowers she sends you, and even though you don't open the cards, I know you are dying to read them."

"So, I like flowers. They brighten up the place. Besides if she is going to waste her money on them, I might as well enjoy them. That doesn't mean I am in love with the sender of the flowers." Chase felt herself blush momentarily. "Besides, I'm kind of talking to someone."

"What?!" Tess jumped off her stool and came around the island. She grabbed Chase by the arms and looked square in her eyes. "Who is it? Where did you meet her? Most importantly, when were you planning on telling me?"

Chase stifled a smile. "Dang nosy. I can't have some privacy in my life."

Tess feigned horror. "Are you kidding me? We have no secrets. Now dish."

Chase rolled her eyes. "Okay fine. Her name is Sam. Well it's Samantha, but everyone calls her Sam. She runs a place a couple of miles up the road. I was out for a run and stopped to check her place out. It's called The Captain's Daughter."

"I know that place. Well the house anyway. I didn't know a lesbian ran it." Tess's eyes narrowed as she tried to take it all in. "Small world."

"So anyway, I was scoping it out and Sam came out and stopped me. She introduced herself as the owner, and I told her that I…we had Serendipity down on the coast. She said she knew it well since she had bid against Avery when it was being auctioned. When she didn't get it, she tried for The Captain's Daughter instead and she's been running it ever since. She invited me in for a cold drink and we just hit it off. The last time I stopped by, she asked me out."

Tess winked mischievously. "Well no wonder your runs have been getting longer lately...I didn't realize you were stopping for extracurricular activities along the way."

Chase blushed again. "Funny. It's not like that. It's...she's really sweet. And she's not really out, so that's probably why you didn't know about her. It was really kind of cute the way she asked me out."

"Oh yeah, what'd she do...hang a sign on the mailbox. Will you go out with me?"

Chase swatted Tess on the arm. "Noooo. That's not how it happened. When we would talk, she was always touching my hand or looking at me intently. I figured she was just one of those types that are really focused in any conversation, so I didn't read too much into it. Besides, I don't even know if I would realize someone was flirting with me."

"There's no question when Jude flirts with you." Tess said pointedly.

Chase glared at Tess. "Will you stop? It's not going to happen, okay." Tess's observation made her think of Jude, especially her eyes. For a moment she felt Jude standing there, her green eyes piercing into hers, silently telling her she wanted to make love to her. The vision took her breath away and she struggled to catch her breath. Chase took several deep breaths, shook her head to clear the vision of Jude and tried to continue. "Anyway, Sam was kind of nervous and cute, fidgeting all over the place. Finally, she asked me if I wanted to get dinner out sometime. And me being as entirely clueless as I am just said sure, that sounds like fun."

"So how do you know that she wasn't just wanting to hang out?" Tess asked. "That she was *interested?*"

"After I left that day, I kept thinking it was just really strange the way she was behaving and the way she asked. So I went back the next day and I asked her, hey are you asking me out as a friend or are you asking me out on a date?"

"What did she say?"

"She said she was asking me out on a date. I said oh, okay. Well then she was all worried, saying forget about it, she obviously read this whole situation wrong. Could we maybe just forget the whole thing happened and go on like nothing happened. So I told her maybe she didn't read it wrong, I am gay…just a newbie so I could understand where she may be confused. And I would love to go out on a date with her."

Tess leaned against the bar and put her palms on the counter. "So when is the big date?"

"Friday night. I am so nervous. I like her a lot but I'm not sure if I'm ready for this whole dating thing." Chase bit her nails nervously.

"So don't go." Tess countered.

"I have too. I already said yes." Chase pushed off the counter and grabbed the salad. She walked towards the dining area. "Besides it's a good first step towards moving on."

#

Jude stepped up to the counter at Hawkes Florists in Bath. She caught the smirk of the woman behind the counter and blushed. "I know, leave me alone will ya?"

"Your usual?" She asked smartly. "It's been what…three months now? Same order every week. How's that working for you?"

Jude rolled her eyes. "How do you think Sheila? If it were working, I wouldn't need to come see you every week. That would certainly cut into my smartass quota for the week."

Sheila burst out laughing. "You know I gotta give you a wicked hard time. I have to say honey, if she doesn't come around soon, I may have to stand in for her." She leered at Jude, smiling wickedly. "She doesn't know what she's missing."

Jude shrugged. "I'm hoping she realizes it soon. I won't stop till she does, but my flower bill is getting *wicked* expensive."

Sheila chuckled at her comment. "I should say so. Although how any woman could resist a bouquet of Oriental Lilies and red roses is beyond me. Same thing on the card?"

Jude's phone buzzed on her hip and she held up a finger. "Hold that thought."

"Jude Stafford." She said in her best lawyer voice.

"Jude, it's Tess. We have a problem."

Jude's forehead wrinkled in concern. "What do you mean?"

"Chase has a date."

"What! With who?" Jude's voice rose and Sheila flinched. "Tess, talk to me. I need to know." Jude paced in front of the counter, her hand shoved in her coat pocket. She felt like someone had punched her in the stomach. All these months waiting for Chase to come around and now she had a date...with some other woman.

"Her name's Sam. She owns The Captain's Daughter, a bed and breakfast down the road."

"Sam? Short for Samantha? Brunette, little shorter than me, nice rack?" Jude's stomach dropped. "Are you sure?"

"I don't know. Chase didn't tell me what she looks like, just that she runs her own place and she thinks she's pretty cute. They are going out tonight."

"Shit." Jude rubbed the bridge of her nose, stressed out by the news. "Where is she taking her?"

Tess was silent for a minute. *"Jude, I'm sorry. I don't know."*

"Don't worry about it. If it's the Sam I'm thinking of, I know." She closed her eyes and took a deep breath, a thought formulating in her head. "And Tess?"

"Yeah?"

"Thanks for telling me. I'm getting too close to losing her for good."

"Don't say that, it's just one date." Tess's voice was a mix of sternness and concern. *"I'm sure it won't go anywhere."*

"You don't know Sam. Unfortunately, she's the perfect woman for Chase."

"Then I guess you better get to her before Sam does."

"I'm working on that." Jude glanced at her watch. "Listen, I gotta run. Thanks again."

Sheila came back to the counter as Jude hung up. "Everything okay?" She watched Jude shake her head side—to—side, sadness in her eyes. "Ms. Flowers got a date?"

"Yeah, yeah she does." Jude said with resignation.

Sheila shook her finger at Jude. "Then I guess you better step up your game."

Jude smiled. "You know, you're right."

"You still want the flowers?" Sheila asked quickly.

"Yep, send her one today and I need a bouquet to go." Jude's voice rose excitedly. "If I go down, I'm going down fighting."

Chapter 37

Chase stared at her reflection in the full length mirror. The last time she had been on a real date was three years ago when she went out with Derek for the first time. She grimaced, thinking of how that had turned out. She wasn't bitter, just sad at the loss of time and the deception. If Derek had actually had a pair, he could have saved them both a lot of trouble.

She looked down at the sleeveless, sky blue shirt with a vee neck collar that dipped low enough to reveal the apex between her breasts. The shirt skimmed the top of her low—slung jeans and accentuated her narrow waist and shapely hips. She ran her hands through her hair, fluffing it out. She licked her lips nervously, hoping that the butterflies in her stomach would go away and she could relax and enjoy her evening. She was fighting an anxious feeling, subconscious doubts nagging her. She took a deep breath and took one last glance. She shrugged noncommittally. *Okay Chase, it's now or never. You gotta get back up on the horse sometime.*

Tess caught Chase coming down the stairs and whistled loudly. "Oh, honey, you are going to wow 'em tonight. You look gorgeous."

Chase smiled shyly. "Do you think so?"

"Hell yes, I do." Tess said emphatically. "I wouldn't be surprised if you turned more than Sam's head tonight."

Chase hugged Tess. "Thank you. I needed that. I'm kinda nervous."

Tess cocked her head and stared at Chase. "Are you sure this is what you want?"

"It's just a date, Tess. It's not like we are getting married. I'm just going to go with the flow and try to have a good time tonight."

"Okay, but if you come back here with a U—Haul, I'm going to lock you in your bedroom." Tess caught Chase's confused look and laughed. "I'm teasing, but at least try not to fall in love on the first date…okay?"

"Yeah, I know. I won't make that mistake again." She shook her head from side—to—side. "But enough of that, I'm not going to think about Jude tonight. Tonight is about Sam and me. She's a wonderful woman and she deserves someone who isn't thinking about another woman."

"You know it is impossible not to think about someone you are in love with. She's here…" She put her hand on her heart. "…it stands to reason she will be here too." Tess pointed to her head. "And believe me, you never really get them all the way out."

Chase rolled her eyes. "I think I will be safe in that regard. I'm not thinking of Jude all the time, it's more like thinking about a situation and the lessons learned in an effort to not repeat them. I'm studying the past to protect myself in the future."

"That's an interesting way to explain not being able to let go." Tess winked mischievously. "So where is the hot date tonight?"

"A place called 83 Townsend."

"You mean 93 Townsend." Tess interrupted.

"Yeah, that's right. Sam said the food is really good." Chase said as she grabbed her purse off a chair in the foyer.

"Wow! I'll say it's good, a little more upscale as far as the menu goes. You will love the food." Tess said excitedly. "Kudos to Sam for that choice. She just moved up in my book."

"Speaking of moving, she should be here any minute." Chase glanced at her watch.

As if Sam knew they were talking about her, she knocked on the front door at that precise moment. Tess winked at the nervous look in Chase's eyes and opened the door. She smiled at Sam, surprised that her heart skipped a beat when she looked into her deep brown eyes. It was disconcerting, but welcome at the same time. She felt alive for the first time in months. She was surprised to see a slightly confused look in Sam's eyes. Shaking it off, she extended her hand quickly. "You must be Sam…I'm Tess."

Sam looked away from Tess's eyes, trying to make sense of her initial reaction to the woman who was Chase's best friend. "Hi. It's nice to meet you." She clasped her hand around Tess's and pumped it firmly, aware of her disarmingly good looks. Sam pulled her hand back quickly and turned to Chase, hoping she hadn't seen the unexpected reaction. "Hi."

"Hi yourself." Chase smiled brightly. "You look really nice. That color looks good on you."

Sam looked down at the turquoise collared shirt she was wearing. She blushed slightly under Chase's scrutiny. "Thank you. You look beautiful." She held her hand towards Chase who curled her fingers in Sam's palm. "Shall we go?"

Chase looked at Tess and smiled. "I'll let you know what I think of the restaurant over breakfast tomorrow."

Sam smiled again. "It was nice to meet you, Tess." She opened the door and led Chase outside.

Tess stood and watched Sam open the door for Chase, then get in the driver's side and pull away. She was somewhat alarmed that Chase's suggestion she wouldn't be home till late bothered her as much as it did, and even more disturbed that when Sam said her name, it sounded like a caress. *This is just what I need, to be attracted to someone else's girlfriend.*

Chapter 38

"…next thing I know, I did a face plant right onto the concrete." Chase said groaning.

"Oh no, were you okay?" Sam's eyes looked concerned.

"Chipped tooth and a scraped up face. Needless to say my parents were not happy."

"I imagine they weren't, they did tell you to stay home." Sam started chuckling. "I was just picturing you with your knees on your skateboard, arms pumping."

"Don't forget the pigtails flying." Chase started laughing with Sam. "I'm sure I was quite a sight, even before the fall."

"I would say it didn't mar your looks at all. You have a beautiful smile." Sam said shyly. "It brightens up the room."

Chase's smile widened at the compliment. She was slowly learning that Sam's flirting was much more subtle than Jude's and while it didn't set her body on fire, it did make her feel good. Just because there wasn't the intense heat with Sam, didn't mean that this couldn't develop into more as time progressed. Sam was very cute and she was one of the sweetest people she had ever met. "Thank you. Being with you makes me want to smile."

It was Sam's turn to blush. "Then it's settled…we make each other smile." She lifted her glass and held it towards Chase. "Here's to whatever comes after that."

Chase was lifting her glass to toast when a movement at the front of the restaurant caught her attention. Her hand stopped in midair, her eyes registered shock. She watched the tall blonde stride quickly towards her with a large bouquet of flowers in her hand.

Sam, realizing that something had caught her attention, followed her gaze, and knew immediately who had made Chase go completely still. She didn't know the exact reason, but knowing Jude she could make a pretty educated guess. When Jude reached the table, Sam stood up. "Jude…what a surprise. We didn't expect to run into you."

Jude answered Sam, but her eyes remained on Chase, who had yet to move from the position she was in when Jude came in the front door. "No, I wouldn't think I would be on your mind tonight." She set the flowers down then leaned forward and put her hands on the table. "Chase."

Chase was silent, a small shake of her head the only sign that she was aware of her surroundings.

"I take it you two are already acquainted." Sam gestured at the chair. "Why don't you join us?" Her politeness was ever present and Jude acknowledged it with a smile. Had someone butted in on her date, she would not have offered them a seat. Instead, she would have shown them the door.

Jude smiled and politely declined. "This won't take long."

Jude's imposing figure and striking good looks had garnered her attention from both men and women. The odd circumstances of the situation had kept their attention, and now they were watching her closely. "Chase, we need to talk."

Chase finally breaking from her stupor, glared at Jude. "I told you already we have nothing to discuss. I am on a date and you're presence here is rude and unwelcome."

Sadness flashed in Jude's eyes, then was quickly replaced by simmering anger. "We have too much history for you to cast me aside like you did. At the very least you owe me the opportunity to say my peace." She stood up straight and motioned her head towards the door. "I would really appreciate it if you would find it in your heart to give me a moment of your time…in private."

Chase continued to glare at Jude. "Whatever you have to say to me, you can say it right here."

Jude let out an exasperated breath. "Chase Berkley, why do you insist on making everything so damn difficult?"

"Jude." Chase said smiling sarcastically. "It's not me that's made it difficult…it's you. I thought I made myself clear by months of ignoring you that I have no interest in what you have to say. You made it difficult. You couldn't just walk away and move on."

Jude's anger was mixing with desperation. She knew that if she was going to win Chase back, she had to lay it all on the line right now, right here, in front of all these people. "Don't you understand? I can't walk away from us. You got inside me and damn it, I can't get you out. I know I don't want to."

"Jude, please don't say something you will regret." Chase pleaded with her. All the months she had spent avoiding Jude were dangerously close to meaning nothing. She knew if Jude kept talking, she might crumble. "Please just go away."

Jude sensed that Chase was struggling to keep her distance. She took a deep breath. *It's all or nothing Jude.* She turned Chase's chair towards her and clasped her hands. "Chase, I've spent my whole life with a wall up, never letting anyone get close. But you shattered that wall and now the only thing I want is to have all of you in here." She put her hand on her heart. Much to Chase's dismay, Jude did something she never thought she would do…she knelt down on one knee. "From the day I met you, I knew that we had something magical. I tried not to see that, I tried to hide from it, all the while loving any opportunity I had to see you, to be with you. Somewhere along the way, I fell in love with you. I'm saying it out loud, Chase. I am in love with you. I can't see my life anymore without seeing you in it."

Chase opened her mouth to interrupt, but Jude put a finger on her mouth to silence her. "Please let me say what I came to say. Then I'll walk away knowing that I played the hand I was dealt, win or lose. For the first time in my life, I want to give my heart and soul to someone. Chase, you have my heart in your hands. It's not mine anymore. And if you don't take it, I don't want it back. Without you, I don't want to feel anymore. I'd rather be dead inside then remember what it feels like to love you with my entire being and not be able to have you." Jude's lips quivered. "Chase Berkley, you're the woman I have waited my whole entire life for and I hate myself for hurting you. I know that if there is even the smallest chance that you could love me, I would spend every day of the rest of my life showing you how much I love you."

Chase swiped at her eyes, tears welling in them. She shook her head from side—to—side in disbelief. "No, no, I can't believe you. I can't hurt like I did." She felt her lip quiver. "Jude, I can't."

Jude's shoulders sagged, and she dropped Chase's hands into her lap. "I'm sorry, I'm so sorry." She put her hand on the table and struggled to lift her body up. She was emotionally exhausted. Her heavy heart seemed to weigh a thousand pounds, making it almost impossible to function. She cupped Chase's cheek in her palm and smiled sadly. "Forgive me, my love." Turning to Sam, her eyes registered apology. "Sam, I'm sorry for the interruption." With that she strode quickly out of the restaurant and out of Chase's life.

Chase stared at the door for what seemed like forever. She kept waiting for Jude to come back in, and insist that Chase give her a chance, but the door never opened. She finally looked at Sam, who had remained quiet the entire time. She smiled apologetically. "I'm sorry for that."

Sam just laughed. "No big deal. I guess you know her better than I thought." She was silent for a moment, her eyes pensive. "So maybe we should call it a night."

"No, that's not necessary. I'm here with you because I like you." She glanced at the door one more time. "Let's just put that behind us and have a good time."

"Good food, good friends, good times." Sam said cheerily. "I've got all three."

Chase didn't miss the emphasis on good friends, and yet it didn't seem to bother her all that much. Tonight it was just what she needed, a good friend to take her mind off of Jude. "Amen!"

Chapter 39

Tess shook Chase's shoulders gently, trying to wake her up. "Chase. Chase, wake up."

Chase woke up and tried to adjust her eyes to the dark. She rubbed her fists on her eyes and tried to focus on the tableside clock. "Tess, what is it? What time is it?"

"It's two thirty." Her voice was urgent. "You have to get up."

"At two thirty, are you crazy? You are going to have to wait until tomorrow to hear about my date." Chase's voice was tired and she wanted to roll back over and go to sleep.

"It's Jude." Tess's voice was low. "She's been in a car accident."

Chase sat up quickly, suddenly wide awake. Her mind raced to Avery and the horrible phone call letting her know her best friend had been killed. "How? Where? We have to go to her."

"I know." Tess straightened up and walked to the door. "Get dressed, I'll fill you in on the way to the hospital."

Chase dressed quickly and within ten minutes they were heading to St. Andrews Hospital. She tapped impatiently on the door. "Tess, what happened? It's my fault isn't it?"

Tess put her hand on Chase's and squeezed. She was just as scared as Chase, but tonight she needed to be strong for her. "No honey, it's not your fault." She was somewhat confused by Chase's belief that it was her fault and did her best to allay her fears. "I don't know exactly. The best that the emergency responders can tell is that she was driving home on Samoset and there was a car that had taken a wrong turn. They were backing out of a driveway and she came around a blind curve and swerved to miss them. She lost control and rolled over several times before landing upside down in the ditch."

Chase's hand flew to her mouth. She felt nauseous and petrified. *Oh God, please don't let anything happen to her. Please don't let the last thing she remembers me saying is I don't want you. I can't lose you Jude.* "Tess, please say she will be okay."

Tess squeezed Chase's hand again. "Oh honey, I'm sure she will be. Jude's a fighter and St. Andrews is a great hospital to be in. Let's not panic."

Twenty minutes later they were sitting in the hallway outside Jude's room. Visiting hours didn't start for another five hours and no amount of coercion was getting them in her room. They waited anxiously for the doctor to come from the room and give them an update on her condition. When the doctor finally came from the room, Chase immediately asked him for an update.

Dr. Stevens, from his name tag, looked at her with sympathetic eyes. "Are you a relative? We've been trying to get hold of her family for some time."

Chase grabbed Tess and propelled her forward. "This is her sister."

Dr. Stevens turned his attention to Tess and gave her a brief rundown of Jude's condition. "Right now your sister is in critical, but stable condition. She broke her left femur and ankle. She also suffered a cerebral contusion. We've gotten her stabilized for now. She will require surgery for the ankle fractures, but it's necessary for us to get the swelling down before we can do that. As you can imagine, I'm most concerned with the trauma to her brain. The first forty—eight hours are going to be critical. We've put her into an artificial coma to help the recovery process, and we will be doing CT scans to make sure that the hemorrhaging doesn't progress and form a blood clot in her brain. In that instance, it would require immediate surgery to remove the clot. We're guarded on her recovery, with this type of brain trauma we can't be sure just how extensive the damage is." He checked his watch. "If you'll excuse me, I've got several more patients to see and then I will be back to check on her again."

Chase watched him walk away before she let the full impact of his words hit her. She felt her knees buckle from the weight of it and she leaned on Tess for support. She let Tess lead her back to the bench. "Tess, I don't know how you did it. I'm going crazy right now. She has to be okay."

Tess put an arm around her and kissed the top of her head. "I went crazy too, pacing around the hospital, begging for someone to just tell me what was happening. And then when they told me that she didn't make it, I died. I don't know what I would have done if

Joe and Barb hadn't been here. I'm not so sure I would have made it through that night. For the first time in my life, I considered taking my own life. If Avery wasn't here, I didn't want to live. I think Barb sensed my despondency and despite her pain, she took care of me. She didn't let me out of her sight for quite some time after that."

"I'm sorry I didn't get here sooner." Chase said softly. "Thank you for being with me tonight."

"I may not love Jude quite like you do, but she means a lot to me. There isn't any place I want to be while I know she's still hurt." Tess pulled Chase's head onto her shoulder. "Why don't you try to rest? I'll wake you up if anything changes."

Chase shook her head. "I won't be able to sleep." Despite her protests, a few minutes later she fell into a fitful sleep. She dreamed that she was walking down the aisle in a wedding dress. Jude was standing at the altar in a white tux, but her face was turned away from Chase. When she finally got to the altar, Jude turned around to meet her, but it wasn't Jude's face, it was a skeleton face. Then she disappeared and Chase was suddenly at a funeral. She walked past the casket and stared into Jude's lifeless face. Suddenly, Jude's eyes flew open and she stared at Chase, accusations in her eyes. Chase stood in horror as Jude sat up and grabbed her hand. "I loved you. You could have saved me."

Tess shook Chase awake. "Chase, wake up."

Chase blinked her eyes open, for a moment confused by her surroundings. "Tess?"

"Shh, shh, honey. I'm here. Are you okay? You were screaming no, no no!"

Chase shook her head. "No, I had a horrible nightmare." She told Tess the whole thing, including the haunted look in Jude's eyes.

"It's okay, it was just a nightmare." Tess rocked Chase against her, trying to comfort the woman in her arms. Maybe she had finally realized that she and Jude belonged together. She wondered why Chase, like herself, was so stubborn that it took almost losing the love of her life to realize she was the love of her life. She smoothed Chase's hair, and held her close, sharing the strength she knew she would need in the coming days.

Chapter 40

Chase sat next to Jude's bed, watching her chest rise and fall evenly. She ran her hand over the tube that led to her mouth, breathing for Jude when she couldn't. She counted the steady drop of the IV as it infused liquids into her body. Tess had gone home hours ago to take care of guests, but Chase couldn't bring herself to leave Jude's side. Dr. Stevens had said she was recovering nicely and they should be able to stop administering the pentobarbital and let Jude start waking up within the next twenty-four hours. So far there had been no sign of swelling and the hemorrhage had not gotten any worse.

"Still here young lady?" Charles Stafford's voice boomed in the small room. He strode in the door and stopped at the foot of the bed.

Chase, not expecting company, jumped at the sound of his voice. "Yes sir, Mr. Stafford. I don't want her to be alone."

"Charles, please. It's Chase right?" He asked noncommittally. He had only met her two days ago, and made little effort to remember her name.

"Yes sir, I mean Charles." Chase tried to hide the annoyance in her voice. She had little respect for a person whose very attitude towards people in general was haughty disdain. The little courtesy she did extend to him she did for Jude, not for Charles. She looked between the two and wondered how on earth anyone as wonderful as Jude could be related to this man.

As if sensing her thoughts, Charles answered the unspoken question. "Jude really takes after her mother." His voice had a insulting tone that raked across Chase's already frayed nerves. "Three children and she doesn't give me one son. What a waste! And on top of that, I've got a lesbian for a daughter."

Chase bristled at the harsh words. She stood up and faced him, eyes blazing. "Why are you here? It's obvious you care very little for your daughter."

He turned quickly, eyes narrowed ominously. "Excuse me? How dare you insinuate that I do not love my daughter?"

Undaunted, Chase stared him down. "Your daughter is lying here in a coma and all you can think about is the fact that your daughter is gay. What kind of father does that? Do you realize what an amazing person Jude is? I lost my best friend in a car accident, but you have a second chance to make things right. You have the opportunity to be the father she deserves. You know a child's only wish is to make their parents proud and have their unconditional love and you haven't given her that one simple thing. If you are going to be ashamed, *Mr. Stafford,* don't be ashamed of Jude because of who she is, be ashamed of yourself because of who you are. Be ashamed of how much you have stolen from your own flesh and blood."

Charles' face was red with fury. No one had ever dared speak to him in such a candid manner. His fists were clenched in rage, and his body trembled with anger. "How dare you..."

Chase's voice lowered to an ominous tone. Her words came out in even, clipped tones. "Do not interrupt me. If I were you I would take the precious gift that I was given and value it. You still have Jude. Don't waste the next thirty—five years holding her at arms length and condemning her because she isn't the son you wanted. And as far as the other matter is concerned, you better come to terms with it very quickly. I love your daughter and if I have anything to do with it, you will be seeing a great deal more of us. Jude is the woman I plan to spend my life with, and that means taking the family that comes with her. Don't risk losing your daughter again by shutting her out because you're a stubborn old man. You need to open up your eyes and realize that this amazing woman is just as much you as she is her mother and she deserves your love and respect." Chase turned around and grabbed her purse off the chair. She walked to the door then faced Charles once more. "Decide which is more important, your daughter or your foolish pride."

Charles watched Chase leave the room and grunted, a small feeling of admiration sparking inside him for the feisty woman that had just given him the verbal lashing of a lifetime. "Women." He muttered softly. He continued to stare at Jude's face intently. He realized for the first time that she bared a striking resemblance to him. Same nose, same mouth, even the same strong Stafford chin. He shook his head, dismayed that he hadn't actually noticed that before. *Has my damn temper too!* He felt his heart catch and a lump form in his throat. Chase was right. He had robbed Jude of a father's love. Her whole life he had berated her mother for another girl, and when she had come out, he degraded her. He hadn't let himself see what a wonderful woman she had grown into, highly driven and successful just like me. He squeezed her good foot and smiled. He suddenly remembered the goofy name her mother had called her when she was younger…Ju—Ju Bean. The thought made him smile, the first genuine one in years. "Ju—Ju Bean, I'm sorry, I haven't been a very good father to you, have I? I just couldn't forgive your mother for not having a boy, and I took it out on you. Your friend Chase is right, harsh, but right. I think it's time your old man starting acting like a father." He chuckled to himself. "Not sure what kind of life you will have with her, but I think you may have met your match in that one. She's feisty! Reminds me a bit of your mother." When he spoke again, his voice was barely above a whisper. "I love you, honey. Hurry up and come back to us." He took one last look then walked out, his hand swiping his eyes.

Chapter 41

Chase hung up the phone and clapped her hands together. Tess called, Jude was making excellent progress in her recovery. And surprise, Jude's mom had arrived finally. She was on a two week cruise in the Galapagos when the accident happened and hadn't been able to leave the cruise until now. Chase took a nervous breath. Was she ready to meet Jude's mom? The possibility that Jude may not want her anymore suddenly hit her. Maybe meeting her mom wasn't such a great idea. Then again, meeting the woman responsible for the wonderful person Jude had grown into would definitely give Chase some much needed insight.

She glanced at her watch and frowned. She was still in charge of the afternoon meal and knew it would be several hours before she could get away. *What's three hours compared to a lifetime...if she still wants me.*

Chase quickly prepared a light lunch of grilled turkey sandwiches with Havarti cheese and artichoke tapenade, zesty pomodoro with beans, and fresh fruit for dessert. She cleaned up the kitchen and with fifteen minutes to spare before three hours was up, she was in the car on her way to the hospital.

Chase looked at the matriarchal figure watching over Jude. She had the same tall, erect stature and quiet dignity that Jude possessed. The woman startled Chase by turning her attention to her and smiling warmly. Chase was mesmerized by her brilliant green eyes and knew this woman was Jude's mother.

"You must be Chase." She walked around the bed and extended a strong hand. "I'd know you anywhere from Jude's description."

"She...she talked about me?" Chase tried to hide the shock on her face, but she could do little to mask the surprise in her voice.

"Of course she did my dear. She's talked of little else the last few months. I'm quite honored to meet the beguiling woman who's stolen my daughter's heart." She let her gaze rove over Chase quickly. "I must say you are stunning. My daughter was accurate in her description of you."

Chase swallowed, embarrassment creeping into her cheeks. "Tha…thank you." She was having a hard time reconciling the patrician woman before her with the woman Jude's father seemed to despise.

"I'm Jude's mother, Caroline Jeffries." Her voice danced melodically, an amused expression in her eyes.

"It's very nice to meet you Mrs. Jeffries."

"Please call me Caroline. Let's not stand on formality." She winked mischievously. "It would seem as though you and I will be much more closely acquainted if my daughter informs me correctly."

"I don't understand." Chase looked really confused. "She and I aren't a…well, we're not seeing…I mean we are not together."

"Then I am more than confused. The last time I spoke with Jude she was planning to propose to you." Caroline lifted an eyebrow and stared at Chase. "I assume she did that."

"She tried to tell me that she loved me, but I wouldn't hear it." Chase looked chagrined. "She was going to propose?"

"Yes, she was. Why wouldn't you listen? You do love my daughter, don't you?" Caroline locked her eyes on Chase, silently requiring an answer.

Chase shook her head slowly. "Yes, I do. I just can't bear to be hurt by her. When I gave myself to her, heart, body and soul, I knew it wasn't forever, but I was prepared to accept the little bit of her she would give me. Then my heart wouldn't let her walk away that easily. I foolishly went after her thinking that if I loved her it would be enough. Somehow I believed that what I was feeling wasn't one—sided. She had to feel it too. But she set me straight pretty quickly and I ran the other way, trying to nurse a broken heart." Chase sniffed softly. "After that, I couldn't believe that she could love me. Every time she tried to talk to me, I ignored her. The hurt was too fresh, too deep for me to let her back in. It wasn't until the night she…well, until the accident, that I realized I came close to losing the love of my life. I have never been so scared in my life of losing someone. So, yes Caroline, I love your daughter very much, and if she will still have me, I plan to spend the rest of my life with her."

Caroline pulled Chase against her and hugged her fiercely. She put her hands on her shoulders, pushed her away gently, and held her at arm's length. "I knew the moment you walked in the door, you were in love with my daughter. I know that you are worried she will break your heart again, but don't be. Jude is very slow to give her heart, but when she does, it's yours forever. I've never heard my daughter talk about a woman the way she does about you. Jude loves intensely, and I can assure you, I've heard the way she talks about you. As a mother, I've learned to read between the lines. Jude fell in love with you the first time she saw you. I know that when she wakes up, she will still feel the same as she did the night she was going to propose."

Chase smiled. "I hope so."

"Ahem."

Both women turned to the sound of someone clearing their throat. It was Dr. Stevens. "Good afternoon ladies."

"Good afternoon Dr. Stevens." Caroline said in a very polished voice.

"Mrs. Jeffries." He nodded at Chase then turned his attention to Caroline. "I believe I have some good news for you. We are happy with your daughter's progress. She doesn't show any signs of additional hemorrhaging and the swelling has gone down enough that she will not need to have surgery."

Caroline smiled brightly. "Oh, but that is good news."

"We are also going to take her off the pentobarbital and bring her out of the coma. The medicine will take some time to leave her body, so it may be a day or longer before she wakes up. At that point, we can begin to ascertain if she has sustained any permanent damage as a result of the trauma to her brain."

Caroline gasped. "Permanent damage?"

Dr. Stevens nodded. "With this type of brain trauma, there is the possibility of lasting damage. Specifically with reaction, attention span, emotions and even memory loss. Again, I should say that it is a possibility and not necessarily a definite. That is something we won't know until she wakes up." He checked his watch and made a few notes on Jude's chart. "Someone will be here shortly to stop the IV then we just watch and wait." He put his hand on Caroline to try and reassure her. "Let's not worry until she's awake and we've run some tests." With that he smiled at the two women and walked out of the room.

Caroline slumped in her chair and put her head in her palm. She sighed wearily. Chase knelt down beside her and put her hand on her arm and squeezed it gently. "I'm sure she will be fine. She's a fighter."

Caroline smiled wanly. "I know dear, that she is. I just know Jude and she won't know what do with herself if she isn't perfect. She is a proud woman, and anything less that perfect would be hard to take." She ran her palm over Chase's cheek softly. "I'm just glad she has you. Your love will make her recovery much easier."

"If she'll still ha…" Chase stopped quickly. "I mean, I'm glad to be here for her too. I'll help her anyway I can."

Chapter 42

Jude tried to force her eyes open. Her lids felt like they were taped shut and her throat was on fire. A faint rhythmic beeping punctured her subconscious and she struggled to break out of the mental haze she was locked in. She finally opened her eyes and blinked them open. Her vision was blurry, and the bright light filtering through an open window made her shut them quickly. She tried to move her hand, but stopped when she felt something attached to it. *God, where am I?*

She lay there several more minutes, listening to the soft beeps coming from somewhere behind her, but close by, muted voices, the sound of her own shallow breathing. This time she opened her eyes slowly, allowing them to adjust to the light slowly. She blinked rapidly, the blurriness slowly clearing to reveal a tiled ceiling above her. She looked down and realized she was lying on a hospital bed.

She looked down at her arm and realized there was an IV running from her hand and up to a bag located just to her left. She tried to remember why she was in the hospital and she couldn't. The last thing she remembered was the restaurant and Chase turning her down. Her eyebrows wrinkled in confusion and she tried to take several deep breaths to clear her mind.

Finally, she looked to her right, towards the window. She saw someone sleeping in a small chair next to the window. She squinted and recognized Chase. Suddenly, all her fear dissipated and she felt a warm calm effuse her body. She no longer cared why she was in the hospital. Her only thought was Chase was here…with her. Nothing else mattered.

Jude watched her sleep. She was slumped awkwardly in the chair, her head resting on the arm. Her hair had fallen in pieces around her face. Jude thought she looked as sweet and innocent and beautiful as anyone she had ever seen. She watched her for what seemed like hours before she saw Chase start to stir.

When Chase sat up, awake finally, Jude saw the dark smudges under her eyes and the tired, haunted look in her eyes. Chase's face broke into a grin when she realized Jude was awake. "You're awake."

Jude nodded. When she spoke, her voice was raspy from being on the ventilator and she struggled to get the words out. "You're…here. I…was…watching…you…sleep."

Chase winced at the horseness in Jude's voice, aware of the effort she was putting into talking. She put her finger on Jude's lips. "Shhh sweetheart, don't talk." She searched Jude's face, her eyes looking for a sign that Jude didn't want her there. All she saw was love, and she wondered how she could have missed it before. She swallowed a lump in her throat when she realized how close she was to losing Jude. "You had a car accident the night of…of the…"

Jude watched tears well in Chase's eyes and she covered her hand with her own, lacing their fingers together. She shook her head from side—to—side, silently telling Chase that everything would be all right. There was no need to dwell on the past.

Chase licked her lips. "You've been in a coma for almost two weeks. You broke your leg and ankle and…" Chase's voice trailed off when she heard the door open. Her eyes met Dr. Stevens and she stood up quickly.

Dr. Stevens nodded to her then glanced at Jude. "Well look who decided to join us. Jude, I'm Dr. Stevens. How are you feeling?"

Jude licked her lips. "Thirsty."

"That's probably because of the ventilator. We'll get you something to drink." He walked over to the bed and began to examine Jude. He took out a penlight and shined it in each of her eyes. Convinced they looked fine, he went on. "Do you remember anything from the night of the crash?"

Jude shook her head no. There was a flash of fear in her eyes and she groped for Chase's hand. Her eyes met Chase's as she locked her hand around hers. She held her gaze momentarily then looked back at Dr. Stevens. "No. I don't even remember the crash."

"I don't know the specific details, but during the crash, you suffered blunt force trauma to the head, resulting in a cerebral contusion. That is probably why you do not remember the crash itself. You have been in a medically induced coma for a little over a week so that the injury didn't get any worse. Fortunately, you didn't develop any other complications and it did not require surgery. You could still have some permanent damage as a result of the injury, but we don't know that for sure. Your femur and ankle were also fractured in the crash. We were able to set the femur without surgery, but the fracture in your ankle did require surgery. Both fractures are going to take several months to fully heal and even then I would be careful on that leg. You're a very lucky woman, Jude. Considering the type of accident, you are walking away with minimal injuries." He jotted a few notes on the chart, and put his pen back in his pocket. "We are going to keep you on the intravenous Demerol for pain control. If you find that isn't enough, let me know and we will consider some alternatives. The Demerol is going to make you sleepy, which is good since you need lots of rest right now." He turned to walk away, but glanced back at the women. "As long as you continue to progress, it's possible you will be able to leave within the next forty—eight to seventy—two hours."

When he left, Chase sat back down and scooted her chair closer to the bed. She smiled at Jude. "How are feeling?"

Jude smiled weakly. "Aside from a pounding headache and pain radiating up and down my leg, I'm fabulous."

Chase winced at the pain that was evident in Jude's voice. "Jude, I'm sorry…"

Jude squeezed Chase's hand. "No, don't. I'm sorry. I should never have thrown myself at you the way that I did. You made it perfectly clear that you weren't interested anymore." She smiled. "If I wasn't so damn stubborn, I may not be lying here right now. I really appreciate you staying here with me. You don't have to stay here anymore. I'll be fine." She pulled her hand away and turned away.

Chase gasped quietly. Of course, Jude thought she was there out of pity. When she didn't leave immediately, Jude turned back, her eyes questioning her. Chase took a deep breath and started talking. "Jude, I love you. I always have. And seeing you lying there…"

Jude's eyes flashed. "I don't need pity love. So what, when the cuts and bruises disappear, so do you? Don't do me any favors. I'm a big girl. I'll heal just fine without you pretending to love me."

"I'm going to attribute your stubbornness to your recent head injury." Chase huffed loudly. "Do you honestly think that is why I am here? That I don't have better things to do than spend the night in an uncomfortable chair waiting around for you to wake up out of pity?"

"But you told me you didn't want me." Jude answered quickly. "At what point in all of this was I supposed to realize you changed your mind?"

Chase chuckled and grazed Jude's cheek softly with her knuckles. "Oh sweetheart, if I'm going to spend the rest of my life with you, you need to realize mind reading is a required skill."

Jude stared incredulously at Chase. "Spend your life with me?" Jude's eyes looked hopeful. "What are you saying Chase?"

"I'm saying I am in love with you. I *love* you!" Chase's voice rose emphatically. "I'm not good at fancy speeches, but this is me pouring my heart out to you. I love you and I want to spend my life with you. I know I told you I wanted to move on and forget you, but I was lying to myself and to you. I didn't want to get hurt again. But the last couple of weeks and lots of Tess's advice helped me to see that even a single moment with you is worth risking everything. I could live the rest of my life in some comfort zone with a false sense of security and rob myself of the chance at happiness or I could throw caution to the wind and give my heart to you." She extended her hand towards Jude, palm up symbolically offering her heart and smiled hesitantly. "I'm choosing us."

A tear streamed down Jude's face and Chase wiped it away with her thumb. She couldn't know that Jude's silence was a result of being overwhelmed. "Please say something."

Jude took Chase's hand and kissed her palm softly. Sparks shot through her body, a pleasant reminder that parts of her were still very much intact. She gently tugged her hand, pulling Chase towards her. Her lips grazed Chase's mouth and she gently tugged her lower lip between hers, holding the kiss as time stopped and their two hearts melded together in a timeless bond. Jude finally broke the kiss and met Chase's gaze, truly happy for the first time. "I don't need fancy speeches, I just need you."

Epilogue

Jude balanced on a single crutch, twisting her body around to watch Chase. The tailored white tux barely fit over her walking boot, but she hardly noticed. The moment she saw Chase, she forgot everything else but her. She walked towards Jude, the silky white material of her dress billowing in the gentle ocean breeze.

Jude held her gaze and smiled warmly, love emanating from her face. Oblivious to anyone else, she smiled from ear—to—ear. It seemed like it took a lifetime for Chase to bridge the gap between them, but finally Jude felt Chase's hand curl around her arm. She pulled her as close as she could, the smile never leaving her face. She leaned over and planted a light kiss on Chase's nose. "Hi." She whispered.

"Hi." Chase's voice was low and sexy and Jude shuddered with emotion.

"You ready?" Jude's eyes searched Chase's. She didn't need a response, Chase's eyes told her all she needed to know. She held her captive a microsecond longer then they both turned forward to face their future.

"Dearly beloved, we are gathered here today to celebrate the union of two hearts..."

Syd Parker was born in California and lives in Indiana with her partner of five years. She loves golfing, biking and spoiling her ten nieces and nephews. She loves to travel and anywhere on the water feels like home.

She loves to read a good love story and thoroughly enjoys writing them as well. "It isn't just about writing a story, it's about creating a world and having the reader climb into it, experiencing it in first person. That's my goal...that's why I write."

Bibliography

Excerpt from *Leaves of Grass* by Walt Whitman, 1867.

Made in the USA
Lexington, KY
14 May 2012